SOUR GRAPES

A SHAKESPEARE IN THE VINEYARD MYSTERY

SOUR GRAPES

CAROLE PRICE

FIVE STAR

A part of Gale, Cengage Learning

GALE
CENGAGE Learning·

Farmington Hills, Mich • San Francisco • New York • Waterville, Maine
Meriden, Conn • Mason, Ohio • Chicago

Copyright © 2014 by Carole Price.
Five Star™ Publishing, a part of Gale, Cengage Learning.

LIBRARY OF CONGRESS CATALOGING-IN-PUBLICATION DATA

Price, Carole (Carole Joyce), 1935–
    Sour grapes : a Shakespeare in the vineyard mystery / Carole
Price. — First edition.
        pages cm
    ISBN 978-1-4328-2920-9 (hardcover) — ISBN 1-4328-2920-3
(hardcover) — ISBN 978-1-4328-2925-4 (ebook) — ISBN 1-4328-
2925-4 (ebook)
    1. Ex-police officers—Fiction. 2. Brothers—Fiction. 3. Re-
venge—Fiction. 4. Murder—Fiction. 5. Theaters—California,
Northern—Fiction. 6. Vineyards—California—Napa Valley—Fiction. I. Title. II. Title: Shakespeare in the vineyard mystery.
PS3616.R525S68 2014
813'.6—dc23   2014019678

First Edition. First Printing: October 2014
Find us on Facebook– https://www.facebook.com/FiveStarCengage
Visit our website– http://www.gale.cengage.com/fivestar/
Contact Five Star™ Publishing at FiveStar@cengage.com

Printed in the United States of America
1 2 3 4 5 6 7 18 17 16 15 14

For my mother, Corelli Watermon, who filled our home
with love and music.

ACKNOWLEDGMENTS

My thanks and appreciation to Five Star/Cengage Publishing. I am grateful for the support I've received from Tiffany Schofield and Deni Dietz and the artist who creates the fantastic covers for my books.

To my husband, Cliff, for his patience and critical eye for consistency throughout my writing, and to my daughter Carla (my web designer) and my daughter Krista who makes me laugh. And Shilo, my precious terrier.

I am again indebted to Sgt. John Hurd of the Livermore Police Department for patiently answering my countless questions. Livermore's Citizens Police Academy continues to give me opportunities to understand how a police department functions, to role-play with SWAT, and to drive a police car. My thanks to Yolanda Magana and Joanna Johnson, LPD Community Service Specialists, for setting me straight about crime scene investigations, and to Christy Boyes for explaining property room procedures.

I'm also grateful to the Alameda County Sheriff's Department for their willingness to share their expertise with me.

Special thanks to my Friday critique group for reading many drafts and for providing helpful insights and constructive criticisms: Penny Warner, Ann Parker, Colleen Casey, Janet Finsilver, and Staci McLaughlin. I'm grateful for the many friends who have encouraged me through drafts and deadlines. Thank you for your friendship. Finally, my heartfelt thanks to my editor, Alice Duncan and to Tracey Matthews, content project editor, for your insightful comments and for steering me in the right direction.

CHAPTER 1

Caitlyn Pepper was startled when her security alarm went off in the middle of the night. Her heart hammered wildly as she sat up, tossed the covers back, and reached beneath her bed for her green canvas bag. She grabbed her Glock and Maglite from the bag, then tiptoed down to the second floor, pressed her ear to the privacy door, and listened before unlocking it.

Hands shaking, Cait switched on the Maglite, stepped into the room, and tracked her Maglite and gun back and forth as the alarm continued to blare. Satisfied no one was on that floor, she continued down to the first floor, shadows mocking each step she took. She hit the light switch for the large front room and hallway. Alert for sudden movement, she backed over to the digital keypad on the wall next to the front door and entered the code to silence the alarm.

Then the landline started to ring.

She ignored the phone while she checked the locks on the door and windows, and then went into the gift shop and grabbed the phone. "Hello?"

"ADT," a man said. "We got a signal there's a disturbance at your house."

"I'm still checking," she said, her gaze darting about the room. "Everything appears to be okay so far, but if you'll hold I'll check the kitchen and office."

"Take your time."

Cait put the call on hold and tiptoed down the hall to the

kitchen. Something soft brushed against her ankles. She gasped and jumped back, blood pounding in her ears. Velcro, the stray cat that had adopted her, disappeared into the shadows. As she reached for the light switch, someone pounded on the back door.

"Who's there?" she shouted, hitting the light switch for the kitchen and back step.

Jim Hart, her new property manager, motioned to her through the window in the door. Cait lowered her gun to her side and walked over and unlocked the door.

"I heard the alarm. Everything okay?" Jim's thinning gray hair stood on end as he peered into the kitchen.

She glanced at the wall clock and saw it was a couple of minutes past three. "I think so. Come in while I check back here. The alarm company's on the phone." She went into the office and picked up the receiver. "My property manager's here now. Everything looks okay. Thanks for calling."

Jim stood in the office doorway. "I'll look around while I'm here."

Cait turned the light on in the office as her gaze swept the room. "I already checked, except for the locks on this window and door. You heard the alarm way over at your RV?"

He nodded. "Surprised us, too. I thought June would jump out of her skin."

"Sorry. You better comfort her so she won't worry."

"She worries about you, too," he said as he checked the locks.

Cait thanked Jim for coming and walked him to the back door. After he left, she secured the door, turned the downstairs lights off, and returned to bed.

Just as Cait felt herself falling back to sleep, the alarm went off again.

She shot up and out of bed. "I don't believe this," she muttered. This time her gun and Maglite were within easy reach on

10

the bedside table. Once again, she went through the same procedure, one floor at a time. She punched in the code on the keypad before ADT could call, stuck her head in each room, and then returned to bed, still feeling anxious. *Maybe Tasha's ghost set the alarm off or this old house is still settling.*

Two months earlier, when Cait inherited the Bening Estate from her aunt Tasha Bening, she'd been a crime analyst in Columbus, Ohio. The estate—a three-story yellow Victorian house on top of a hill, two Shakespearean theaters, and a vineyard—was located in Livermore, forty-five miles east of San Francisco. After a tumultuous settling-in period, Cait felt she could go forward with Tasha's beloved Shakespeare festival and the vineyard. The first thing she did was have a security system installed in the house and the theaters. If someone tried to break into the theaters, she might be able to hear the alarm but wouldn't know which one had been compromised.

When she went downstairs later that morning, she found Marcus Singer, her recently promoted festival manager, staring at the computer screen in his office. She told him about the alarm scare during the night and asked that he have ADT send someone to check the system.

"Could be the wind," Marcus said. He pulled a file from one of the desk drawers. "I'll call now."

June Hart, Jim's wife, knocked on the back door. She usually wore her blond hair in a knot at the top of her head, but today it was clipped at the nape of her neck. She reminded Cait of her mother: five-three, trim frame, a ready smile. "Sorry about the alarm," Cait said. "I had no idea it could be heard way over at your RV."

"Startled us," June said, "but it's a blessing in disguise in case there's real trouble. Being alone in this big house would scare anyone. You need a guard dog."

"So I've been told." She thought about the plays opening that weekend—*Hamlet* at the outdoor Elizabethan theater and *Macbeth* at the small indoor Blackfriars theater. "You know I couldn't manage the festival without you and Jim. I would've had to close the theaters."

"Nonsense. Why would you think that? From what I've heard, you managed *Tongue of a Bird* like a pro last month."

"Only because Tasha had made all the preparations. I didn't have to do anything but smile and greet people when they came to see the play."

"All's Well that Ends Well," June quipped, with a glint in her blue eyes. Retired after four decades as a Shakespearean actor, she loved to slip quotes from Shakespeare into conversations to amuse and confuse her friends.

Cait nodded. "*Hamlet* is different. It reminds me that Tasha had been chosen to be the play's associate artistic director at the Oregon Shakespeare Festival, if she hadn't been—"

"Don't go there, Cait. What happened to Tasha was no fault of yours. I'm happy I can help you with the festival and not have to compete with the much younger actors. Too darn much drama on and off the stage."

The doorbell rang.

"That should be ADT," Marcus said, entering the kitchen from his office. "I was told they were already working in the area."

Cait glanced at the clock as she slid off her stool: 9:30. "I'll get the door, Marcus."

When she opened the front door, a tall black man smiled and displayed his ID. "Morning, ma'am. ADT."

Cait glanced over his shoulder and noted a white and blue panel truck in the driveway, then compared the man's face to the one on his ID tag. "Thanks for coming so soon." She held the door open for him to enter.

She explained about the two late-night alarms.

"I'm sorry," he said. "Would have freaked me out, too. Probably a bug in your new system."

"That's what I thought. Let me know if you need anything." She left him standing by the security panel and went into the kitchen where June and Marcus were discussing the alarm system.

Marcus dunked a teabag in his cup. "I hate the nuisance of an alarm, too, Cait, but we'll get used to it. It's for your own protection."

"I know."

"Hope it's just a loose wire. We don't need more trouble around here." Marcus swept his hand over his spiked sunbleached hair. "I'll be in the garage. Still work to do on the platform before the Green Show."

Cait watched him go. She marveled at the change in Marcus, an ex-con Tasha had taken under her wing as her secretary. In exchange for giving him a second chance in life, he'd done everything she'd asked, even taking her to appointments because she didn't like to drive. When Cait inherited the estate, Marcus had been indifferent to her, sometimes ignoring her, but after she declared her right to make changes on the estate, they came to a mutual understanding.

"Ma'am?"

Cait jumped at the deep voice behind her. The security technician stood in the doorway.

"Nothing's wrong with the keypad," he said. "I'll go outside, walk the grounds around the house, and check the lights. Could be a short setting off the alarm."

"Thanks. I don't want to go through another night like last night."

"Could be a mouse," June said after the technician left.

Cait shivered. "*That* possibility gives me the creeps."

13

June turned to leave. "Let me know if he finds anything. I'm going to see what Jim's up to."

Concerned the Harts would take their RV back on the road now that both were retired, Cait asked, "Is Jim happy here?"

June rolled her eyes. "He's settled in like a rock. You may have to kick us out to get him to leave." She stepped closer, her voice low. "I know Jim told you he's a carpenter, but that's just one of many hobbies. Jim and his partner ran a small security firm specializing in stolen art. He still keeps his nose in the business, but only as a silent partner. He's like a modern-day Indiana Jones."

Cait raised an eyebrow. "Why didn't he tell me?"

June grinned. "He's a private, modest man. He would never have told you himself, unless you asked, but I thought you should know."

The back door opened. "Ma'am, would you mind stepping outside? I need to show you something."

Cait's heart lurched as she stared at the technician. *This means it's not a mouse interrupting the system.*

Cait and June followed him around to the west side of the house where he directed their attention to the two windows from the gift shop. Pry marks scuffed the wood beneath one of the windows, and a deep gouge was cut into the other window-sill.

"Those are fresh marks," the man said. "Looks like someone attempted to open these windows and tripped the alarm. Maybe a kid. Too sloppy for a professional burglar."

Cait's breath caught as she stared at the damaged window-sills. *Kids wouldn't climb up here to break in.*

"There's also this. I found it outside the back door and stumbled over it." He pulled an object from his tool belt and held it out to her. "Not your usual burglar's tool."

Cait frowned, took the unfamiliar ornate object, and turned

it around in her hands, careful not to cut herself on the sharp point. "I wonder what it is."

The man pointed to the rose bushes beneath the windows. "There's also a knife. I didn't think I should touch it."

Cait leaned over and stared at the knife caught in the thorny bush, then found a tissue in her jeans pocket and carefully reached to pick it up.

"Ma'am," the ADT man continued, "you should call the police."

CHAPTER 2

Cait wrapped the tissue around the handle of the knife and picked it up. *Looks like a military knife,* she thought, noting the green handle and serrated blade. She stared hard at the knife. *This looks vaguely familiar.*

June held her hand out. "Can I see that metal piece?"

Cait had forgotten she was holding it. She stood and handed it to June.

June grimaced. "Christ on a broomstick. I hope I'm wrong."

Cait laughed. "What?"

June shook her head, her eyes intent on the object she held.

"At least we know nothing's wrong with your alarm system," the technician said, "but don't hesitate to call if you need service."

"Thanks. You've been helpful." *More than you know.*

After the man left, Cait and June went around to the back of the house. "Do you recognize it?" Cait asked, referring to the metal piece. "What is it?"

June nodded. "I think so, but I want to be sure. I'd like to research it. Okay if I take it with me?"

"Sure, and while you're doing that, I'll call Detective Rook." Inside the house, she held the knife close to one of the lights mounted beneath the cabinets. Her gaze dwelled on the initials "HD" etched into the three-inch steel blade. A knot tightened in her stomach. "Impossible," she blurted. The knife slipped from her hand and pinged against the granite counter.

A slow burn rose in her chest. *But what if—*

The wall clock struck ten, jarring Cait from her thoughts. She reached across the counter for her cell phone and called Detective Rook.

"Rook," he answered.

"It's Cait Pepper. I think I need your help."

"What's it about?"

"Someone tried to break into the house in the middle of the night and set the alarm off."

"It can be windy on that hill—"

"The wind doesn't leave pry marks on windowsills," she snapped. "ADT just left. The technician found a knife in a rose bush beneath the window."

"Now you've got my attention," he said. "Did you call the sheriff's department?"

"No. I wanted to talk to you."

"I'm glad you called, but remember your property is in the sheriff's jurisdiction. If they're overwhelmed with calls elsewhere, they'll sometimes call the LPD for help."

"I know."

"Tell you what. I'll come out, but their detectives will do any follow-up unless they don't have time. Maybe an exception can be made since I was previously involved with the estate."

"Thanks." Cait appreciated the friendship that had developed between her and the detective during the investigation into murders at the estate a couple of months ago. After another hard look at the knife, she went into the gift shop to examine the windowsills, but found no damage on the inside. Everything on the shelves—drama masks, T-shirts, cards, games, books, puzzles—could be replaced if stolen. Her anxiety was the knife and what the initials meant to her.

He's dead. I know, because I shot him.

★ ★ ★ ★ ★

Cait crossed the hall and looked into the second room used as a gift shop. The shelves were filled with more souvenirs—sweatshirts, ball caps, pillows and throws, Shakespeare busts, and other paraphernalia. Having a gift shop in the house where strangers could wander was not an ideal situation, but it would be awhile until a new shop could be built. She walked out and returned to the kitchen to wait for Rook.

When the detective arrived, he was dressed in a dark gray suit and a lavender shirt and tie as if heading to court. Marcus followed him into the house. Rook stood at the counter looking at the knife. "Interesting knife." He picked it up, careful to hold the handle with the tissue.

Marcus stared at the knife. "Where did *that* come from?"

"Our burglar's tool of choice," she said.

Marcus ran his fingers through his spiked hair. "So that's why Detective Rook is here."

"I called him." Cait knew, even if Marcus didn't, that he ran his fingers through his hair every time something disturbed him. Like the attempted break-in.

Rook turned the knife over. "Ah, here's what I like to see but seldom do. All we have to do is find someone with the initials 'HD' and match them to fingerprints on the knife."

Cait doubted it would be that easy. "Let's go outside. I'll show you where it was found and the damaged windowsills."

Rook nodded. "I'll take the knife with me when I leave."

She expected Marcus to follow, but as soon as they stepped outside, he took off in the opposite direction. She wondered if it was because of his past record that he still felt intimidated in the presence of police. Cait led Rook around the side of the house and pointed to the windows.

Rook avoided the prickly rose bushes and concentrated on the ground around them. "The grass has been trampled a lot."

"Sorry about that. I wanted a closer look. The technician also found an odd-looking object."

Rook turned. "Where is it?"

"June has it. She thought she recognized it and took it to her RV to research it."

"Who's June?" Rook asked.

"Sorry. June Hart is a retired actress and is the woman from Ashland who put me in touch with Kenneth Alt. He's the actor and director at the Oregon Shakespeare Festival, the man Tasha would have worked for as his artistic director for the play *Hamlet.*"

"I remember, he's the guy who called me to confirm your identity. So how does June Hart enter into this?"

"June and her husband, Jim, were Tasha's friends and offered to help me with the festival. Their RV is parked in that clearing on the other side of the house where RT parked his trailer."

"I'd like to meet them after I look at the windowsills." He snagged his jacket on one of the rose bushes in an attempt to get a closer look. "Good thing you've got that alarm. It wouldn't take much to get in these windows." He backed out of the bushes. "I've seen enough. Let's go see your friends. The next time RT calls, I'll let him know you have someone staying up here with you."

Cait was thinking about the knife as they walked and almost missed what Rook said about RT.

"Do you know where he is?"

"No, but I suspect somewhere unsavory." He smiled. "I think RT calls me because he feels responsible for my brother's death. RT was in charge of the mission they were on in Afghanistan."

Cait thought often about RT and why he chose to be a Navy SEAL as a career. He wanted a job where expectations and demands to perform were high and would push him to be the best he could be. The same reason she became a cop after college.

They found June and Jim sitting outside their Fleetwood Fiesta RV in a serious discussion. They stood when Cait and Rook approached.

Cait made introductions. "Detective Rook wants to see that metal object you were going to look up."

"I'll get it." June went into the RV and returned moments later. "It's a halberd."

"Never heard of it," Cait replied.

"A halberd is a weapon used in Elizabethan times," June explained. "This iron head was probably attached to a long wooden pole. But modern fencing matches, especially those presented on stage, use a lightweight buttoned foil. If a foil needs to be drawn on stage, a scabbard to hold the foil is made from tin piping and covered in leather and used to protect the actor." She handed it to Detective Rook.

Confused, Cait asked, "A foil?"

June smiled. "It's a type of sword with a thin flexible blade with a button tip to prevent injuries. The points can be made out of wood and silvered over to look like the real thing." She pointed to the metal object in Rook's hands. "I don't know where that head came from, unless it's part of Tasha's collection of unusual period weapons. Audiences don't know the difference between a foil and the real thing, but the old halberd heads were heavy enough to injure an actor when the halberd was drawn from their scabbards."

"Impressive. Thanks for the educational information," Rook said, turning the halberd around in his hand.

"I hope it helps," June said. She glanced at Cait. "Is something wrong?"

Uncomfortable thoughts swept over Cait. "Someone involved with the festival is my burglar or . . ."

"What?" Rook asked.

Or someone from my past life as a cop tried to break into my house. Before she could answer him, an urgent phone call caused Rook to leave abruptly.

CHAPTER 3

That night, Cait left her Glock and Maglite on the nightstand in easy reach. Although comforted knowing the bedroom door was locked, she stared at the shadows slinking over the bedroom walls as if they were bearing down on her.

She'd had every intention of telling Detective Rook about the knife and what the initials, HD, on the blade could mean, but when he received the phone call, he'd left in a hurry and took the knife and halberd with him.

She slept fitfully. Her mind wandered into forbidden territory—forbidden because she refused to dwell on her shooting someone to defend a fellow police officer. She'd gone through three sessions of therapy at her department's request. The therapist convinced her that she'd been doing her job, even if it meant someone had to die. Not long after the episode, she was promoted from a cop who patrolled the streets to a crime analyst, and the incident was thrust into the far reaches of her mind.

Cait woke in the morning with a head full of cotton from lack of sleep but immediately phoned Detective Shep Church. She'd met Shep ten years earlier in her rookie year as a cop in Columbus, Ohio. He'd been with the Columbus Police Department for a dozen years, starting as a young cadet. While her formal education was at Dennison University in Ohio, Shep's came from the school of hard knocks. She couldn't have had a better mentor. She rolled over, found her cell next to her gun, and called him.

"Good morning, Cait," Shep answered.

She sat up on the side of the bed and then got to her feet. "Do you have time to talk?" She crossed the bedroom and stood in her pajamas looking out the bay window at the sun-streaked vineyard below.

"For you, yes." Shep worked in the investigative subdivision and conducted in-depth investigations of crimes that, due to their nature or complexity, could not be investigated by uniformed officers.

She turned away from the window and sat on the edge of her wicker chaise. "Remember that bank robbery two years ago, the one that went terribly wrong?"

"Of course. You were a mess for a few days after shooting the bastard."

Restless, Cait rose and stood in the shaft of sunlight. "Hank Dillon."

"That's right. He's dead, Cait. How does he concern you now?"

"He *is* dead, isn't he?"

"Yes. What's going on?"

"The security alarm went off during the night a couple of times. A technician from ADT came to check on it but found nothing wrong with the system. But he did find scuff marks and a gouge on the windowsills."

Cait heard him draw in a deep breath before asking, "Someone tried to break in? Any evidence left other than the damage to the windowsills?"

Protecting evidence was always Shep's priority at any crime scene. Heaven help anyone who destroyed it. "A halberd and a knife."

"A halberd? Where would someone get a medieval weapon?"

"I don't know, unless it was stored in one of the theaters.

23

When the alarm went off, the guy must have dropped it and ran."

"What about the knife?"

"It's military. The initials HD are engraved on the blade." She waited for his reaction.

After a moment, he said, "I know what you're thinking, Cait. Hank Dillon is dead. There have to be a zillion people with those initials."

"I know, but would you mind pulling his file?"

"Cait—"

"It's a military knife! The blade is serrated and folds into the handle, exactly like the one found on Dillon after the bank robbery."

"Calm down. Even if it is the same knife, how would Dillon have gotten access to a military knife, and how did it find its way to California?"

"I have no idea. Hank was adopted. Maybe his adoptive brother brought it back from some war zone he was working in and gave it to him as a souvenir."

"I'll pull his file and have someone check the property room for the knife. But, Cait, you went to Dillon's funeral."

"Yes. I stood outside in the rain. Let me know what you find out."

Cait was in and out of the shower in three minutes and then called Detective Rook. As she sat at the desk towel-drying her wet, black hair, memories of the bank robbery forced their way to the front of her mind. If someone was looking to avenge her shooting Hank Dillon, why wait two years? She hoped Rook had an answer because she sure didn't. "Okay if I come by?" she asked when he answered. "I won't take much of your time."

"Sure. Sorry I had to run off like I did yesterday. I was going to call you later."

"I'll see you soon."

"Cait, if it's about the knife or the halberd, I don't know anything yet. It's too early."

"I didn't expect you to." She hung up and dropped her phone into her bargain-priced Vera Wang handbag, slipped into her sandals, grabbed her keys and went downstairs.

Marcus was in the office leaning over the keyboard and staring at the screen. He looked up when Cait walked in. "Going somewhere?"

"Yes, to see Detective Rook. Ilia and Fumié should be here when I get back. She's helping him with his new photo book, but maybe they won't mind doing a walk-through with me at the theaters to make sure they're clean and supplied with necessities before the actors get here Thursday to rehearse."

Marcus leaned back in his chair, hands behind his head. "Ilia's a terrific photographer." He sat up straight in his chair. "Do you think he'd include my horse in one of his photo shoots?"

Marcus kept his horse at the Bening Ranch in Livermore. Cait knew how much his horse meant to him. "Ask him. He'll be spending a lot of time at the ranch researching his next book."

His cheeks pinkened as he looked back at the screen, as if he were embarrassed to ask for a personal favor. "I'll think about it."

Cait left and went around to the garage where her new nocturne-blue metallic Saab sport sedan was parked. When she inherited the estate, she also inherited Tasha's older Jaguar. Marcus loved the Jag and had meticulously maintained it for Tasha. Since it wasn't Cait's style, she gave it to him.

She opened the car door, slid into the buttery leather seat, turned the key, and inhaled the newness of the car. At five-eight, she loved the car's extra headroom and how it accommodated her long legs. She backed out of the garage and drove down the steep driveway, careful not to brush the chardonnay and cabernet vines and the rose bushes.

The Livermore police station stood between the library and city hall, a short drive from the Bening Estate. Detective Rook was waiting for her in the lobby when she walked in, and he led her to a private interview room.

Rook shut the door and motioned toward a chair at the table. "Have a seat." He pulled out another chair and sat down across from her. "I still don't know anything about the weapons."

Cait pulled her chair up close to the table. "Are they still here?"

"Yes, in the property room."

She drew a deep breath. "I'm positive that knife is the same one found on a bank robber in Columbus a couple of years ago. I'm waiting for a call back from a detective friend of mine. He'll let me know if the knife is still in their property room."

Rook raised his eyebrow as he leaned his arms on the table. "Did that robbery have anything to do with you?"

"You could say that. I shot the perpetrator."

"This happened two years ago?"

"Yes, when I was a cop."

"What makes you think it's the same knife?"

She drummed her short nails on the table, anxious to get this over with. "Because of the initials on the blade, HD. Hank Dillon."

Rook reached inside his jacket and removed a small pad and pen. "Hank Dillon was the bank robber?"

"Yes. He was outside the bank holding a gun to the neck of an officer. I was close enough to see his finger move on the trigger. I made a split-second call and shot to kill. The knife was found in his pocket."

Rook frowned. "This was the first time you killed someone?"

She nodded. "First and last. I became a crime analyst soon

26

after the incident."

"Did the shooting have anything to do with your changing jobs?"

She thought about the question and how best to answer it. "No. My transfer was already in the works. I was married at the time. My husband didn't like me working the streets."

"I see."

I doubt it. It was selfishness on Roger's part. She inched closer to Rook in her seat. "What are the chances of that knife turning up here in Livermore? If the knife isn't in their property room, then I'm in real trouble."

Rook frowned as he wrote on his pad. "If this guy is dead, who else could be after you?"

She thought for a moment before answering. She'd learned the hard way that it was best to cast a wide net in order not to overlook any potential suspects. "I don't know. A single parent raised him. When he was twelve, he was adopted—the family was white, he was black. He had a record and had been in and out of trouble a lot. Hank's mother considered him a bad influence on his younger brother. Dillon was twenty-four at the time of the robbery."

They were silent while Rook wrote. He looked up. "What do you know about the family who adopted him?"

"Very little. We were told his adoptive brother was a journalist working in Afghanistan, but returned to the States to attend Dillon's funeral." She hesitated. "I heard the adoptive brother accused me of discrimination—killing Dillon because he was black—and he intended to look into the matter the next time he was in the States."

"Have you heard from him or anyone else in the family?"

"No. Unless one of them tried to break into my house."

"Sloppy work, leaving two pieces of evidence behind. You said there's a younger brother? What's his name? How old would he be now?"

Cait thought back, trying to remember what she'd known about him. "I don't know his name, but I think he was eight and Hank twelve at the time of the adoption. I asked Shep to pull Dillon's file. When he calls, I'll ask him for the brother's name and to confirm their ages."

"You think it could be the younger brother?"

"Who else could it be?"

"Hard to say. I'll check with your neighbors, see if anyone's had a break-in. I may want to talk with your detective friend sometime."

Cait reached in her handbag for her cell phone, pulled up Shep's number, and recited it to Rook as he wrote it down. "He'd be happy to talk with you."

Rook pushed his chair back and stood. "I don't need to tell you to watch your back."

Cait rose. "I may be out of my former line of work, but I'm not out of the habit of protecting myself."

Rook smiled, and a slight blush touched his cheeks.

"I am concerned about this weekend. With two plays going on simultaneously, people will be all over the place, even in the house because that's where the gift shop is. Actors' Equity will be breathing down my neck if there's trouble."

Rook opened the door for her. "I'll see to security. I know it won't be easy, but take precautions and tell your friends to do the same." He walked her to the front doors. When she was outside, he called to her. "Cait, you can't avoid or forget some things in life, but you learn to move on."

She understood. Rook was referring to her shooting the bank robber. She thought she had moved on—until now. She raised her hand in acknowledgment and walked to her car. She set her phone in the tray between the seats in case Shep called, then turned the ignition key and drove out of the parking lot.

Moving on is easier than forgetting.

CHAPTER 4

Cait drove with a tight knot in her chest. Cops knew fear like any ordinary citizen. She'd wasted no time replacing her police-issued Glock .22 with another after moving to California.

Hands tight on the wheel, she thought about the Mannings and wondered why they adopted Hank Dillon, a troubled boy, when they already had a grown son. There was no doubt in her mind the knife found in her yard belonged to Hank Dillon. What she wanted to know was why whoever it was waited two years to come after her.

Ilia's yellow VW bug and Fumié's Jeep were parked in the driveway in front of the house when she returned. Cait continued on and pulled up in front of the garage, hit the electronic door opener, and eased the car inside. A sudden flash of white pain, like lightning, pulsed in her right eye. She shut the engine off and squeezed her eyes shut against the pain. *Not a migraine! Not now!*

She left the garage and went to the back of the house. Feeling light-headed, she entered Tasha's meditation garden and sat on the marble bench, warm from the sun. She rested her head in her hands until the spell passed, and then she admired the white marble dolphin perched atop a pedestal surrounded by a patch of fragrant lime thyme, blue-red lupine, peach-colored Peace roses, and royal larkspur. Velcro appeared at her feet, her china-blue eyes gazing up at Cait. As Cait stood, she caught sight of a golden eagle in liquid movement across the blue sky and remembered RT's parting words before he left for another assignment—"A golden eagle is an omen of good things to come."

Or signifying the advent of change in a foreboding sense.

Or when fate rears its ugly head and swoops down upon you and plants itself in your path.

Her ringing cell phone interrupted her thoughts. Shep's number was displayed in the window. "Shep. Any news?"

"He's dead, Cait. Hank Dillon's family visits his grave every month on the same day he was shot. I talked to the detective in charge of the case and then called the family that adopted Dillon. I have his file in front of me."

But what about the knife?

Shep continued. "I asked Mrs. Manning about her son Calder. She assumes he's still out of the country because he hasn't been there in awhile to see his daughter. Being a war correspondent puts him out of touch for long periods of time."

"Tell me about the knife."

"It's gone, Cait."

She had hoped she was wrong and that the knife was still where it belonged in the property room. She shut her eyes and massaged her temple. "They keep records. Who signed it out?"

"No one. Unfortunately, an inventory hasn't been done for several years. I'm sorry. I know you're disappointed."

Understatement. "How do you lose a knife? There's a process you go through to remove anything from property."

"I know. Someone screwed up. It's possible a family member, maybe Hank's younger brother Wally Dillon, requested the knife be returned. All that's needed to get it back is to fill out a form. If approved, it can be returned. I asked one of the clerks to see if a request had been made and granted. I'll let you know when I hear back."

"Doesn't matter," she said. "It's the same military combat

knife. I've seen it before. Just didn't want to believe it." She heard voices drawing close. "Thanks. At least we know Dillon was in that coffin. I'll tell Detective Rook. He has your phone number. He may want to talk with you."

"One more thing. I researched Calder Manning. You should do the same. He's written interesting articles from war zones, and there's a photo of him in army fatigues. He's wearing a helmet, so you won't see much of his face, but you might get a vague idea of what he looks like."

"I'll look at it." She noticed Ilia and Fumié approaching. "Maybe Manning wanted the knife since it's military."

"He shouldn't have trouble getting another one. Be safe, Cait."

Ilia and Fumié waited for Cait to end the call.

"Did Marcus tell you about doing a walk-through with me at the Blackfriars?"

"Yes. No problem," Ilia said.

She nodded. "I'll meet you there in a few minutes. I have a call to make."

Cait watched them leave. Fumié's long hair flowed out like a raven's wings in the breeze. She thought they made a perfect couple, even if they didn't know it yet. A Japanese-American graduate of UC Davis, Fumié Ondo had been accepted at a school in Santa Rosa for park rangers but was on hold until her mother recovered from breast cancer. Ilia was a professional photographer.

She phoned Rook. "Shep said the knife is not in their property room. Guess we know what that means."

Cait heard him release a sigh. "I'll round up extra officers for your festival this weekend. I'd also like a copy of the schedule of the plays and the names of the actors. And it would be a good idea if you'd get to know them. We don't want just anyone dressing up in those fancy costumes." He hesitated. "Keep your phone handy and your gun loaded."

"You don't need to remind me. I used to be a cop, remember?" She left the garden and turned down the brick walkway through the towering cypress trees. "I don't mean to be flip, Rook, but I am responsible for the Bening Estate. I'll do what I have to do to protect it." She thanked him for his advice. When she opened the arched gate that led into the theater complex, she cringed at the squealing hinges. "I'll have Marcus send the information you asked for."

"You might warn your friends, the Harts, and ask them to keep an eye out for trouble."

"I will. June knows most of the actors. She can introduce me."

Cait found Ilia and Fumié waiting outside the Blackfriars theater. She reached into her pocket for the keychain remote. With a touch of her finger, she disarmed the theater. "Watch your step," she cautioned as she tried to open the door. It appeared to be stuck but eventually gave way. Cait felt along the wall for the light switch.

She loved the intimacy of the theater, with its black painted walls and stage. Wooden shutters, screens, and trellises had been positioned to block sunlight. Tiered benches surrounded the small stage, providing seating for 140 people. The theater reminded Cait of the old fantastical Duke of Dark Corners who disguises himself in *Measure for Measure*.

"I love this theater," Fumié said. "It's romantic. It reminds me of the original Black Swan Theater at the Oregon Shakespeare Festival in Ashland."

Cait stepped up onto the stage and looked out over the seating. "I think Tasha had that in mind when she built this one." Cait had studied Shakespeare at Dennison University, had even tried acting, but couldn't control her giggling whenever she looked at herself in the mirror and saw all those layers of Elizabethan costumes. She'd chosen a different path after graduation, one in law enforcement. It's amazing, she thought, how those two paths had merged here in California.

Ilia snapped her picture. "You look so serious."

She smiled. "Lost in thought."

"Tasha would have had my head if I'd tried to take her picture," he said. "Why would someone in the public eye be shy about having their picture taken?"

Cait didn't know. She'd never met her mysterious aunt. "Good question. RT's mother gave me an old photo of Tasha taken when they were aspiring actors, and I have a publicity picture of her dressed as Lady Macbeth." She looked around the small theater. "It shouldn't take long to go through, but I want to make sure it's ready by the time the actors arrive." She jumped down off the stage.

Ilia bent over and picked up a scrap of paper off the floor. "Other than trash, anything in particular we should look for?"

"Loose cords, burned-out light bulbs, cracked benches, anything I could be sued over. I'd prefer to stay on the good side of the stage manager, Ray Stoltz. Fumié and I will be in the back."

Ilia slipped his camera from around his neck and carefully set it on the stage. "Okay."

Fumié checked the dressing rooms backstage while Cait checked bathroom and kitchen cupboards for essentials. In the space delegated for the kitchen, she found coffee supplies and enough water bottles to last a month, but she used her electronic notepad to remind Marcus to order more.

Back at the front, she found Ilia on the stage videotaping the room. "You going to use this theater in your next book?"

He grinned. "I'm thinking about it. Free publicity for your festival. I didn't see anything needing to be repaired, but these windows don't look very secure, and the door is about an inch off the floor."

"I know, but the building is alarmed, Ilia."

He shrugged. "Just saying. At least there's a high wall around part of the Elizabethan theater."

Cait turned out the lights and alarmed the theater after Fumié and Ilia went out through the door.

"Do you want to go through the Elizabethan theater now?" Fumié asked.

Cait rubbed her aching temple. "I'd rather wait until tomorrow. It will take much longer."

"Are you feeling okay, Cait?" Fumié asked.

"Just a headache," she said. "You two go on. I'll see you later."

Cait stayed behind to spend a few precious moments in her favorite place, a place where she could open her heart and her mind among the wildflowers in quiet reflection. Tasha had her meditation garden; Cait preferred the serenity behind the Blackfriars theater, where she felt like she was sitting on the edge of the world. A meadowlark trilled. A sudden gust of wind whipped through her hair and over the orange California poppies and carpet of yellow mustard. As she sat on the grass, she rested her chin on her hand and gazed at the majestic and alluring contour of Mount Diablo to the north, she promised herself that some day she would hike the trails all the way to the top and visit the observation deck for a glimpse of the Sierras.

Her phone beeped.

Unable to ignore a ringing phone, she withdrew her cell from her pocket. "Hello?"

After a short silence, the caller hung up.

It rang again.

This time she heard heavy breathing. She stayed on the line until the caller hung up.

CHAPTER 5

When Cait returned to the house, the landline was ringing and Marcus wasn't in his office to answer it. She left a note on his desk to order water and coffee for the Blackfriars theater as the answering machine picked up the call. If someone wanted tickets for the plays, Marcus would know more about that than she would.

A gruff voice said, "I know where you are."

Cait froze. "What the—"

Then someone knocked on the back door and startled her. She peeked around the corner and was relieved to see June through the door window. When she opened it, June rushed in carrying a covered plate and set it on the counter. "I made enough lasagna for an army—too much for Jim and me." She removed the foil from around the plate and sat down. "You have all these fancy stainless steel appliances but never use them."

The aroma of tomato, cheese, and sausage curled up Cait's nose, sending her stomach into spasms. She opened a drawer, took out a fork, and sat next to June. "It's not that I can't cook. Sometimes I get busy and forget to eat."

The phone rang.

"The answering machine will get it. I had crank calls earlier." She told her about the hang-ups on her cell and the landline. "The last was threatening. In case anything comes of these calls, there's something you should know." She told June why

36

the initials on the knife concerned her.

"Good lord, I hope you told Detective Rook."

She nodded. "I stopped by the station to tell him. When Shep Church, my friend at the Columbus PD, checked their property room, the knife wasn't there." The more she thought about the calls and the knife, the angrier she became and the tighter the knot in her stomach. "Detective Rook wants you and Jim to watch for anyone acting suspicious this weekend . . . someone wandering away from the crowd. There will be about four hundred here for the plays, but Rook's promised extra security."

"I'll tell Jim to keep his gun with him."

Cait didn't know Jim had a gun. "I'm sorry. The last thing you and Jim expected were cops and robbers when you came here, and it never crossed my mind I would become a target for something that happened two years ago on the job."

"Fiddlesticks. Excitement keeps us on our toes."

"Hank Dillon's younger brother Wally would be twenty-two now. Maybe he made the calls and tried to break into the house."

"How could he get the knife? He couldn't just waltz into the police station and ask for it, could he?"

"No, but he could request it and fill out a form."

"Oh, that easy?"

"Depending, after a period of time and if it hadn't been involved in a homicide." She cut into the lasagna. "Another possibility is Calder Manning."

"Who?"

"Manning's family adopted Hank Dillon, a black kid, who'd been in and out of trouble with the law. Calder Manning, their son, is a war correspondent."

"That would keep him out of the country a lot, so he couldn't be a suspect. 'The croaking raven doth bellow for revenge.' " June grinned. "Sorry. Sometimes I can't help myself. You can take the actor out of the theater, but you can't take Shakespeare out of the actor, or something like that. That was taken out of context from *Hamlet*. Jim and I didn't come here to drink wine and bask in the sun. We need to be useful. Tell us what we can do to help you."

The landline rang again.

They exchanged glances and waited to hear a message, but one wasn't left.

Then it rang again.

Cait jumped up and grabbed the receiver. "Who is this?" When the line went dead, she punched *69, but wasn't surprised when she didn't see a number. "Every criminal's favorite toy. Disposable phones."

June slid off her stool. "I'm going to tell Jim what you've told me. Don't answer the next time it rings."

After June left, Cait finished eating, turned off the lights, and went upstairs.

Cait logged onto her laptop and searched Calder Manning's name. What she read surprised her. Not his undergrad degree from Ohio Wesleyan or his grad degree from Northwestern University, but the in-depth articles he'd written from war zones and his narrow escapes from certain death. Covering stories in the midst of a war zone took guts, she thought as she read more of his articles. One in particular, in which he wrote about unnecessary deaths, the aftermath of car bombings, and the misery and futility of the war, touched her. Cait didn't think he sounded like someone with time to waste tracking down a police officer, even one who killed his adopted brother during a bank robbery.

For the first time, she wondered if her inheritance had something to do with the attempted break-in, someone coming out of the woodwork demanding his or her share. She shook her head. *But that wouldn't explain the knife and the initials.*

Cait leaned back in her seat. She seldom experienced loneliness, not even after she left her husband. She savored privacy, yet her life was fulfilled with work and friends. But everyone she loved and trusted was either dead or in Ohio. Her thoughts turned to Royal Tanner, the Navy SEAL she'd met when she'd first arrived in Livermore. His work took him around the world, but after a shaky start, they'd parted as friends. When he left a month ago, she opened an account on Skype to stay in touch with her best friends, Samantha and Shep, but secretly hoped RT would look her up on it. So far she hadn't heard from him.

She refocused her attention on the screen, and after much searching she found the picture Shep had mentioned of Manning wearing a helmet and a flak vest strapped over his clothing. Even without a weapon, she thought he looked intimidating. She decided this illusion must be caused by the fatigues and the soldiers surrounding him with their massive weaponry. She wondered if journalists who had been drawn to the hot zones of the globe were driven by a notion that they have a role to play in an historical period. As much as she admired Manning's bravery, she wondered if his real mission was to draw the attention of the world to the evil committed by malicious forces against helpless victims—like a global crusader.

She reviewed military weapons and found the knife the police discovered on Dillon after he was shot, which was identical to the one found outside her house. The one distinguishing feature she'd missed when she'd described the knife to Detective Rook was the double bevel that ran down the center of the blade. It was listed as an Applegate Combat Folder, which was considered to be best-of-class among tactical knives.

Cait relaxed, satisfied with her finding. The screen began to blur before her eyes. She closed the document and pushed away from the desk when an electronic chirping stopped her. She clicked the mouse and saw Shep on Skype.

She smiled, her own image displayed in a tiny window in the upper left corner. "Hey you."

"You must have been at your computer," Shep said.

"Yes, and I found that photo of Manning you mentioned and I also identified the knife."

"Cait. I have something to tell you."

"Okay." *This can't be good.*

"I talked with Commander York about the knife. After Dillon's funeral, someone came to the station and asked about the officer who shot Dillon. The guy refused to give his name but did say he was a journalist."

The skin on the back of her neck tingled. "Calder Manning."

"Maybe. When the officer he talked to wouldn't give him your name, he left. Protocol has to be followed in the case of any officer shooting. Your name was kept out of the papers until after the full investigation had been conducted. The officer Manning talked to reported the incident to his sergeant."

"I should have been told," she said.

"You're right. Remember Chuck Levy? He retired a couple of years ago."

"Sure."

"He kept meticulous notes in his infamous black journal. Stuff like conversations nobody else thought important, details like why the hall lightbulb at a murder scene had been removed. When he retired, he turned the journal over to his commander and then told him about an incident that happened days before he retired."

She fidgeted in her seat. "What incident?"

"Levy was having what he called a celebratory Johnnie Walker after work at that place around the corner from the station."

"Ah." She had fond memories of the old police hangout. Her department had given her a party there to celebrate her promotion to crime analyst and again when she got her inheritance.

"Well, what Levy thought was an accidental bumping of elbows at the bar at the time, turned into an interrogation. This other guy drank along with Levy, got him talking about his retirement. Levy later noted in his journal he made a mistake by saying he wished he'd inherited a vineyard in California like one of the officers in his department and letting your name slip."

Cait stared at the screen and the grim look on Shep's face, but couldn't find the words to console him for being the bearer of bad news. "Something else I wasn't told. But lots of people hang out at that bar, Shep, and cops know they must be tight-lipped when they're in there."

"Yep, they sure do, but you know alcohol loosens the tongue."

"I don't suppose Levy gave a description of the guy in the bar."

"No, but at least he reported it when he realized his mistake."

"I'll let Detective Rook know what you've told me."

"I already talked to him, since this involves both of our departments. Cait, I'm thinking about coming out there."

She hesitated, not wanting to hurt him. "Please wait to see if anything comes from this. You're my only contact there. Rook will have cops here during the festival. My concern is Actors' Equity coming down on me again. Last time there was trouble, they threatened to remove their actors from what they considered a dangerous environment for them to work in."

His face serious, Shep touched his finger to the screen. "Okay, but leave this thing on so we can stay in touch. I'll catch a flight if you need me. Be safe."

The window faded, as did her hopes of a festival without danger.

CHAPTER 6

The Wednesday morning sun streamed through the bedroom windows. Cait hadn't slept well, unable to shake off thoughts about the knife—like a bad dream.

The Bening Estate was her home now, and she would protect it the only way she knew how: using her training as a police officer. She would not become an easy target for the person behind the phone calls and the attempted break-in. She would carry on with her routine but would have her gun and cell phone with her at all times.

She was up and out of the shower by seven. As soon as she got downstairs, the landline rang. Marcus wasn't around so she picked it up. "Bening Estate."

Heavy breathing came through the phone.

Cait slammed the receiver down, rubbing her left ear as if his breath had touched it.

She opened the refrigerator to study its contents as Marcus and the Harts walked in the back door. She took the milk out and closed the door. "Marcus, there was another crank call. We may have to change the number, but for now the phone company can set up Call Trace to track down the calls. If you enter star-fifty-seven on the phone, the call is automatically traced, but it only works within the local service area." She reached for the box of cereal and a bowl.

Marcus ran his finger around the collar of his sports shirt as if it were too tight. "Then what happens?"

"Any information collected is turned over to the police," Cait said. "Problem is, if the caller uses a phone booth or one of those toss-away phones, the police may not get enough information to take action on. The other option would be to change the number."

"Did the caller say anything this time?" Jim asked.

"No, just more heavy breathing." She opened a drawer for a spoon and then pulled out a stool and perched on its edge.

"Why not change the number now?" Jim asked.

"Because it's the number for the festival reservations." She looked at Marcus. "I'm hoping whoever's calling will give up, but you might want to start making a record of all calls. I'd hate to have to change the number during the festival." She started eating. "The same goes for my cell phone." She sighed. "To be on the safe side, keep your phones with you and turned on. I'll tell Ilia and Fumié when they get here. The last thing I want is for any of you to get hurt because of me."

"You said Royal Tanner used to walk the grounds every evening when he was here," Jim said. "I'll do the same. I have a gun, and I won't hesitate to use it."

"Jim, you're retired. That's expecting a lot . . ."

"Nonsense. I worked many years in the world of art recovery. I'm not a novice at skullduggery business. I know which end of a gun to point." A grin broke across his face. "Besides, I've always had a zest for adventure. That's why I got into the business I did."

Cait's heart swelled with affection for this kind, gentle man. She stood and gave him a hug. "Thank you."

"I forgot," Marcus said. "Ray and Jay Stoltz are waiting to get in the Elizabethan theater. I'm surprised Ray's not pounding on this door."

"He can rant and rave all he wants. I thought he was coming Thursday. I planned on a walk-through today."

Marcus dragged his hand through his spiked hair. "Must have changed his mind. I thought I should wait to let them in until you came downstairs."

"I'll go while you call the phone service about Call Trace. I could use a little fun with Ray Stoltz."

"We'll go with you," June said, "in case we need to tear you two apart."

They located Ray leaning against the white plaster and dark-timbered theater. Instead of barking at Cait for keeping him waiting, he bowed, sweeping his hand in front of him in a swashbuckling manner. "Nice to see you again, Cait. Not expecting trouble this weekend, are you?"

Cait smiled at the gesture, so out of character for brawny Ray Stoltz. "Now why would you think that?"

He shrugged and looked down at her from his six-three height. "Just sayin', but you have to admit trouble follows you."

Unfortunately, that's too true. "You're a day early."

"I'm a busy man. Two plays running simultaneously this weekend means extra work. Let's see what needs fixing to keep the actors happy. Happy actors make good performances, something I'm sure you're interested in. Working with cranky directors isn't easy either, nor the costume designers, scenic designers, lighting staff—"

"I got the message, Ray." She disarmed the theater and held the door open. "Let me know if you need anything."

"I promised Tasha everything would run slick as grease. The same goes for you." His eyes shifted to June and Jim. "Who are these people?"

June poked a finger at Ray. "Put your glasses on, Ray Stoltz. I can be your worst nightmare, so show a little respect for your elders. Maybe you don't recognize me when I'm not wearing a wig and layers of gowns at the Oregon Shakespeare Festival."

Ray's brow arched over a wicked smile as he looked down at

June. "Oh, yeah. Knew you looked familiar. What I remember most about you and those other actors who retired from being on stage to work behind the curtains is how you loved to boss everyone around." He rubbed the stubble on his chin. "So what are you doing here at Cait's festival?"

Cait suppressed a grin. *Oh man. They're on a crash course already.*

June slipped her arm through Jim's. "This is my husband, Jim. We're here to help Cait with the festival. Since Tasha and I had been friends forever, I thought it would be fun to work at her festival. So you be nice to Cait, or you'll have me to answer to."

Jim looked at Cait. "You obviously know this character."

"Of course," Cait said. "Ray mistook me for one of his hired hands when we met," she said as she punched the code on the security panel. "What can we do to help, Ray? Follow you around like minions while you check for shoddy housekeeping?"

"Hey, bro," a familiar voice said from behind Cait.

Cait turned and saw Jay, Ray's brother. "Hi, Jay."

"You ready for the weekend, Cait?"

"Depends on your brother."

Jay glanced at Ray. "Want me to bring the boxes in from the van?"

"Yeah, go ahead." Ray raised his eyebrow at Cait. "No surprises like last time, I hope."

Cait assumed he was referring to a shotgun that was missing from one of the props trunks. She considered telling Ray about the attempted break-in at the house and the phone calls, but wanted to get the walk-through over with first. She shielded her eyes from the sun and looked out over the 250 seats in the outdoor theater, and she prayed that rain had ended for the summer.

She turned to the Harts. "Let's go in the back." She ran up the short flight of stairs and onto the stage, pushed the red velvet curtain aside, and entered the green room. The room had been set up with two dark brown leather sofas for the actors, so they could relax and watch the monitor mounted on the wall for their cue to go on stage. Adjacent to the room were the wig and makeup room, costume room, dressing rooms, and props room.

"Bro," Ray said, "before you get the boxes, go up to the loft and see what shape the gobos and gels are in. The actor who plays Hamlet can be difficult to satisfy. If he doesn't like a particular design covering the stage floor or the colors splashed across the costumes, I'll hear about it. Some may have to be replaced." He turned to June. "If you're willing to work, check the wig and costume rooms, something you're most familiar with. A couple of wheels fell off one of the rolling clothes racks at the Blackfriars theater during rehearsal for *Tongue of a Bird*. It crashed, bringing down costumes and tearing some. Make sure that won't happen again."

June raised her eyebrow. "Am I supposed to repair broken wheels?"

Cait bit the inside of her cheek to keep from laughing.

Ray ignored June and looked at Cait. "Come with me." His cell phone rang.

When Ray stepped away to answer, June winked at Cait. "Ray's a teddy bear under all that tough exterior," she said. "I know our Hamlet, Chip Fallon. He can be difficult and is a perfectionist, but I admire him and so did Tasha. He adored her. I'm sure he signed on to play the role as a favor to her. He studied at the American Conservatory Theater in San Francisco, one of the best acting schools in the country. I'll introduce you when he gets here."

"I feel useless," Jim said. "It makes more sense for me to help

Marcus with the picnic tables. They're almost ready to set up in the shade of the old oak trees. You need anything, call."

Cait followed Ray around the green room while June looked into the costume room. In spite of his sometimes-tempestuous disposition, she liked him. She liked his attention to detail as he examined the fire extinguisher, the first-aid kit, the large white-board and accompanying pens, and his concern for the actors' safety.

"Do you have plenty of bottled water?" he asked.

She pointed to a closet next to the half-sized refrigerator. "In there."

"Coffee?"

"In the closet."

Ray kneeled to examine a cord running across the floor when a loud thump came from overhead.

Cait glanced at the stairs to the loft. "Maybe we should check on Jay."

"He's a big boy. If he needs help, he'll holler. Lots of boxes are stored up there. Maybe he tripped over one."

"I don't know what all is up there since I've only been up a couple of times," she said. "I donated some of Tasha's old costumes to the festival. They're hanging in clothes bags in the loft. It would be nice if they could be used."

Ray rose and looked at Cait with compassion in his eyes, something she rarely saw from him. She wasn't sure how to react. *He may not be a teddy bear like June said, but he sure had a soft spot for Tasha.*

He turned his back on her, as if embarrassed. "I appreciate you didn't toss her costumes out. Most of what's up there are souvenirs from the theater she collected over the years, things that had special meaning to her—a dress form, medieval weapons, pieces of scenery, and an old Singer sewing machine

Tasha actually used. Jay's used it, too, to repair costumes. Damn lucky none of it was burned when some idiot set fire to the theater a few months ago."

"You must have known Tasha pretty well."

"Yeah, a long time."

"I'm going up there," she said, just as Jay tromped down the stairs.

Jay swiped his dusty hands along the sides of his jeans. "Gobos and gels look okay. Not sure what's with that box of weapons though. Tape's been ripped off and the lid partially opened." He looked at Cait. "Hard to tell if anything's missing."

"Hey, don't look at me," she said, as a prickling sensation spread across her brow. "I haven't been messing around up there."

"Damn!" Ray said. "It's always something!"

June came out of the wig room. "What's all the commotion?"

"Tampering in the loft," Ray said, "that's what."

"You don't know that," Cait said, thinking he might not be too far off the mark. "Maybe the trunk was moved to avoid someone falling over it."

Ray looked at his brother. "Was the packing slip still in the box? Use that to see if anything's missing."

"No packing slip. I looked," Jay said.

Packing slip? Cait thought. *If the halberd wasn't from Tasha's collection of old weapons, where was it from?*

Ray drew a handkerchief from a pocket in his jeans and blew his nose. "As usual, we'll find out what's missing when it's needed." He glanced around the room. "Okay, bring in the boxes from the van."

June rolled her eyes and slipped back into the wig room.

Cait was left standing alone in the green room, not sure what she should do, when her cell phone rang. She unclipped it from her waist and glanced at the screen. "Sam?" she answered.

"Oh, Cait? You're okay?"

Samantha Barnet, an ER doctor, never called during the day while she was working. Cait longed for a heart-to-heart talk with her best friend in Ohio. She visualized Sam frowning over her wire-rimmed glasses, which made her look bookish. "I'm fine. Why wouldn't I be?"

"You won't believe this, but Penny was just here."

Penny, a reporter for the *Columbus Dispatch,* was one of their friends. "Is she okay?"

"Yes, but . . . Cait, you know she sometimes writes obits for the paper?"

Cait sat down on one of the sofas. "I remember. She hates it."

"Right. Uh . . . prepare yourself. She received a call to write an obit about . . . oh, God . . . I can't even say it."

"Sam, just tell me."

"Your obit."

Cait almost dropped the phone. "What?"

"Someone called in wanting to place an obituary in the paper about your death. Obituaries are only accepted from funeral homes or customers with verification of death. When Penny tried to explain this to the man, he hung up. She was too shaken to call you herself, and came here to see if I'd heard from you recently. What a cruel joke. Any idea who would do such a thing?"

Oh, yeah. "Sam, remember the time I shot a bank robber to save another officer's life?"

"Of course, a couple of years ago," Sam said. "You were miserable afterwards."

"I was. Apparently, someone's looking to avenge the shooting." She explained about the attempted break-in, the calls, and the knife with the initials etched on the blade.

"My God, Cait. I'm sorry. Does Shep know?"

"Yes. And we've both talked with the detective here."

"Sorry. Gotta go. I'm being paged," Sam said. "But there's something else you should know. When Penny tried calling the phone number back, she noticed the call came from the same area code as yours. It rang and rang but no one answered. Cait! He's in Livermore! Promise you'll be careful."

"I promise." Cait looked over her shoulder as if expecting to see someone with a gun aimed at her back. "Doesn't surprise me the call came from here. Thanks for letting me know. Now go tend to your patients, Sam. I'll be in touch soon."

June walked into the room as Cait finished the call. "The look on your face tells me something happened."

Cait nodded. "Someone tried to put a nail in my coffin. Literally."

CHAPTER 7

"Seize on him, Furies, take him unto torment," June said on their way back to the house.

Cait shook her head. "You got me with that one."

"I can't help myself. *Tragedy of King Richard III*. Richard's brother, the Duke of Clarence, says that to a jailer in the Tower of London. It relates to a dream in which he drowns, goes to hell, and meets the spirits of those he murdered or betrayed in life." She smiled. "That tragedy wouldn't happen to be on the festival's agenda, would it?"

"No, but maybe it should be."

"Seriously, Cait, if you need to go to the grocery store, take Jim. Two guns are better than one. You have to protect yourself, not the whole world."

"I know how to protect myself, but I also have a festival to run, a vineyard to tend to, and a class to learn how to manage it. Which reminds me, I have a class tonight."

"Cancel it."

Cait smiled. "I want to go. Before RT left, he arranged for a temporary manager to care for the vineyard. If RT comes back, I want him to know I'm making an effort to learn the wine industry, one class at a time. Tasha and Hilton and RT's parents were friends. I don't want to disappoint anyone by neglecting the vineyard."

"Do it for yourself then, not to please others. What's this class about?"

"How to operate a vineyard—viticulture practices for spring and summer, pest control, soils, irrigation practices, and a whole lot more. I'm actually enjoying it, but sometimes it's hard to concentrate while the festival's going on."

June touched Cait's arm. "Jim's secret passion is to learn the wine industry. That's why you'll sometimes find him in the vineyard talking to Kurt Mathews. Maybe he should go to class with you. I'm going to check on the guys to see how they're coming along with the picnic tables."

Cait watched June until she disappeared inside the garage where the guys were working. When she entered the house, she heard faint noises from the gift shop and tiptoed down the hall and peeked around the doorframe.

Fumié stood on a small step stool with a dust cloth and was rearranging plaster busts of Shakespeare on the shelf. She didn't see Cait until she stepped down. "Oh, hi. I hope you don't mind, but I thought the shelves could use a little reorganizing. Marcus let me in."

"No problem. There's something I want to talk to you and Ilia about."

Fumié brushed her hands off. "I hope I'm not in trouble. I'd work for free just to be part of the festival."

Cait looked at Fumié's shiny black hair, her sparkling dark eyes, and porcelain skin and wondered if she would lose her after she told her about the phone calls and the break-in attempt, but Cait knew she needed to warn Fumié to stay alert in case of serious trouble. "It's nothing like that. Is Ilia around?"

"Yes. He's taking pictures for his new book."

"Great. Let's go in the kitchen. I'll call him."

Ilia was peeking in the door window when they walked into the kitchen. Cait opened the door. "I was going to call you. Pull out a stool. I need to talk to both of you." She took three Cokes from the refrigerator and passed them out. "Someone tried to break in Monday night."

Fumié gasped.

Cait told them about the alarm, halberd, knife, and the significance of the initials on the blade. "There've been phone calls and hang-ups. I want you to keep your phones on when you're here in case there's an emergency."

"My camera is always with me," Ilia said. "I can take pictures if I see anything suspicious."

"Just be careful."

"I grew up on a ranch," Fumié said. "My dad taught me to shoot when I was twelve. I could borrow one of his guns."

Cait smiled. "That won't be necessary, but it may be useful when you become a park ranger. This may go no further than annoying phone calls, but you need to be careful and alert. Detective Rook will have security here this weekend." She pulled the tab on her Coke and sipped from the can. "Jim Hart and I will also be armed."

"I know how to shoot," Marcus said from the office doorway.

Cait hadn't heard him come in through his office door. "You're on probation." The crestfallen look on his face almost broke her heart. Marcus had served time for burglary before Tasha hired him as her administrative assistant. It had taken Cait awhile to bond with him, but now she would trust him with her life. "I need you to make yourself available to the actors and those attending the plays. That's a huge responsibility."

He nodded. "You shouldn't go to that class tonight."

"I have a business to run, and I can't do it if I don't know how. It will be okay."

"I could take you and wait for you."

Cait thought Marcus worried too much about her. "Thanks, but that won't be necessary." She took a long swallow of her Coke. "Want to walk through the vineyard with me?" She'd been thinking of asking him if he was interested in taking viticulture classes at the local college.

"Sure," he said.

She opened the door then hesitated. "Ilia, I know someone who would be happy to let you take pictures of his horse to use in your book."

Ilia looked confused, then grinned. "Sure. Anyone I know?"

Cait tipped her head at Marcus. "He keeps his horse at the ranch."

"Now why didn't I think of that," Ilia said.

"That was cool," Marcus said when they were outside, "what you said back there."

"You can thank me when his book comes out," she said.

A rush of Spanish greeted them when they reached the front of the house. Trailers were hitched to trucks parked in the driveway, while workers filled burlap bags scattered about the driveway and at the ends of several rows in the vineyard.

"Hey, Ms. Pepper," a man called to her.

Cait held her hand up to shield her eyes from the sun. Kurt Mathews, the temporary manager RT arranged to help with the vineyard, caught up with her. "Hi. How's the vineyard looking?"

"Good. We finished the suckering."

She smiled. "Someday I'll know what that means."

He pushed his ball cap up on his head. "Sorry, ma'am. That's the removal of shoots that originate on the trunk of the vine and below the ground. They diminish the vigor of the trained position of the vines."

Oh, boy. "Thanks, but no need to apologize, Kurt. And please call me Cait."

He smiled. "You'll only learn if you ask. To prevent mildew we need to keep up the spray schedule to dust the vines with sulfur about every ten to fourteen days. I can get you a copy of the schedule if you'd like."

She sensed uneasiness between Marcus and Kurt, but couldn't put her finger on the problem. "I would, thanks. RT did say something about mildew, but I didn't understand it."

"Any grower who neglects a spray schedule will pay dearly. The vines will be stunted in growth, the flowers may not go to berries, or the berries will be damaged. Good berries make good wine."

"Then I better let you get back to business while I study for my viticulture and winery technology class tonight." She turned away, then over her shoulder asked, "You wouldn't be interested in a full-time job would you, Kurt?"

Kurt's eyes flicked on Marcus. "Depends. We can talk about that later."

As they wound their way in and out of rows where the workers weren't working, Cait said, "RT said you knew Kurt."

"Yeah, a long time ago," Marcus said.

"Were you in school together?"

"Livermore High until I dropped out my junior year. Kurt was part of the *in* crowd." He started to walk away. "I better get to work on the picnic tables. Jim'll be wondering where I am."

Cait watched him go, shoulders drooped, head down.

Ilia and Fumié were gone when Cait entered the house. She left her unfinished Coke on the counter and looked into the fridge: black olives, sliced cheese and ham, and crackers looked good. She prepared a tray and took it upstairs to the apartment where she settled on the lounge in the bay window and opened her book on viticulture to look up the term "suckering."

Several chapters later, her eyes closed and the book slipped from her hand. She slept for two hours until the muscles in her neck cramped. She sat up and checked her cell as she picked up the book and discovered it was already after four-thirty.

"I'm going to be late," she mumbled. She ran to the bathroom. Minutes later, she grabbed a jacket, her shoulder bag, book, and keys, and hurried downstairs. She left a light on in the kitchen, went out the door, and around to the garage, where she found Jim and Marcus staining a picnic table. "I'm late for class." She opened the middle garage door, jumped in her Saab, and backed out, careful not to bump Marcus's Jag.

Traffic was heavier than usual as she crossed the overpass to the north side of Livermore. She had to drive around a couple of times until she found a parking space. She hurried into class and found a seat at the back just as the instructor began his lecture.

Cait focused her attention on the instructor and not on the knuckle-cracking guy sitting next to her. She concentrated hard to absorb everything that he presented. She wrote in her notebook and used her yellow highlighter to mark specific words and phrases in her book. They took a fifteen-minute break, and when she returned to the classroom, the knuckle guy was gone. She looked around at the rest of the students in the room and was surprised to see how many were her age or older.

Class ended at seven. Cait dropped her books into her shoulder bag, found her keys, and slipped out of the room ahead of the rest of the students. The sun wasn't as bright as when she got to class. A couple with their arms around each other walked ahead of her. Their voices drifted back to her in the breeze. Keys clutched in her hand, she looked about as she picked up the pace, anxious to get inside her car. The lot was full; the cars cast shadows down each row. She wove between the cars until she found the row where she'd parked her car.

Over her right shoulder she heard the sound of a car braking as if to make a sharp turn. Her attention had been on finding her car, but she whipped her head around to see a pickup coming toward her at a ridiculous speed.

She threw herself against the car parked next to hers seconds before the speeding pickup flew by, missing Cait by inches.

The couple who had been walking ahead of her ran over. "Are you all right?" the guy asked. "Are you hurt?"

Shaking uncontrollably, she felt her shoulder bag slip to the ground.

"I'm fine," she said, as she gathered her belongings. "That pickup must have been out of control."

"Looked to me like he meant to hit you," the man said. "He was headed right at you." He pulled out his cell phone. "Want me to call the police?"

"No, whoever it was is long gone. Did you happen to see the license plate?"

"Sorry, it happened so fast."

"It was black, a Ford I think," the girl said, "with those big tires."

Cait thanked them and unlocked her car and got in. She waited a few moments to settle down before starting the car. She wanted to believe it was an accident, a student in a hurry to leave, but couldn't help wondering who was behind the wheel.

CHAPTER 8

The next morning, Cait flashed back on the parking lot incident and what Sam told her about the obituary, and then called Detective Rook. "There was an incident last night you should know about," she said when he answered.

"At the house?"

"No, at school. Someone tried to run me over in the parking lot."

"I didn't get a message. Did you call it in?"

"No. Why bother? He was long gone. I didn't get a plate number but it was a black pickup, maybe a Ford."

"If this harassment continues, I'll have to put you in protective custody."

"Very funny."

"We can only speculate at this point, Cait, you know that. But let's assume it was Wally Dillon, Hank's brother. The next time he might not miss, whether his choice of weapon is a car, a gun, or whatever. You should consider dropping out of class until he's caught."

Cait's anger boiled in the pit of her stomach. "Not going to happen. I might go back to the school and explain why I need to carry a gun to class."

"You can't carry a gun within a hundred feet of a school."

She sighed. "I know. What was I thinking? I'm going out to the ranch and spend the afternoon with Bo Tuck and his family. I need to get away from this house, the theaters, and . . .

58

everything. You can call Marcus if you need anything."

"Do they know what's going on?"

"Of course. Well, except for last night. Everyone needs to know so they can protect themselves." Then she remembered the obituary. "There's something else."

"What?"

"My obituary."

"Your what?"

"It's good to have friends in all the right places, Detective. Someone tried to put my obituary in the *Columbus Dispatch*. He couldn't because he didn't have authorization. That doesn't mean he won't try elsewhere."

"Jesus! Did this friend of yours get a phone number?"

"Yes, and when she tried calling no one answered. It was a local call."

"You mean Livermore?"

"That's right, the same nine-two-five area code."

"That's two more reasons to increase your security. Have you talked with Detective Church?"

"Not today. I'll call him."

"You do that. In the meantime, I haven't been on a horse in awhile. I could change into jeans and pick you up in twenty minutes."

His pretense didn't fool her. She didn't want a bodyguard at the ranch, but she liked Rook and didn't want to insult him. "You're welcome to come along only if you promise not to tell Bo what's going on. Their daughter Joy is exceptionally smart for a ten-year-old. She'd pick up immediately that there's a problem."

"You don't think Bo deserves to know you're being stalked? What if someone follows you to the ranch?"

She hesitated. *Am I being selfish? The ranch is the only place I can go to relieve the tension I'm under.*

"They've been through a lot with Tasha and Hilton's death. I'd rather not burden them with my problems, but if the moment's right, I'll tell them. I'll make sure I'm not being followed. Will that satisfy you?"

"Okay, but I better not hear you had a riding accident."

Despite what she told Rook, Cait wasn't going to the Bening ranch to ride. All she wanted was a little time away from the house, a nice visit with Bo and his family, and to see Hilton's beautiful horse, Faro.

With a heavy heart, Cait checked the rearview mirror before turning onto Mines Road. The last thing she wanted was to bring trouble to the ranch, but the comfort and pleasure she always felt there outweighed any fear she might have of being hurt by Wally Dillon or whoever was stalking her. She had her Glock, and Bo had his rifle. If there was trouble, she was confident they could handle it.

It was a weekday and traffic was light, but she kept her eyes on the mirrors for a black pickup. She hadn't gone far when she slowed and pulled onto a dirt road, where she soon encountered a flock of turkeys. She remembered RT telling her about Murrieta's Well winery. Since it was on her way to the ranch, she decided to buy a bottle of wine to take to Bo. After a short distance, she exited from a clump of trees and saw a beautiful barn. Its exterior concrete exposed patches of creek stones in myriad colors. It was built into the hillside adjacent to the property's well, where Joaquin Murrieta, the famous Gold Rush–era bandit, watered his band of wild mustangs.

Sun sparkled over the grapevines and shiny foil strips blowing in the breeze. Cait parked in front of the old stone building, stepped out of her Saab, and paused to admire the early California architecture. She turned her face up to the sun and inhaled the scent of roses mixed with the slightly dusty summer breeze.

As she mounted the staircase adorned with Mexican tiles and entered the high-ceilinged tasting room, she wondered if the Tucks preferred red or white wine.

The man behind the bar pointed to opened bottles. "Would you like to taste one of our wines?"

"Not today, thanks. But if you could suggest something for a gift, that would be helpful. I'm guessing a red, but I have no idea what their preference is."

"Glad to." He held up a bottle to show her. "Murrieta's Well produces a great red, or if you prefer, Meritage, our white blend of bordeaux varietals, which has aromas of blackberry and blueberry with hints of well-integrated oak. Do you think your friends might enjoy something like that?"

Cait laughed, not being a wine connoisseur. "I've no idea, but I'll take it."

"Will there be anything else?"

"No, that will do." She pulled out her credit card and handed it to him.

He glanced at the card, then at Cait. "Are you a club member?"

Confused, she asked, "Club?"

"Our wine enthusiasts."

"Oh, no. Sorry."

He rang up the sale and returned her card, along with the packaged bottle. "Hope your friends enjoy it."

She smiled. "I'm sure they will. Thanks."

Cait left the winery and continued out Mines Road for about three miles. When she reached the tall arch with BENING RANCH and a horse emblazoned in cast iron across the top, she pulled in and drove slowly to keep dust from rising on the dirt and gravel lane. Pristine white fencing lined the left side of the lane and eucalyptus trees the right. When she reached the red barn, she parked off to the side next to a dusty white trailer with a horse's head decal on the side.

Cait stepped out of her car and gazed out over the ranch that had been Hilton's until his death. The ranch wasn't part of Cait's inheritance; it was part of the Hilton family's trust that couldn't be sold. Hilton had left it to his veterinarian, Bo Tuck, to live in with his family as long as he wished.

Bo appeared from the side of the barn, dressed in jeans and a blue denim shirt with the sleeves rolled up. His black Stetson shielded his eyes from the sun, and his smile was broad. "Hey, stranger," he said. "I thought you'd forgotten about us."

"Never, Bo. How have you been?"

"Just dandy." He walked over to her car. "Looks like you got yourself some new wheels."

She grinned. "I'm not the Jaguar type. Marcus appreciated it more than I did, so I turned it over to him."

"He told me." He pushed his Stetson back. "Joy's got a horse picked out for you when you're ready to ride."

"I don't know, Bo. I'm a city gal. I'm here today to get away for awhile and to see you and your family. I don't mean to interfere with your busy day, so I'll just wander about and visit Faro, if that's okay." She reached in her car's open door for the bottle of wine. "Brought you something." She handed it to him.

He took it out of the sack and glanced at the label. "Ah. Murietta's Well. I haven't tried their Meritage. Thanks, but you didn't have to do that. You know you're welcome here any time."

She nodded. "I know." She'd come to love the Tucks, the quiet, and the peaceful wide-open spaces of the ranch. And Faro.

Bo draped his arm over her shoulder. "Something bothering you, Cait?"

Pulled back from her thoughts, she shook her head. "No. Just wondering why I waited so long to come."

"Then let's go on up to the house before the family tans my hide for keeping you to myself."

They rounded the barn and crossed the footbridge over the dry creek bed. She loved the house Hilton built and how it backed up to a hill. It looked more like a small lodge, with its pencil-reed balcony across the front. "What a great place, Bo. You're so lucky to live here."

"Don't think I don't know it. Hilton was a generous man." He held the screen door open for her.

The house, with the rustic feel of its interior—knotty pine tongue-and-groove floors, cathedral ceiling, and immense soot-blackened fireplace—was the warmest and most welcoming home she'd ever been in. The spectacular view of the hills and pasture through the tall windows filled Cait with a peacefulness she was missing at her own house. Not that the hilltop estate wasn't lovely, but the constant threat of danger surrounding it made it difficult for her to relax and enjoy it.

"Cait, have a seat. I'll get the family," Bo said.

Cait preferred to walk around the cozy room. She went over to their upright piano to look at the photos of Joy straddling her horse's back, jumping barriers, and accepting trophy ribbons before her accident.

A soft whooshing sound caught her attention. She turned and smiled as Joy rolled into the room. With her tousled smoky black hair and crackling deep-set violet eyes, she was a vision of beauty at ten years of age.

"Cait! You're here!"

"I missed you, Joy." She knelt in front of the girl. "How are you?"

"Super. You want to ride? I picked a horse gentle enough not to scare you."

The time has come, Cait thought. She couldn't bear the

thought of disappointing Joy again. She liked horses, from a distance. She glanced up at Bo.

He shrugged. "Up to you."

"What is?" Khandi, Bo's wife, walked into the room. She wore her tight jeans with a soft pink low-cut T-shirt that accentuated her trim figure and soft cocoa complexion. Her long sable hair flowed down her back. She gave Cait a hug. "Are they ganging up on you already?"

Cait rose. "Yes, and I'm weakening." *Maybe, if I concentrate hard enough on staying on the horse, I'll forget about the bad stuff going on in my life and have fun for a change.*

Joy grinned from ear to ear. "You mean it? What are we waiting for? Let's go."

Bo looked at Cait, his eyebrow raised. "Should we go see your horse?"

Cait nodded, glad she'd worn jeans. "What have I got to lose but my pride?"

"Yippee!" Joy shouted.

Bo pushed Joy's wheelchair down the ramp and across the footbridge while Cait and Khandi talked about Faro.

As they approached the barn, Cait remembered her gun was in the car. "I need to get something from my car. I'll catch up with you."

"We'll be out behind the barn," Bo said. "Your horse is there."

Oh, man, I hope I don't embarrass myself too much. She opened the passenger door and reached into her shoulder bag. Before taking the gun out, she looked around to make sure she hadn't been followed, then she backed out of the car and nestled the Glock at the small of her back. She pulled her red plaid shirt down to cover it, then reached back into her bag and grabbed a package of black licorice that Joy loved.

Cait met up with the Tucks and received a huge smile from Joy when she gave her the licorice. To delay the agony of climbing on a horse, she asked, "Can I see Faro first?"

"Sure," Bo said. "He's out this way."

Behind the barn and Bo's clinic, Cait admired the fenced fields, a small group of paddocks, and a couple of wooly llamas. A pair of golden retrievers barked and danced around Cait's legs.

When she first met Faro, he wouldn't venture close enough for her to see his silky bay color and sleek, long extended neck. The last time she was there, he came closer to the fence, as if he was beginning to trust her. Today, he stood at the railing as if expecting them, a compact horse with massive muscles and big liquid eyes bright with curiosity.

Bo slipped Cait a butter mint. When she offered it to the horse, it quickly disappeared.

"He's beautiful," she said.

"Yes he is. Hilton always had quarter horses on his ranch in Colorado. Said they could work cattle almost on their own." He chuckled. "He liked to say they could turn on a dime and toss you back nine cents change. Ready to meet your horse?"

"Sure. Let's do it," she said.

"There she is." Joy pointed to a small paddock where a lone horse gazed out at them.

The closer Cait got to the paddock, the larger the horse appeared. Nonetheless, she was determined to do this—to avoid appearing wimpy, but mostly to please Joy. Maybe she'd even like it. There weren't many things she feared—two were tight places and animals bigger than she.

"Isn't she beautiful, Cait?" Joy said.

Cait nodded. "Very. Big, too," she said.

"She's a paint horse," Bo said. "A sweet, gentle mare, well trained, and great for the beginner or intermediate rider. She's five years old."

Cait eased closer to the fence, her eye on the horse with its large patches of brown and white. "What's her name?"

"Peaches," Joy said. "Don't worry, Cait. She loves to be on the trail and takes care of her rider. And she loves attention."

Bo opened the gate. "Ready?"

"I'll get my saddle for Cait," Khandi said.

Bo handed Cait a butter mint to offer the horse. It disappeared quickly.

Khandi returned carrying a brown leather saddle and tossed it onto Peaches's back.

Bo secured the straps and stirrups. "Okay, Cait." He helped her place her left foot in the stirrup and then told her to swing her right leg up and over the horse. "I'll walk you over to the ring. When you're feeling comfortable on the horse, we'll take to the trail."

"You'll stay with me?" she asked, sitting rigid in the saddle.

"Yep. Right along beside you." He handed her the reins and explained what to do to get the horse moving and how to stop her. "Nice and easy."

Cait glanced over at Joy, who stuck a piece of licorice in her mouth and flashed her a thumbs up. She relaxed and was surprised to learn she enjoyed being on the horse. After several turns around the ring, she was brave enough to break into a trot.

Joy and Khandi applauded from the sideline. "Ready to try the trail?" Bo asked.

"I guess so."

He motioned Khandi over. "Wait with Cait while I get my horse."

"Looking good up there, Cait," Khandi said. "How does it feel?"

"Surprisingly comfortable. I might even learn to like this."

"Peaches is a nice horse. No bad habits or vices."

Cait heard commotion from the barn and turned to see Bo

trotting toward her on a familiar black horse.

Bo reined his horse close to Cait. "Remember Cash from the last time you were here?"

"I sure do. He's beautiful," she said. "Not quite as scary looking as when I first saw him."

Bo laughed. "That's because you were clinging to the fence; now we're sitting even. Ready?"

Khandi backed away. "Relax and have fun, Cait."

Bo stayed beside Cait as they left the ring. "Just do what you were doing in the ring and you'll be fine. We'll pick up the trail behind the house."

Cait trotted along with Bo, feeling more excited than scared. *What would RT think if he saw me now?*

"Doing okay?" Bo asked.

Cait slipped her sunglasses down from the top of her head to shield her eyes from the intense sun. "This is fun. Thank you for giving me this opportunity to ride."

He smiled. "My pleasure."

They crossed the bridge over the creek and went around the right side of the house. Cait kept her eyes straight ahead, her hands tight on the reins.

Bo pointed. "That wooded area ahead is where the trail begins."

The dogs followed but dropped behind as they approached the trail.

They rode slowly and aimlessly along the narrow trail that led through the middle of a large dense growth of trees.

Cait grew anxious. The farther they rode, the more the trail looked familiar. "Bo, isn't this where Hilton fell?"

He looked at her and nodded. "Yes. I wondered if you'd remember."

She sat up higher in the seat and looked around, as if expecting someone to charge them from the trees.

They sat side by side on their horses for a few minutes, remembering Hilton. Bo spoke first. "Something you should see up ahead."

As they rode, the horses kicked up dust on the trail. Bo pulled his horse to a stop and jumped down.

As Bo helped Cait down, her foot caught in the stirrup and she began to fall. Her shirt rode above her waist, her gun in full view.

Bo frowned. "Why are you carrying a gun?"

She froze for a second, embarrassed. "I promised Detective Rook I would bring it with me." She sighed and looked off into the trees. "I didn't mean to involve you and your family, Bo, but someone's stalking me."

He kicked the dirt with the toe of his boot. "Well, damn, Cait. Any idea who it is?"

"Maybe. It goes back a couple of years when I was a cop. Bo, I was careful coming out here. I made sure no one followed me. Can we leave it at that? At least for now?"

He removed his Stetson and slapped it against his leg. "Can't do that. You're like family. But first, come over here. I want to show you something." He directed her to one side of the trail and stooped in front of a large rock at the base of an old oak tree barren of leaves. "This is why I brought you here."

At first, Cait thought it was just a rock with a little moss, but when she looked closer she saw engraving on it and realized what she was looking at. She kneeled beside Bo, suddenly overcome with emotion for a man she'd only heard about. "How lovely, a memorial for Hilton," she said softly.

"Yes. Joy asked us to place a marker where Hilton fell. She wanted a rock engraved with a cowboy hat, his initials, and the date he died." He looked at Cait and smiled. "She got her wish."

"Your daughter is uncannily wise for her age." She ran her finger over the engraving and wondered if Tasha had done the same thing, but hesitated to ask.

"He was like a grandfather to Joy," he said as he stood.

Cait rose. "Thank you for bringing me here."

He put his hat on. "You're welcome. Let's head on back. You can tell me why you're being stalked and what I can do to help."

Khandi and Joy were waiting at the barn. Bo helped Cait down and then took the horses inside the barn.

"Peaches is a fine horse," Cait told Joy.

Joy grinned. "Did Daddy show you Hilton's rock?"

"He did. That was the perfect thing to do."

"I'm glad you like it. Sometimes Daddy takes me with him on his horse to visit Hilton's memorial."

"And sometimes we all ride out with a picnic basket," Khandi said.

Joy reached up and took hold of Cait's hand. "I'm glad you got to ride Peaches and see the rock."

Cait squeezed her hand and smiled. "Me, too."

"Riding makes me happy," Joy said. She tipped her head up at Cait. "I don't think the ride made you happy."

Cait stooped in front of Joy. "Why would you think that?"

"I think you're worried. Is it something you can fix?"

Cait felt a hand on her shoulder. She looked up and saw Bo. She kissed Joy's cheek. "I'm sure going to try."

Or die trying.

CHAPTER 9

Cait made the tough decision not to return to the ranch until Wally Dillon, or whoever was stalking her, was caught. The last thing she wanted was to inflict more suffering on Bo and his family.

The vineyard crew was gathering their equipment and trash bags when Cait returned to the house. The garage doors were open, and she pulled into the middle space. Marcus and Jim looked up from their work.

"Have a nice visit?" Jim asked as she stepped out.

Cait limped over to look at the bench they were staining. "It was fun. I got on a horse and rode with Bo on a trail behind their house."

A faint smile crossed Marcus's lips. "That's why you're walking funny."

Cait groaned. "You think? Don't you dare laugh." Then she remembered Marcus had his horse at the ranch. "I should have asked to see your horse while I was there."

"We'll go to the ranch together sometime and I'll introduce you to Spade."

"Did I miss anything while I was inflicting pain on my body?"

"Well, let's see. A bunch of bandits rode through searching for gold," Jim quipped, "but I told them they were a century too late." He winked.

Cait laughed.

"You looked like you could use some levity," Jim said.

That's not all I could use, she thought, thinking of a hot tub of water. "Do you know where June is?"

"Probably at the Elizabethan. Ray was looking for you, then he and June started squabbling but they left together."

"I think they enjoy provoking each other." She rubbed her lower back. "I better see what Ray wanted."

The door at the Elizabethan was open. Cait found June in the green room, her ear pressed against the wall outside the costume room. When June saw her, she put her finger to her lips.

Cait stood quietly on the other side of the doorway and listened to a man's voice reciting:

"O earth. What else?

"And shall I couple hell? O, fie! Hold, hold, my heart;

"And you, my sinews, grow not instant old,

"But bear me stiffly up. Remember thee!

"Ay, thou poor ghost, while memory holds a seat

"In this distracted globe. Remember thee!"

Cait heard heavy footsteps on the wooden floor inside the room. The door was cracked open and Cait chanced a peek inside.

A man, tall and lean with a rangy runner's body, paced about the room, head down, hands behind his back, animated by the role he was rehearsing. His head shot up; he faced a mirror.

Cait ducked back and listened to his next disjointed words:

". . . put an antic disposition on." Then, "The time is out of joint! Oh cursed spite, that ever I was born to set it right . . . Nay, come, let's go together."

The door flung open and the man stalked out and tripped over the cat.

Cait gasped. She had no idea Velcro had followed her into the theater.

June grabbed the man's arm to steady him.

71

Instead of being angry, the man reached down to pick up Velcro, but the cat scampered off. "I hope I didn't hurt him."

"He's fine," June said.

He looked up. "Mrs. Hart! What are you doing here?"

June grinned. "The same as you, Chip. I'm helping Cait with the festival." She reached out for Cait. "Chip Fallon, meet Cait Pepper, Tasha's niece."

Chip smiled and extended his hand. "It's a pleasure to meet you." His unruly sandy hair hung over his ears, giving him a deceptively youthful look. His eyes were so green, she wondered if they were contacts.

As they shook hands, Cait said, "You're our Hamlet, I hear."

"I am indeed. It's the greatest play ever written. Everyone loves a mystery. My life is on the line every time I play the part—a huge challenge, but one I welcome."

Confused, she said, "I don't understand."

He posed with his hands on his hips. "Everyone knows Hamlet's journey and ultimate fate. It's my job to bring something different to it, some new experience for the audience. I read the text many times, which is what I was doing just now, and alter the emphasis on the words."

Cait had seen the play many times, but her interest grew as she listened to Chip's deep voice as he talked about preparing for the role. She thought him to be intelligent and philosophical, the qualities of Hamlet that were part of his undoing. "I hope you don't mind that June and I were listening at the door."

He laughed. "Not if you tell me what you thought about what you heard."

"I wasn't here long, but I thought I recognized part of a conversation with Hamlet's ghost," Cait said.

Chip raised his eyebrows. "Ah, you do know Shakespeare. That's good if you're going to run this festival."

"I studied it a little in college, but Tasha would shake her head at how little I've retained. But *Hamlet* is one of my favorite plays."

"Yours and many others." Anger suddenly flashed across his face. "Tasha's death was a tragedy."

She nodded, amazed by the transformation on his face.

"I assume you and Tasha were close for her to leave you the theaters."

Cait sighed. She hated the awkward moment of admitting she'd never met Tasha. "Unfortunately, no. I never met her." *I didn't even know she existed until two months ago.*

He narrowed his eyes, as if he didn't believe her. "How is that possible?"

"It's complicated, and I'd rather not go into it." She sensed he wanted to ask why she'd never met Tasha, but was too much of a gentleman. She changed the subject. "You probably know Tasha was expected to be *Hamlet*'s associate artistic director at the Oregon Shakespeare Festival."

He nodded. "I recommended her. I cared a great deal for Tasha and her talent, and apparently she felt the same about me. She asked me to be Hamlet at her festival. I couldn't refuse."

"Do you know if her replacement's been found?"

Chip frowned, shifted his feet, and said, "No. Please excuse me. I need to rehearse before Ray Stoltz kicks me out."

Cait wondered what caused his mood change. "We'll get out of your way then."

Ilia ran over with his camera held high. "Mr. Fallon, how about a picture?"

Chip looked at Ilia as if he had horns sprouting from his head.

Cait smiled. "This is Ilia Kubiak, a professional photographer and friend. He's great at promoting the festival."

Chip's genial attitude returned. "Oh. Sure." He relaxed against the doorframe and smiled into the camera.

Ilia snapped his picture, thanked him, and left.

Chip slipped back in the room and closed the door.

On their walk to the house, Cait said to June, "Chip's an engaging man."

"He has a rare talent for mixing explosive anger with brooding charm, but everyone likes him, particularly girls." June hesitated. "But there is one exception."

"Isn't there always?"

"Chip's name was on the same short list of candidates as Tasha for that associate artistic director's job. Even though he recommended her. You noticed how quickly he changed the subject when you asked about it."

Shortly after Cait had come to California, Kenneth Alt, one of the directors at the Oregon Shakespeare Festival, had given her three names on that list, but Chip Fallon's name hadn't been one of them. "Alt didn't mention Chip."

"He wouldn't. He removed it from the list."

Cait turned to June. "Why would he do that?"

"Chip has always wanted to direct, but Kenneth doesn't like him and carries a lot of weight. Jealousy, I suppose. Both played Hamlet numerous times, and they're both great actors. Each brings something new to the role. Yet every time they're in the same room, sparks fly." Her hands flew out as if to express fiery particles in the air.

"Then I hope they never meet here."

"Amen. 'Time is the old justice that examines all such offenders.' " She smiled. *As You Like It.*

CHAPTER 10

"You had a phone call," Marcus said when Cait returned to the house. He handed her a slip of paper.

She glanced at the note. "Dawson? I don't know anyone by that name."

"Parker-Dawson vineyard," he said. He leaned against the kitchen counter. "They were here in April for the tea."

Cait marveled at Marcus's memory, but then he had grown up in Livermore and knew many of the residents. "Oh, the tea." She had vivid memories of the guests who had attended the tea—city officials and winery owners curious to see who had inherited the Bening Estate—but she couldn't put a face to every name. "I tried to memorize everyone's names and their businesses but didn't do too well."

Marcus worked his cuticles. "It was a tough time for all of us."

Yes, it was. She thought back to the tea six weeks ago. In a short speech to the guests, she'd admitted she knew a lot more about law enforcement than running a festival or growing grapes. She wanted her guests to know she was committed to carrying on with Tasha's plans for the estate.

"I suppose I'll have to continue the teas every year at the start of the festival."

He straightened up. "Only if you want to keep your promise, but it's up to you now."

Marcus's clipped tone didn't escape her. He would always be

sensitive to changes at the estate. Cait understood. He wanted to stay loyal to Tasha, not betray her wishes, even if it meant stepping on Cait's toes occasionally. But she resented being on the defensive. "Let's have breakfast tomorrow, eight o'clock. I'll let the Harts know. We're all on edge over the attempted break-in, the phone threats, and my apparent stalker. I'll ask Ray Stoltz, too. I'm sure he'll have ideas on the actors' safety."

"He always does."

Someone knocked on the door. When Cait opened it, Fumié grinned. "Hi."

"I thought you'd gone home."

"Change of plans. Ilia and I went to the cave so he could take pictures of the Native American petroglyphs."

Cait shivered at the thought of the cave on the back property and felt stirrings of claustrophobia. "Marcus is protective of the cave and the drawings on the walls."

"They already asked me," Marcus said. "I have no objection if it's okay with you."

Confused, she said, "I thought you and Fumié were concerned about the laws to protect national treasures."

Fumié shook her head. "Photographing those lovely horses, dogs, and warriors won't hurt them."

"I'm not opposed to sharing what the Ohlone Indians created, as long as the cave doesn't become a tourist attraction, but I thought that's what you were concerned about, Marcus."

He shrugged. "Not anymore."

"I'll let Ilia know." Fumié reached into her pocket for her cell and followed Marcus into his office.

Cait looked at the note Marcus had given her and called the number. "Hi, this is Cait Pepper returning your call."

"Cait. Trish Dawson. We met at your tea."

"Oh, yes. I remember."

"We're having a party at our winery Sunday. I'd like to hire the young woman who sang at the tea. I know it's the last minute, but the entertainment we had planned fell through."

Cait walked over to the office. "You can ask Fumié yourself. She's here." Cait handed her cell to Fumié. "Her name is Trish. She wants you to sing at her party."

Cait indicated for Marcus to follow her out of the office so Fumié could talk in private. "I saw a flyer about the rodeo coming to town. Will that be a problem for the festival?"

"Why would it? The rodeo doesn't start until next week, but some of the riders come early."

"You're right, it's not like we're across the street from the rodeo grounds."

"Why are you worried about the rodeo?" he asked.

"Because someone tried to run me down on the campus. Maybe it was someone from the rodeo."

Marcus stared at her, his face paler than usual. "What was he driving?"

"A black pickup," she said. "I didn't get the plate."

"Probably hundreds of those around. Did you have your gun with you?"

"No guns allowed on campus, Marcus."

"It had to be your stalker, not some guy from the rodeo. You shouldn't go to class until the jerk's caught."

Fumié returned Cait's cell phone. "Trish asked me to sing and play the guitar at her party."

Cait smiled. "Congratulations."

"But I can't, at least not now. I'm going to work in the gift shop. The more souvenirs we sell, the less we'll have to move when the new shop is built."

"Why not entertain our guests?" Marcus said.

"Good idea, Marcus." Cait looked at Fumié "How about it?"

Her eyes sparkled. "Sure. I'd like that."

"Then it's settled. Can you come for breakfast tomorrow at eight?"

Cait remembered she'd left her gun on the kitchen counter when she knocked on the Harts' door. Their RV took up a lot more space than RT's twenty-four-foot Airstream trailer.

Jim opened the door. "Thought I heard someone knocking." He helped her up. "Where's your gun?"

She felt like a kid who'd forgotten to go to school. "In the kitchen."

"Not going to do any good there if your stalker's waiting behind some bush."

"Leave her alone, Jim," June said as she set a plate of chocolate chip cookies in front of Cait. "I'll take some out to the actors later. So, you liked Chip?"

Cait bit into a cookie and then licked chocolate from her lips. "He's polite and good-looking."

"Tasha adored him and was excited when he accepted her invitation to be part of the festival."

"I can see why." Cait hesitated. "I have something to tell you. Someone tried to run me down on campus yesterday."

June's jaw dropped. "What?"

Jim frowned. "I don't suppose you had your gun with you."

Annoyance simmered just beneath the surface. Not at Jim, but at the situation. "No. Weapons aren't allowed near a school. I'm not dropping the class. I'm not putting my life on hold because someone decides to come after me for doing my job. I'll get to the bottom of this, but I'm not going to hide while I wait for the police to get him!"

June placed her hand on Cait's arm. "We understand your frustration, but no one would blame you if you went into hiding for a while."

"I never hide from a problem."

June nodded. "Okay. What are you going to do? Maybe you could sit in the audience and observe."

"I'll be on the sidelines or the back of the theater so I can move about. I want to see Chip in his role of Hamlet on Saturday, and then I'll catch *Macbeth* Sunday afternoon. I'll spend as much time as I can at both plays."

"Then I'll see *Macbeth* on Saturday and *Hamlet* on Sunday," June said. "I've been in both of them, and I'll hang out backstage with the actors." She grinned. "My voice carries. If there's a problem, I'll scream."

Cait smiled. "That will work. I'm confident my stalker is Wally Dillon, but I'm not eliminating anyone yet. What concerns me is if he disguises himself as one of the actors. The theaters have to be unlocked. Anyone could walk in." She bit into her cookie. "Marcus wants to help. He isn't exactly Delta Force, and he can't carry a weapon, but he could help guard the doors."

June nodded. "What about Calder Manning? Could he be your stalker?"

"I looked him up on the Web. He went into the police station and asked about me. He's a distinguished war correspondent and he has a young daughter. Why would he waste time on me? He could jeopardize his job. That leaves Wally."

"You're probably right, but take art theft, for example," Jim said.

When Cait thought of art thieves, she thought of Pierce Brosnan or Sean Connery.

"Why would anyone steal a painting like a Vermeer?" Jim continued. "It couldn't be sold, but it might be swapped for drugs."

Cait thought about it. "Your point?"

Jim leaned on his elbows. "You're not sure it's Wally, but in all likelihood he's involved. Maybe it's not you he's after. Is there anything of real value in the house that could be sold or traded for drugs, diamonds, or even artwork?"

She shook her head. "I haven't torn through the walls to look, but I doubt it, Jim. He's after me."

"Just trying to cover all possibilities. At least think about it."

"I will. Before I forget, you're invited to breakfast. Eight o'clock."

Marcus had left by the time Cait returned to the house. She picked up her gun from the kitchen counter and went upstairs for her shoulder bag and to call Shep.

"I was going to call you," he said.

Cait stared out the window at the golden hills. "Sam called."

"I know. She told me about the phony obituary. She's worried about you and begged me to track down the guy who called it in. He might try other newspapers, but I don't think he'd succeed, because most require confirmation of death. He's jerking your strings, Cait, to frighten you."

"He's doing a damn good job of it." She paced the bedroom, and then settled on the edge of the bed. "Did Sam tell you the call to the paper came from this area code?"

"I recognized it. If it is Wally, he's got help. If it's Calder Manning, he has the means to track you down. I hope you're keeping your gun close."

She slipped her hand in her shoulder bag and gripped the cold, hard Glock. "Of course."

"Every time you go outside?"

"You know how awkward that is? I'm careful, okay?" She closed her eyes for a moment against her frustration. "I'm sorry, Shep." She pulled a book out of her purse. "I'm taking a class at the local college."

"Make it a day class."

"I can't. I have a festival to run, and if I'm going to grow grapes, I have to know how to operate a vineyard." She smoothed her hand over the downy ivory and green duvet.

"You can't take a gun to class."

She sighed. "I know. I'm not dropping the class because of Wally Dillon or anyone else." She paused. "There was an incident last night after class."

"What happened?"

"Someone tried to run me down in the parking lot."

"Jesus, Cait. Come home. You can get your job back."

"That doesn't sound like you, Shep. Neither one of us are quitters. Besides, if I did go back I'd be right where this mess started."

"Just saying. I'll look into Wally Dillon's background and call you back."

She stood and picked up her bag. "Thanks. I'm going to the store. The cupboards are bare."

Cait checked the area before she got out of her car at Trader Joe's. The lot was crowded for a Thursday evening and she had to park farther away than she would have liked. She locked the car and hurried inside. She grabbed a handbasket and bought what she needed for tomorrow's breakfast, along with a couple of Lean Cuisine dinners and desserts.

She paid for her groceries and went outside, looking over her shoulder as she walked. Part way to her car, something made her hesitate. The skin on the back of her neck prickled, but no one was behind her—still, she sensed someone watching her. When she got closer to her car, she paused to reach into her shoulder bag as if looking for her keys. She gripped her gun, using the opportunity to glance surreptitiously at a man lighting his cigarette by the car next to hers; the rolling smoke dissipated as it rose through the early evening air.

The man looked up, made direct eye contact with her, and sauntered off. Instinctively she knew this was her stalker. But was it Wally Dillon? Average height, baseball cap, dark-skinned, wearing a black muscle T and black sweats.

She unlocked her car, got in, and released a long sigh. After another glance around the parking lot, she called Detective Rook.

He answered right away. "Detective Rook."

"It's Cait. Have you got a spare officer who wouldn't mind spending a day in the warm sun tomorrow, maybe absorb a little Shakespeare?"

"I thought you'd never ask. What happened?"

She turned the key and started the engine. "I was followed to Trader Joe's."

"Describe him."

"A black man like Hank Dillon, or he's spent a lot of time in the sun. I don't want to wait until Saturday for police protection at my house. I want it now." When Rook didn't respond, she continued. "One actor's already arrived; the rest will come tomorrow to rehearse. The theaters will be open, giving anyone ample opportunity to walk in."

"I'll have someone there in the morning. I'd like an officer with you every time you stepped out of the house, but that's not possible."

"I don't want someone with me twenty-four-seven. It would drive me nuts."

That night, Cait fell into a sound sleep until the landline rang. It was after midnight according to the luminescent dial on the alarm clock. She grabbed the receiver.

"Hello?"

When no one spoke, she knew.

"I saw you." She tried to keep her voice steady. "And one day I'll get you."

CHAPTER 11

Bright sunshine spread across Cait's face early Friday morning. She was out of bed by seven, showered, and dressed in jeans and T-shirt and downstairs twenty minutes later. By the time everyone arrived for breakfast, the aroma of cheese, peppers, and sausage omelets drifted throughout the kitchen.

Cait filled coffee mugs and set one in front of everyone gathered around the black speckled granite counter. "I dare anyone to tell me I can't cook."

"Not me. I like my job," Marcus said. "Besides, this is delicious."

"To good food and fine friends," Jim said, raising his steaming mug of coffee.

There was a loud knock on the back door.

Cait turned to look and saw Ray through the window.

Marcus got up to let him in.

Ray hesitated in the doorway. "Okay if I come in?"

Marcus moved aside to allow Ray to enter.

"The theaters are locked," he grumbled.

Cait slid off her stool. "Of course they are, Ray. I'll give you a remote for each theater so you can come and go. Just let me know when everyone leaves so I can reset the alarms. Are you hungry?"

Ray stepped into the kitchen and sniffed the air. "Do I smell sausage and peppers?"

"Yep. I'll fix you a plate."

"Can't stay," he said. "Got people waiting to get in the theaters, but I could take it with me."

"You can take some for Jay, too."

Ray stroked his chin. "If there's enough—"

"There's plenty." Cait opened a drawer and took out a couple of heavy-duty paper plates and a tray. While she prepared the plates, she was wondering whether it was time to let Ray know someone had tried to break into the house and about the halberd found outside the door. "Ray, was anything missing from those boxes in the loft, like a weapon?"

Ray scowled, his powerful arms crossed over his chest. "What do you know about that?"

"Jay said tape had been ripped off a box in the loft. I was wondering how someone would know to search the loft for a weapon."

"How the hell—uh, heck should I know? It's your theater."

Cait turned with two plates of food in her hands. "I have remotes to open the theaters." She glanced at Marcus. "Would you get one for Ray, please?"

Marcus went to the office. When he handed one to Ray, he said, "Don't leave it lying around."

Ray slipped it into his shirt pocket. "You realize, don't you, that all of us will be in and out all weekend? They shouldn't have to track me down every time they need to go inside. I want them to remain open until the last person leaves for the day."

Cait covered the plates with foil, placed them on a tray, and handed the tray to Ray. "I'm aware of that, but there's something you need to know." She told him about the break-in attempt and the halberd. "Someone is stalking me. Goes back a couple of years to the time I was a cop. I don't like it any more than you, but I'm dealing with it. My concern is keeping everyone safe."

Ray stared at her as if she had two heads. "I do not f . . .

freaking believe this!"

"That makes two of us," Cait said. "June identified the halberd on the Web and it's now in the hands of the police. There was also a knife. Detective Rook promised officers would be here this weekend." She paused to let the information sink in. "It's possible the suspect could disguise himself in a period costume, so pay attention and be sure you recognize each actor and crew member."

"How come trouble follows you?" Ray asked. He rolled his eyes heavenward. "Tasha's probably up there shaking her head and asking herself if she made a mistake putting her estate into your hands."

Cait looked at Ray and wished she could tell him the whole story. Instead, she said, "I'm handling it, okay? Do you check IDs when everyone arrives on a set?"

"No, after years in the business most of us know each other." He glanced at June. "Isn't that right?"

June nodded.

"But do it here," Cait said.

"This little gig you got going normally wouldn't draw troubles like yours," he said, "but if it will make you happy I'll look everyone in the face twice."

Cait grinned. "Thank you. That would make me very happy."

"Don't be a fool and go get yourself killed," Ray warned.

"Better a witty fool than a foolish wit," June responded.

Ray looked puzzled. "Who said?"

June grinned. "Shakespeare, you silly oaf. You should recognize *Twelfth Night*."

Cait had never seen Ray blush. She thought back to when she'd first met him and how he'd treated her as hired help until he'd learned who she was. "Jim Hart and I will be armed and our cells will be on. Give me your cell number so we can call if there's an emergency." She pulled her phone from her waist-band.

Ray set the tray of food on the counter and reached into his pants pocket for his phone.

After they exchanged numbers and Ray left, Cait sat back down to eat. "Ray doesn't need to know about the incident at the school, but should it come up when you're talking with him, go ahead and tell him. No reason not to."

"Believe me, he'll pick up on it sooner or later," June said. "My knowing the actors will give me an excuse to hang out backstage, like going undercover."

Jim smiled. "You go, woman. And Marcus and I can look busy setting up picnic tables and benches. There's always something that needs fixing."

Cait glanced at Marcus, his clean white shirt unbuttoned part way to his fancy belt buckle, crisp blue jeans, and polished tan cowboy boots. His daily uniform—except today his spiked, sun-bleached hair was relaxed without the mousse he normally used. She liked the softer touch and wondered if there was a girl he wanted to impress.

"I brought my horse and trailer over this morning," Marcus said.

Cait raised her eyebrow. "Really?"

Marcus shrugged. "In case I get a chance to lasso a bad guy."

Cait laughed, almost choking on her coffee. "Lasso?"

"You bet."

"When I'm not working in the gift shop, Ilia and I could hang out at the theaters, too," Fumié said. "I'm probably the last person anyone would take seriously as a watchdog. And I can shoot with the best."

Petite Fumié could fool anyone. "You're a one-person army, Fumié. You'll make a terrific park ranger, but don't bring a gun here. And no heroics. Call me or tell a police officer if there's a problem."

Cait was clearing the dishes after everyone left when her cell beeped. She checked the display. "Good morning, Detective Rook. Where's the officer you promised?"

"I'm all you're going to get this morning. See you soon."

Cait glanced at the wall clock—9:15—and then at the leftover sausages on the griddle. "I know babysitting me is not your responsibility, but perhaps some leftovers from breakfast will help ease the pain."

He laughed and hung up.

Cait went upstairs to collect her gun and was about to go back down when she heard a chirp from her laptop. She went over to the desk, clicked on a key, and Shep's face popped up on Skype.

"You there, Cait?"

She sat on the edge of the chair. "I'm here, Shep. You got news?"

"A little about the Dillon boys. Hank belonged to a gang that would kill for hubcaps. Wally is in a gang I'm way too familiar with. The usual stuff: gun battles between gangs, kids shot. Hank was ten when he first got involved in one of those battles, but he was already a juvenile delinquent at eight. His mother, a single parent, was afraid his little brother Wally would turn out the same if she didn't do something about it. That's how Calder Manning's parents got involved. Both parents went to the same church. The Mannings offered to adopt Hank because they thought a home environment with more love and attention than his mother had time to give him would have a good effect on him. They thought it did, for awhile."

"I get the picture." She watched frown lines crease Shep's forehead and knew he sensed her disappointment. "It's something to think about, but keep me posted if you find out

87

anything that might affect my situation." She put her finger up to his face, not ready to let him go. He'd helped her through plenty of tough times—her parents' plane crash, her divorce. They were close friends but never lovers as some thought.

"One more thing. I met Manning's three-year-old daughter. His mom takes care of her when he's out of town."

Cait nodded, always sensitive when it came to children. "He should be home caring for her," she said.

"We do what we have to, Cait, to make a living," said Shep, who'd lost his fiancée to a brain tumor several years ago.

"I know."

"Have faith and be safe."

Cait watched the screen go blank before she closed her laptop. She tucked her Glock at the small of her back, picked up her keys, and went downstairs. Outside, she wondered how anything bad could happen on a sunny day like today. The intense heat had turned the hills from green to the color of wheat. Yellow roses spilled over the rim of half wine barrels flanking the back door. She took the shaded brick path between the tall cypress trees and thought about the Dillon brothers and Manning's little girl. Cait was unable to have children, and it always depressed her to hear of parents not having the time or money to devote to their own kids and having to depend on others to care for them. Powerless to shake this sudden despair, she paused at the gate beneath the trellis to smell the trailing ivory-colored roses.

Voices penetrated the funk Cait had found herself in. She opened the gate and saw a man and a woman standing in the middle of the courtyard. They glanced her way and then continued their conversation. Instead of going around to the back door that would take her directly into the green room at the Elizabethan theater, she entered at the side door.

The sun spread across the empty seats in the open-air theater.

She went up the side aisle so she could stand at the rear of the theater and look down upon the stage as if seeing it through the eyes of an audience. The curtains had been drawn back, and different scenery lowered from overhead, creating an expectant feeling that the actors might appear on stage at any moment.

Cait's heart overflowed with pride. Without realizing it, she had stopped thinking of her inheritance as an anchor around her neck and started appreciating her legacy as a gift. *Who would have thought my English lit degree would be so useful?*

It took her a few moments to notice movement next to the orchestra pit.

She stared at the man, his back to her, and wondered how long he'd been there. Slowly, she started down the aisle. "May I help you?" she asked as she drew closer to him.

He ignored her and continued to stare at the stage. Then he glanced over his shoulder. "Who are you?"

In profile, his sharp, well-chiseled features reminded Cait of someone, but she couldn't recall who it could be. She studied his six-foot frame, heavy eyebrows, and auburn hair streaked with gray. Definitely not the man she'd seen at Trader Joe's. "I could ask you the same thing. Are you an actor?"

He tossed his head back and laughed, a dry humorless laugh that provoked Cait. He rubbed his hand over his chin hair. "Scholar, actor, director, mentor, teacher. All the above."

Cait stepped closer. Intrigued by the intensity of his dark brown eyes and formal speech, she asked, "What's your name?"

He eyed her, from her head to her old tennis shoes, taking his time before he spoke. "Kenneth Alt. And you are—"

"Cait Pepper." She held out her hand as she recognized the name. "We spoke on the phone last month."

He reached out to shake her hand. "So we did. I apologize. I should have known it was you, but I was caught up in my own thoughts."

"Why didn't you tell me you were coming?"

"I only decided a couple of days ago." He glanced around the theater. "This is a nice setup, much better than I'd imagined. But then, Tasha always liked nice things. She was the consummate Shakespearean actress. What a shame she isn't here to appreciate the performances she took pride in scheduling for her little festival." He looked back at Cait. "Since you're here, I assume you're planning on staying and carrying out her longtime dream."

"I've given up a job I loved," Cait said. "So yes, I'm staying."

He frowned. "Right. I believe you said you worked in law enforcement. I wasn't totally clear what it was you did in law enforcement."

Cait didn't know how much Detective Rook had told him when Alt called him in April to verify her identity. "I was a police officer and later became a crime analyst."

He nodded, his eyes glued to Cait. "I see. Has anyone ever told you how much you look like Tasha? Astonishing, considering she was your aunt." He stroked his chin again. "How old are you, Cait?"

"Why, Mr. Alt, you know better than to ask a woman her age."

The curtain was pushed back and June walked on stage. "I thought I heard a familiar voice." She stared down at Alt. "What are you doing here, Kenneth?"

He looked up at her. "June Hart? What the dickens are you doing here?"

She trotted down the steps to greet him. "It's not my ghost. Jim and I retired. We're living in our RV now and helping Cait with the festival. Aren't you supposed to be in Ashland directing the next *Hamlet*? Or did you come here looking for tips on how it's done?"

Cait squirmed, hoping she wouldn't have to stand between

them to ward off blows.

Alt frowned. "June and I go way back, Cait. When I heard Chip Fallon was appearing at Tasha's festival, I had to see for myself if his acting skills had improved."

"Don't you dare cause trouble, Kenneth," June snapped. "You know damn well Chip is a fine actor, and he'd make a fine artistic director if given the chance."

Cait watched Alt's face turn red and his hands clench at his sides.

"He's not on the short list," Alt said.

"Of course he isn't. You removed his name!" From out of nowhere, their cordial conversation turned dark.

Alt stormed off until he reached the door, then he looked back. "He isn't ready to direct. He may *never* be ready."

My problems continue to multiply.

CHAPTER 12

"Whoa," Cait said when the door slammed behind Alt. "That man's got a temper."

"And a whopping ego," June said. "He's definitely not the warm and fuzzy type, but everyone admires him because he's such a great actor."

"I wonder why he's here," Cait said.

June raised one shoulder. "Maybe to get into Chip's head and screw him up."

"Why?"

"To distract him, like a wasp buzzing you."

Cait shook her head in disgust. "I talked to him last month after you gave me his number. I wanted the names on that short list for associate artistic director. He wouldn't give me the names until he confirmed with Detective Rook that I was who I said I was. Can he remove a name just because he doesn't like the person?"

"Apparently. It was probably for the best, because the two of them working together would be like a fire in a forest after a drought."

"That bad, huh? One of my professors said there were two Hamlets in the play. One the sweet prince who expresses himself in poetry and is dedicated to the truth, and the other a barbaric Hamlet who treats Ophelia cruelly. Not hard to guess which Hamlet would fit Alt."

June laughed. "*Hamlet* is a grand poetical enigma." She took

Cait's arm. "Come on, I'll introduce you to the actors. This is fun for me."

Cait followed June up the stairs and behind the curtain into the green room. The people in the room vibrated with an undercurrent of energy, but Chip Fallon's attention was riveted on a young woman obviously in distress, her hands flying around as if trying to make a point.

June said, "Father Chip's at it again. That's Toni Behren he's talking to. She plays Ophelia, who Hamlet's mother hopes will be his bride."

Cait raised her eyebrow. "*Father* Chip?"

June nodded. "Chip went into the Josephinum Pontifical College in Ohio right out of high school to become a priest. He dropped out during his third year. People heard about it and, much to his chagrin, started to address him as 'Father.' It stuck. Sometimes it embarrasses him, but he's sensitive to others' feelings and tries to help if they ask."

"I'm familiar with the college. It's in Worthington, outside of Columbus," Cait said, her eyes on Chip. "I wonder why he dropped out."

"The tuition's high, but my guess is Chip missed girls." June pointed to a woman entering the wig room. "That's Paula. She plays Gertrude, Queen of Denmark and mother of Hamlet. I'll introduce you."

Cait glanced around, expecting to see more actors. "I know this is a small festival compared to Oregon's, but shouldn't there be more actors?"

June nodded. "A few more will come, but actors play multiple roles, even in a single play. Trust me, it can be a feat of dramatic gymnastics. Don't ask the actors how they keep their heads straight—or their lines. It's in their job description, but they love what they do. I did and so did Tasha."

"I'm glad I chose a different path and became a cop after

college," Cait said as she followed June into the wig room.

"Paula," June said to a woman who was adjusting a wig on a Styrofoam head.

The woman spun around.

"Sorry, I didn't mean to disturb you," June said. "I'd like you to meet Cait Pepper, Tasha's niece. Cait inherited the Bening Estate."

Tall, blond, and striking in white shorts and red tank top, Paula smiled and held her hand out to Cait. "I was devastated when I heard about Tasha. She mentored me and shared her secrets for remembering lines. I was honored when she picked me to play Gertrude."

Cait shook Paula's warm hand. "I'm looking forward to seeing the play."

"Tasha couldn't have chosen a better location for her festival on this hill with spectacular views of the valley," Paula said. A frown crossed her face. "I hope you plan to continue the festival. It meant so much to her."

Cait still struggled when asked about her inheritance. "I gave up my job to come here so, yes, those are my plans, but I don't know how to entice actors to come here since I'm not in the business."

Paula's eyes lit up. "Didn't you know? Plays are scheduled for two more years. Tasha knew which actors she wanted and booked us a long time ago. I'll be here each year." She glanced over Cait's shoulder. "I have to go. It was nice meeting you, Cait."

Cait watched Paula leave. "I had no idea there was a three-year plan in place. Had I known, I wouldn't have worried. Marcus never mentioned it."

"He probably thought you knew," June said. She picked up a blond wig and set it on her head, turning her head back and forth in front of a mirror at one of the vanity tables. Her voice wistful, she asked, "What do you think?"

Cait adjusted the wig on June's head. "You'd make a perfect Gertrude."

June replaced the wig, a twinkle in her eye. "That's good, because I played her many times."

Cait remembered June saying there were few roles for aging actors. "Sometime you'll have to tell me about your acting career."

"I'd love to, but not when you're tied in a knot over Wally Dillon."

Outside the room, Cait heard Ray Stoltz's booming voice barking instructions about lights and sound to a crew of technicians.

"Ignore Ray," June said. "A stage manager's job never ends. Right now, he's in the middle of the information wheel, communicating with everyone to make sure all changes are noted and taken care of." She looked at Cait. "If you're thinking he's ruthless now, just wait until the seats are filled and the audience brings their own energy. It changes everything. A good stage manager reacts to an audience and takes notes. Trust me, Ray is one of the best at what he does."

"I never thought about it like that," Cait said. "What about his brother, Jay? I don't see him anywhere."

"Oh, Jay's job can be stressful, too. You'd never know to look at him, but Jay is the go-to guy when there are problems with the costumes. Brawny as he is, he has magical fingers with a sewing machine—turns out gorgeous dresses and blouses in satins and silk. You should see the shawls he's knitted."

"I'd like to," Cait said, with a bit of a chuckle as she pictured big Jay with tiny knitting needles.

June grinned. "Remember, never judge a book by its cover. Let's see what's happening at the Blackfriars theater. I'll introduce you to the *Macbeth* actors."

They crossed the courtyard, where half a dozen people were pulling suitcases behind them. Cait watched the group, looking for signs they didn't belong to the theater. "I should have called Stanton Lane, Tasha's attorney, about the furnished apartments Tasha leased. I don't know if it's up to me to see they're cleaned before the actors get here." She reached into her handbag for her new electronic notepad. "If I don't write it down, I'll forget to ask Marcus when I get back."

"Don't stress over it. Believe me when I say they'll let you know if they need something. Actors are not shy."

When they reached the small white building that housed the Blackfriars theater, Cait heard laughter through the open door. "I see Ray's already opened this theater." She stepped through the doorway, aware of tape that had been used to cover the electrical cords during last month's play, *Tongue of a Bird*. The last thing she needed was to be sued for carelessness.

Cait hadn't before seen the theater so well lit. Floor lights had been set up around the stage. The bright lights spread over the black walls, stage, and tiered benches, but the wooden shutters, screens, and trellises remained closed to block outside sunlight.

"Tasha was brilliant to think of building this theater," June said. "It's scaled similarly to Oregon's Black Swan, perfect for those experimental and risky productions that are coming into their own these days."

"And now *Macbeth*."

"Yes indeed." June waved to someone across the room. "Sit down, Cait, in the first row. I want to demonstrate something." She took a big step up onto the stage and stood at the edge. "How do you feel?" she said, looking down at her.

"Vulnerable."

"Good—that's how an audience feels this close to the actors. Isn't it wonderful? This intimate seating allows you to immerse

96

yourself into the play and into the minds of the actors."

Cait nodded, but thought she'd prefer to sit a couple of rows back. "Where's the scenery?"

"Tasha talked with me about that before she died. *Macbeth*, in this intimate setting, is meant to focus on the psychology of the characters. The props are simplified to two chairs, two goblets, and the crown." She blinked a few times and turned her head away. "Sorry."

It was times like this that reminded Cait of how close June and Tasha had been. Cait had her own moments regretting she'd never had the opportunity to know Tasha, but she took comfort in small things, like Tasha's meditation garden and the view of Mount Diablo and the valley below. But sometimes, when a breeze touched her shoulder as she sat in the garden, she wondered if Tasha was sending her a message.

June cleared her throat. "As I was saying, the crown is seen as the central image to the play, the reason Macbeth commits that first murder."

Cait wondered if June missed acting more than she admitted.

Ray Stoltz walked in from the rear of the theater. "You wouldn't happen to have a pair of roller skates hanging around, would you? I'm feeling my age every time I race back and forth between the theaters."

"I thought Jay was your assistant," Cait said.

"He is, but he has his own problems to deal with." He pulled a radio from his belt of tools. "This is how we communicate."

Cait pointed to a disc in the middle of the stage with what appeared to be a pool of blood at its center. "Remind me about that."

He stared at Cait. "Do I have to explain everything to you? If you're going to run a Shakespeare festival, maybe you should go back to school. That's a disc painted to work with a special lighting design to convey changing moods of the play's most dramatic arc. When you see the play, pay attention to how the pool of blood seems to glow from within."

Cait ignored Ray's comment and looked closer at the disc.

"The blood will be used as a weapon and a prop." Ray wiggled his bushy eyebrows. "Do I need to tell you how it ends?"

She shook her head. "I know how it ends, Ray. The characters' stark white costumes will be splattered with blood."

"Kudos for you," he said.

"But on this small stage and without a caldron for the witches—"

"The pool of blood *is* the cauldron, Cait," June explained. "The round stage is also a cauldron." She nudged Ray on his arm. "Have you seen Kenneth Alt? He's here for some reason. He and Chip Fallon don't get along. Maybe you should keep an eye on them."

"Now I'm supposed to babysit two hot-tempered actors?" Ray said. "We've got two plays going on at the same time. Hire a couple of rent-a-cops, for Christ's sake." He jumped down from the stage and stormed off.

"He's right," Cait said. "He's got his hands full."

"Don't worry about Ray," June said. "He'll come through. He always does." She paused before a black curtain that stretched across the width of the rear of the theater. "We have six actors—Macbeth, Lady Macbeth, and Banquo, Macbeth's ally, and three women who play the other roles. The small stage is perfect for hearing the language and getting into the heads of the characters." She held the black curtain aside for Cait. "Looks like we're in time for dress rehearsal. Let's find Betsy Ryder; she plays Lady Macbeth."

Cait bumped into a clothes rack on wheels and caught it before it rolled away.

June went up behind a woman and tapped her on the shoulder. "Hi, Betsy."

Betsy turned. She grasped June in a hug. "I saw you when you came in the door. What are you doing here?" She glanced at Cait.

Cait stared at the tall woman dressed in layers of sheer white materials, her long dark curly hair clasped behind her head. She looked exactly like the magazine photo of Tasha that Stanton Lane had given her.

"Jim and I came here after we retired," June said. "This is Cait Pepper, Tasha's niece."

Betsy beamed at Cait and held out her hand. "Hi. It's so nice to meet you."

Cait shook Betsy's hand. "The feeling's mutual, I assure you. I have a picture of Tasha dressed in a costume like the one you're wearing."

She looked down at her costume. "This is from the wardrobes at the Oregon Shakespeare Festival." She looked over Cait's shoulder. "I'm being summoned. Let's talk later, Cait." As she rushed off, hems of her layered dress dragged across the floor.

"They're about to start rehearsing," June said. "We should get out of their way."

Outside, Cait watched one of the crew push a cart across the courtyard. "I'm going to look for Rook."

"Okay. I'll hang around here for awhile."

Cait scanned the yard as she walked. She slowed when she noticed a tall man in jeans and pale blue T-shirt standing in the meditation garden. She reached for her gun.

He turned. "Hello, Cait."

She nearly collapsed with relief and grinned—Royal Tanner was back!

CHAPTER 13

Cait's heart raced. "RT," she whispered, his name caught in her throat. The air between them quivered with tension. He'd been gone a month, and she hadn't heard a word from him.

RT walked toward her.

"I didn't expect to see you again," she said.

"I said I'd be back." His eyes drifted lazily over her.

"Where were you sent this time?"

"You know I can't tell you."

Cait tried to appear casual as her gaze swept over him, from the dark stubble on his cheeks and chin to his dusty boots as she looked for signs he'd been injured. When she first met RT in April, he was still recovering from a back injury he'd received while on a mission. As he stood before her now, he looked fearless, brawny, and too damned attractive. Seeing him again left her breathless, yet she managed to ask, "How did your mission go?"

A thin line creased his forehead. "We got the job done."

She nodded, hating small talk. "That's good."

RT reached out and gripped her hand in his, pulling her to him. "Rook told me what's going on. I'm sorry I wasn't here for you, but maybe I can help now."

He smelled fresh and clean, as if he'd just stepped out of the shower. "He said he'd talked to you," she said.

RT nodded.

"Does he usually know how to reach you?" Cait remembered

RT and Rook went back a long way, to when Rook's younger brother and RT were on a SEAL mission together.

RT's deep blue gaze locked onto Cait's. "Not exactly. I called him when I arrived in San Diego three days ago. He told me someone from when you were a cop was stalking you and that you'd shot and killed the guy's brother. I've been given a couple of weeks off. Rook and I will go after this guy."

"What about Mindy?" She had met RT's five-year-old daughter when his parents dropped by in April on their way to Utah. "She's your first priority."

"She is, but we spent three fun days together, went to Disneyland, reread my books on treasures from the bottom of the sea, rode horseback, and walked through my vineyard." He smiled broadly. "Before I left San Diego, she asked if I was going to see the pretty lady who lives in Tasha's yellow house. When I explained why I needed to come here, she wanted to give you a present."

You're the only present I need, she thought, but asked, "A present?"

"She picked it out just for you. It's in my trailer."

"Oh! June and Jim Hart's RV is parked there now."

He laughed. "I know. I saw it. I'm parked in the visitors' lot. Rook explained everything, about the Harts and that you've got a couple of plays going on this weekend."

"Rook said he'd be here. I was looking for him when I saw you."

He tugged on one of her dark curls. "You get me instead."

His touch felt like an electrical charge; his lips hovered over hers.

"This must be the infamous RT," June said, walking up behind them with Detective Rook.

Cait pulled her hand from RT's, feeling like a teenager caught kissing behind the school. Her cheeks flared with embarrassment. *My God, I've never been drawn to another man as I am to RT. Not even my late ex-husband when we first met.*

Rook smiled and shook RT's hand. "You look damn good for someone who's been on a volatile mission."

Cait wondered if Rook knew where RT had been for the past month. "RT, this is June Hart, Tasha's friend. When June and her husband retired, they offered to help me with the festival."

RT smiled and reached out to shake June's hand. "I met your husband a few minutes ago. He mistook me for Cait's stalker until Marcus stepped in and introduced us."

"Lucky for you Marcus was there," June said.

Cait looked at Rook. "I promised you lunch. If anyone else is hungry—"

"Nothing for me, thanks," Rook said. "I had a sandwich at my desk."

"I stopped for a bite outside of town," RT said. "I want to hear everything that's happened since I left, who this guy is, and what kind of security is planned." He shot Rook a questioning look. "You got a plan to pick this guy out from a couple hundred strangers?"

"I'm working on it," Rook said.

Cait watched RT, his intense body language and his focused blue eyes, as she thought about the very private world SEALs worked in. He was a warrior; she wondered if he could turn that aspect of himself off and live a normal life.

They settled in the kitchen where Jim, Marcus, Ilia, and Fumié joined them. Detective Rook had briefed RT earlier about Cait's situation. She filled in the details, including her recent conversation with Shep about the Dillon brothers and his meeting Manning's daughter.

"Shep is investigating Calder Manning thoroughly," Cait continued. "He asked Manning's mother for a picture of her son, but she refused. Because he's a journalist reporting from war zones, she wanted to protect him from the public and protect his young daughter. Shep didn't press it because the little girl was in the room." She looked at RT. "Have you heard of Calder Manning? I've only seen a shadowy image of him in fatigues on the Web."

"Depends on his assignment and the location he's assigned to," RT said. "Don't believe everything you see in the news or the Web. Manning could be working exclusively undercover."

Her eyes bright with interest, June asked, "You mean like a secret agent?"

One corner of RT's lips curled. "Anything is possible. I'll collect on a couple of favors and see what comes up. No guarantees, but I might be able to get a photo of Manning."

Cait relaxed at the kitchen counter, more content than she'd been since RT left a month ago. *If he says he'll do something, he will.*

"I want to meet the actors and stage crew," RT said, sliding off his stool. "But first, let's head over to my trailer." He winked at Cait. "To see your present from Mindy."

Cait wondered what RT was up to, but she secured the house and walked with the others to RT's trailer.

Cait stopped and pushed her sunglasses up on her head at the sight of the familiar silver vintage Airstream trailer hitched to RT's black Hummer. The sun sparkled off the twenty-four-foot 1970 trailer, which was parked in the back of the lot away from cars and trailers belonging to the actors and crew. Seeing his home away from home stirred memories that were best left alone—memories she didn't want to dwell on, because RT would leave again in a couple of weeks, or sooner if recalled. Never enough time to build a lasting relationship.

"You coming?" RT asked.

She slipped her sunglasses over her eyes and closed the

doorway to her emotions. "I'm used to seeing your trailer on the other side of the house."

"I hope it doesn't take up too much space," he said. "I could move it—"

A sudden banging of doors and loud swearing interrupted RT. "Dammit! I'll have someone's ass for this!"

Fumié jumped.

"Ray's blowing off steam again," June said. "I wonder what's wrong this time."

Everyone hurried to a large white panel truck and found Ray Stoltz leaning inside the door. Ray slammed his hand against the truck and continued his ranting. "This place is a damn nightmare. Nothing's safe."

"Calm down, Ray. What's wrong?" Cait asked.

"What does it look like? Someone broke into my truck!" He reached into his shirt pocket for his cell phone. "I'm calling the police. If I were you, Cait, I'd forget all about the festival and hightail it back to wherever you came from. This place is one giant headache."

"You'd miss me if I left. You wouldn't have anyone to pick on," Cait said.

Rook stepped forward before Ray could call 911. "I'm Detective Rook. We've met before, but I don't remember your name."

Ray stared at the detective for a moment. "I remember you. I'm Ray Stoltz, stage manager of this festival."

"Was anything stolen?" Rook asked.

"Obviously, or the door wouldn't be standing wide open like this. I know I didn't leave it open."

"You checked to see if anything is missing?" Rook asked.

"No, but I will," Ray said.

"You do that while I look up front." Rook opened the driver's door. "Did you leave the windows down?"

Ray grunted and glanced at Rook. "It's hot. I left one open a little. The doors were locked. Dammit! My best hammer's not in the tray where it belongs!" He ducked inside the truck.

"Maybe you left it in one of the theaters," RT said.

Ray turned. He smiled at RT. "Where did you come from? Maybe you can catch the smartass who stole my hammer."

"That's the plan, Ray," RT said. "Keep looking and let us know if you find your hammer or if anything else is missing."

"Found scratch marks on the inside of the door," Rook said. "Looks like someone used a hanger to reach in the window and slip up the lock." He glanced up with a smile on his face as he held up a gum wrapper. "You chew Dentyne Ice, Ray?"

Ray shot Rook a look as if the detective had lost his marbles. "Never touch the stuff."

Cait wondered what had gotten into Ray. She'd never seen him this uptight. She watched Rook pull a small plastic bag from his back pocket and drop the gum wrapper inside.

Ilia whispered to Cait, "What do you think is going on with Ray besides his truck being broken into?"

"I don't know," she said.

Rook closed the driver's door. "I'll be here for awhile. Let me know if you want to file a police report."

When they went to RT's trailer, RT said, "Wait here." He unlocked the door and disappeared inside long enough for Cait to wonder if he'd fallen asleep.

After a few minutes, Ilia knocked on the trailer door. "Need help in there?"

The door swung wide open.

Out jumped a dark brown dog restrained by a leash in RT's hand.

Cait's jaw dropped. Nothing could have surprised her more.

RT led the dog over to Cait and handed her the leash. "His name is Niki. He's a chocolate lab retriever, six months old."

He grinned. "Mindy's gift to you. She worries about you being alone up here and picked this pup just for you."

CHAPTER 14

Cait had never experienced such a tender gesture from a child and instantly fell in love with Niki. The dog pawed at her jeans, his soulful brown eyes begging for attention. She crouched in front of him. "You're beautiful." Overwhelmed, she looked up at RT with tears in her eyes. "Please thank Mindy for me the next time you talk to her."

"I will."

Everyone gathered around Cait and Niki, talking and laughing while the dog bounced around, barking at the attention he'd drawn. RT released the leash from Niki's collar, pulled a dog treat from his pocket, and gave it to Cait. "Give him this."

"Won't he run away?" Cait asked, as she offered the treat to Niki.

"No, he's trained to follow commands. I've got his food, bowls, and favorite pillow in the trailer. I'll bring them to the house later."

The dog grabbed his treat and ran with it.

Cait rose, her eyes on Niki. "I've never had a dog."

"In case you're wondering," RT said, "he's house-trained. Take him upstairs with you at night."

"About time you got a dog." Ray Stoltz walked over, and his face softened into a smile as he watched Niki. "Maybe now this place will be safer."

Is this the same angry Ray from a few minutes ago? "I'm sure it will be. There's lots of space for a dog to explore."

Ray turned to Detective Rook. "All that's missing from my truck is the hammer. No need to file a report."

Rook nodded. "Let me know if you change your mind."

Cait wondered what turned Ray from Godzilla into a friendly human being. Was it Niki?

RT closed the door on his trailer and locked it. "Time I met the actors." Niki ran up to him. "You too, buddy. Maybe you can sniff out the bad guy, if he's around." He pulled another treat from his pocket and gave it to Niki.

"Jim and I should set up the benches," Marcus said. "We could use help. How about it, Ilia? Think you could put your camera down long enough to help carry tables and set them up under the trees?"

"Sure," Ilia said.

"I'll help, too," Fumié said.

Cait hung back while the others went ahead. She looked over the golden hills sloped in shadowy patterns beneath the late-morning light. *This is my world now, far from city traffic, streets packed with people rushing to their destinations, and the smell of pollution. But I'm responsible for the mayhem that followed me to this valley, and it's up to me to solve it.*

She caught up with RT, Rook, and June. "I'll be at the Elizabethan. I want to talk to Ray." She wanted to get him alone. If he had another problem besides his truck being broken into, she wanted to know, particularly if it had anything to do with the actors or crew.

Cait entered the theater through the side door and waited while it closed with a soft wheeze behind her. She heard raised voices from the back of the theater and looked up the aisle, but whoever was there was hidden in the shadows. When the voices became heated, she tiptoed up the aisle and slipped into a wall recess to listen.

"Why else would you come here except to check on me?"

Cait thought she recognized Chip Fallon's voice.

Someone laughed. "I'm not here because of *you*. You're not worth my time. But since I am here, I'll see the play and hope you don't screw up. Hamlet deserves the best to play him. Trust me, that's not you."

Cait cringed at the harsh words directed at Chip.

"You arrogant bastard, Alt! You probably consider yourself to be the best," Chip said.

Cait peeked out from her hiding place. *Oh no. Kenneth Alt? Chip? All I need is hostility between the two men to ruin the festival.* She was about to confront them when Alt continued.

"If you'd paid close attention, you might have learned something when I was Hamlet," Alt said.

"Ha. Then explain why Tasha invited me here and not you," Chip said.

"Because I'm too busy getting ready to direct *Hamlet* at OSF. She must have been under a lot of stress at the time she asked you," Alt said. "Don't forget, she *was* murdered."

"We don't know that for sure. You must be desperate for roles now that you're getting up there in years where roles are fewer and further between."

"That's totally absurd! I've got more requests for my services than I can handle."

"Tell me why you're here," Chip demanded. "To gloat that you removed me from your short list? I would have made a better associate artistic director than you would as a director."

"Time will tell," Alt said. "It always does."

"What the hell does that mean? Don't you dare do anything to screw up this festival. Cait's got enough on her mind after inheriting this place."

"As I said, time will tell."

"I know what your problem is, Alt. You're a jealous has-been."

Cait heard a shuffling of feet and what sounded like a thud.

Suddenly, the gun at her back felt heavier. She pulled her cell from her belt in case she'd need to call Detective Rook to intervene. She hoped Alt and Chip could resolve their problem before she'd be forced to evict them from the premises. But then what would she do without someone to play Hamlet?

"Go rehearse your lines," Alt said. "I'm sure you need to."

"And I'm sure you should go back to Oregon," Chip snapped.

Cait heard feet approaching and slipped out the door. She waited a few seconds and then went back in as if she'd just gotten there and didn't know what had taken place between Alt and Chip. She hoped she would learn more by playing innocent, unless the situation progressed too far.

Alt stopped dead in his tracks when he saw Cait. "I didn't know you were here."

She smiled. "Just came in." She glanced over his shoulder and saw Chip walking down the aisle behind Alt. "Were you rehearsing?"

"No, I'm not in the play," Alt said.

Of course you're not, she thought. *So why are you here?*

"Cait," Chip said. "I want to talk to you. Got a minute?"

"Sure."

"Let's go backstage," Chip said.

Cait felt Alt's eyes on her back as they went up the stairs. Before they slipped behind the curtain she glanced back, but Alt had disappeared.

Chip ushered Cait to a far corner of the green room, surprisingly empty of actors and crewmembers. His voice rushed, he asked, "Cait, did you invite Kenneth Alt to come here?"

"Of course not," Cait said. "Why would I? I'd never met the man." She wondered if she should tell him about her phone conversation with Alt a month ago, when she'd asked for the names on the short list, but she decided to wait and see where this conversation was going.

Chip nodded, his unruly blond hair falling across his forehead. "Don't get me wrong. There's no denying Kenneth Alt is a great actor, about as good as they come. He's going to direct *Hamlet* this season at the Oregon Shakespeare Festival. That's a big deal, and I admit he's earned it." He glanced around the room. "But he's got some hidden motive for coming here. I don't trust him, and I don't think you should, either."

Surprised by his warning after he'd praised Alt's work, she said, "Those are strong accusations, Chip. If you know why he's here, please tell me. If not, I'll find out myself."

He shook his head. "I don't know, other than to torment me." He brushed his hair back. "Look, it's no secret Alt and I don't like each other. We weren't rehearsing. I wanted to know why he was here. I don't want him to spoil your festival or for you to get hurt."

She drew in a deep breath. "You think he'd hurt me?"

"Not physically."

"Well, I assure you I'll be safe and so will you and the rest of the actors. Several police officers will be here this weekend." She considered telling Chip why Alt was the least of her worries unless his reason for being here affected the festival. Then Chip flashed his dimples, and she didn't want to spoil his day with more bad news.

"Good," said Chip. "I was happy to see June and Jim Hart. They're fine people."

"All right, everyone," Ray said, loudly and firmly, but not sounding unfriendly. "On stage."

Actors streamed into the green room from several directions. Chip stepped close to Cait and whispered, "Jim Hart worked in the art recovery business—still does, I think. He's smart. You can trust him with your life."

Chip hadn't told her anything she didn't already know, except to keep her eye on Kenneth Alt. Her list of candidates to watch had grown.

Cait grabbed Ray's arm before he got away. "I need a minute."

He wiped his dusty hands on the front of his shirt. "What's on your mind?"

She glanced around the room, which was buzzing with activity. "Can we step outside?"

Ray scowled, but followed Cait out the back service door and into the bright sunlight. "Make it quick. Actors are an impatient bunch."

As are you, she thought. Her eyes swept the trees and shrubs for any sudden movement; she needed this moment of privacy with Ray. If he had a problem with the plays, the actors, or the theaters, she wanted to know. "It's obvious something is going on with you other than your missing hammer. Can I help?"

Ray wiped his brow with his sleeve and looked off into the distance. "You don't mess around, do you? I like that you're direct, but it's personal, okay? I can handle it." He opened the door and slipped back inside without giving Cait a chance to respond.

Before the door closed, she grabbed it. "Does it have anything to do with your brother or one of the actors?"

"You're way off base."

Cait let the door click shut. *What is it with these people? Kenneth Alt and Chip Fallon, and now Ray Stoltz. Is it this place or their work that brings out the worst in them?*

She wondered if RT, Rook, and June were still waiting for her at the Blackfriars. She went around the theater and saw them heading toward her. She started to cross the courtyard as something hissed past her and slammed against a tree, a few feet from where she'd been standing, sending bark flying. The faint click of a rifle's action told Cait the direction from which the shot had come.

"Gunshot!" Cait screamed as she threw herself on the ground. She reached for her gun and scraped her left palm as she crawled for cover behind a shrub.

There was a scurry of critters racing for cover.

Damn, this can't be happening.

Another bullet pinged against the bricks near her feet, sending chips shooting in the air. She scooted back to get out of the line of fire.

A few people ran out of the theaters.

"Stay back!" Cait yelled.

"Everybody down!" RT and Rook yelled. RT dodged his way over to Cait with his gun drawn. Niki barked at the commotion. Rook covered RT with his own weapon as RT dropped down beside her. "Are you okay?" he asked as he scoured the area.

"Yes," she said, breathing hard. "Oh, God! What about the actors? The crew? Anyone hurt?"

"I don't think so. They've gone inside."

Rook crouched beside them. "Let's wait, then spread out and look for this sucker. If he's smart, he's running."

They cautiously got to their feet. No shots were fired. Cait pointed across the courtyard. "The shots came from over there, by that oak tree." She brushed her scraped palm down the side of her jeans. "I don't know where Ilia and Fumié are. Or Marcus. I have to call and make sure they're okay." As she reached for her cell phone, June ran up to her.

"I called Marcus and the kids," June said. "Everyone's okay." She looked Cait over. "What about you?"

"Fuming." Cait held her gun down by her right leg. "Would you please go inside the theater and see if everyone's okay? They must be frightened. I'll explain everything to them later, but right now I'm going to help look for this jackass."

"He can't be far if he's on foot," Rook said. "I didn't hear a motor start up, but I'll head over to the parking lot anyway. Or maybe he left a car on the road and ran back down the hill."

RT reached into his pocket and pulled out a knife. "I want that bullet."

Rook stood watch as RT dug the bullet from the tree.

Ray Stoltz ran out of the theater. "Holy crap, Cait. I was so caught up in my own problems, I underestimated the seriousness of yours. You okay?"

She pursed her lips and nodded. "I'm afraid the actors will freak out after hearing gunshots, and when Actors' Equity hears about this, I could be forced to close the festival."

"I think I can help you with that," Ray said and hurried off.

"Well, well," June said. "Big Ray to the rescue. Cait, I told you he could be counted on when times got tough."

"He's a stage manager, June. How much influence could he have with Actors' Equity?"

June glanced back at the theater. "I don't want to know, but he seemed confident."

"Look at this," RT said. He held up the bullet he'd dug out of the tree.

Cait stared at it. "From an AK-47?"

"Or a variant of it that uses the same type ammo," Rook said. "Cheap, used on the street, and easy to get."

Cait took a deep breath to shake off chills running through her body. She looked over her shoulder several times, a nervous survival habit she'd acquired on her job. "Wally Dillon means business. Maybe Marcus was more intuitive than I realized."

"What do you mean?" RT asked.

"Marcus brought his horse this morning. Let's ask if he's up for a ride."

CHAPTER 15

Marcus searched for the shooter for what seemed like a long time to Cait before he returned to the house, disappointment written on his face. Detective Rook called for backup to look for anyone on foot or a suspicious car parked on the side of the road at the bottom of the hill behind the theaters.

While the search continued, Cait returned to the Elizabethan theater. June summoned the actors and the crew so Cait could explain what had happened and what the police were doing to find the shooter. They congregated in the green room. A few drank bottled water; some sat on the sofa, others on the floor, while a few remained standing. They inundated Cait with questions the moment she walked in.

"Hold on," Ray yelled. "If you stop badgering her, she'll explain." He handed Cait a bottle of water.

"Thanks," she said. She appreciated Ray stepping in, as the questions came fast and furious without giving her a chance to answer. She glanced around the room, then took a deep breath. "Okay. What happened was directed solely at me. I hoped it wouldn't come to this, but since it has, I owe you an explanation." She cracked the seal on the water bottle and took a swallow. "Two years ago, while I was still a cop, I was called to a bank robbery. I shot and killed one of the robbers to save the life of another officer. I had no choice."

"Two years is a long time," someone said.

"Yes it is, but time means nothing for someone who craves

revenge. We believe a family member of the person I shot is stalking me. How this person tracked me from Ohio to California boggles my mind, yet there's no denying he, or she, is here." She was positive the shooter was Wally, but she didn't want to go into details at this time. She studied her audience's faces and looked for signs of fear, anxiety, or anyone ready to make a quick exit. Her greatest apprehension, aside from a bystander being killed, was that Actors' Equity would learn of the shooting and force her to close the festival.

No one made an effort to leave.

"Our concern for Tasha carries over to you, Cait," Chip Fallon said.

"If you're worried about us abandoning you, you needn't be. We're here for the duration," said Toni Behren, the actress who was playing Ophelia.

"Tell us how we can help," said Betsy Ryder, the Lady Macbeth actress.

"There are more of us here than him," said a man Cait hadn't met yet.

"Right," another man said. "Our critical mass will kick his ass."

Laughter erupted.

Their empathy brought a lump to Cait's throat. She looked up and saw RT and Detective Rook standing in the background and motioned them forward. Niki trotted over and sat at Cait's feet.

She stroked the dog's neck. "This is Niki, my new dog. And this is Detective Rook from the Livermore Police Department, and that's Royal Tanner. RT is a Navy SEAL on leave, who came from San Diego to help. While he's here, he'll be staying in the silver Airstream you've probably seen in the parking lot."

"Love the Hummer it's hitched to," someone said.

Everyone laughed.

"Yeah, me, too," RT said.

"RT and I are armed," Rook said, "as is Cait, so go about your business as usual, but stay alert. Your safety is our priority. Your support for Cait means a lot to her, but please, no heroics. There will be plenty of police present this weekend in plainclothes and in uniform. If you're suspicious of anyone, let us know immediately." Rook withdrew a business card and set it on the coffee table.

"When can I ride in the Hummer?" Chip asked.

More laughter.

"Maybe after we catch the SOB who's after Cait," RT said.

Cait left the theater and walked back to the house, her mind jumbled with memories. Her job as a cop had been to protect and serve, which was the reason she joined the police force. If she'd thought there was pressure then, her new life as proprietor of a vineyard and a Shakespeare festival was a million times worse—and growing.

At times, she wondered where she'd be if she'd refused to accept her inheritance and wondered what her parents would think of her now. She'd been consumed with guilt over their deaths for what seemed a lifetime. Would they be alive if she'd been able to prevent them from boarding the plane that later went down in the ocean? Would her ex-husband still be alive if she'd stayed with him and been able to give him the child he'd always wanted? She shook her head to dispel the unhappy memories. She opened the gate and continued walking. Up ahead, Kenneth Alt stood in Tasha's meditation garden. As she approached, he turned, the sun striking the auburn in his graying hair.

"What's that about?" he asked, pointing to the small copper sign at the edge of the garden.

"Exactly what it says," Cait said. "This is Tasha's meditation garden."

"When did Tasha take up meditation?"

Cait thought Alt looked tightly wound, held together by sheer willpower. Tension showed in his shoulders, in the fine lines across his forehead and around his mouth.

"I'm the wrong one to ask," she said. "I'm told she had morning tea in the garden, but I didn't have the privilege of knowing Tasha. Since you did, maybe you could tell me about her habits."

Alt arched a dark eyebrow and looked baffled.

Amused by his lack of comment, Cait said, "Look, all I know about Tasha came from others who did know her. I don't know your history with her, but if you'd like to come in the house, I'll fix coffee and we can sit down and talk. What do you say?"

He smiled slightly. "I was hoping to see the inside of the house Tasha last lived in and perhaps sense her presence."

What an odd thing to say. She reached in her pocket for the remote to unlock the door, then held it open for Alt to enter. She felt his eyes on her as she punched the security code into the panel. "Have a seat while I fix coffee."

Alt remained standing in the middle of the kitchen. "Are the theaters alarmed?"

Cait turned. *Why would he care?* "Yes."

"I just wondered because people have been going in and out all day without an alarm going off."

"It would be inconvenient to constantly lock and unlock the theaters while everyone is here, don't you think?"

"Yes, I suppose you're right. Skip the coffee. Would it be all right if I looked around the house?"

A warning bell rang in Cait's head. Something about Alt didn't add up. She hadn't forgotten the intense argument between him and Chip Fallon. The diamond studs he wore in his ears glittered from the overhead fluorescent lights as he dragged his fingers over the black speckled granite counter. "I can show you the first floor." She led him down the hall. "The gift shop is temporarily housed in these two rooms."

Alt peered in them. "They're not convenient to the theaters."

"No, but I'm having a shop built in the theater complex."

"Hmmm. Sounds like you plan on staying."

Did I detect disappointment in his voice? "This is my home now."

He stepped inside one of the rooms. "Is a gift shop really necessary for such a small venue?"

"Apparently Tasha thought so." She observed his intense interest in the pictures on the walls, but then he walked out and went into the front room where he paused before each Shakespeare picture. He didn't mention the lack of furniture in the room, but he struck a few chords on the grand piano. "Nice. Do you play?"

Cait smiled. "Not a note. Obviously, you do. Sit down and play if you'd like."

Alt pulled out the bench and sat on the edge. He placed his hands on the keyboard and stared up at Cait. "I can't get over how much you look like Tasha."

Cait froze but quickly recovered. "So I've heard. Had you known her a long time?"

He blinked, frowned, and began to play. "Yes."

Cait recognized the music from *A Midsummer Night's Dream* and wondered if there was some significance to the haunting song he'd chosen. Any other time she might have enjoyed it; today it gave her the chills, being alone in the house with Alt. When she'd had enough, she interrupted. "Mr. Alt, it's time we talk about Tasha."

Alt rose. "I thought we were. It's a fine piano. You should learn to play."

They returned to the kitchen and sat on stools at the counter drinking sparkling mineral water.

"What would you like to know about Tasha?"

"How about where and how the two of you met?"

He smoothed a crease from his trousers. "New York City. I was twenty-three and Tasha twenty-nine. I was rehearsing my role when she walked in and lit up the room."

"Shakespeare?"

"Actually, no. I was with the Acting Company of New York at the time. Tasha was there to audition. Trust me, that can be a soul-baring experience, a stripping down of humanity. Tasha had a lovely voice but was as nervous as a hummingbird."

"Did she ever talk about her family?"

He drank half his water. "She said she had a twin brother."

Cait waited and wondered how far she should press him for details. "You became friends, like a confidant?"

Alt set his bottle of water on the counter. "Very good friends." He pursed his lips. "Look, what can I tell you? She was lively, beautiful, and everyone was in love with her."

Cait cocked her head. "Including you?"

His jaw dropped. Before he could answer, someone pounded on the back door.

When Cait opened it, Niki ran in ahead of RT and Detective Rook.

RT looked over her shoulder. "Who's that?"

She turned and was surprised by the look of amusement on Alt's face. "Kenneth Alt, this is Detective Rook. You called him last month to verify I was who I said I was. And this is Royal Tanner. Kenneth is with the Oregon Shakespeare Festival and was a close friend of Tasha's."

Kenneth shook Rook's hand. "Cait hasn't told me the reason the police are here, but I assume it has to do with the gunshots I heard." He looked at RT. "Are you also with the police?"

RT didn't shake hands with Kenneth. He crossed his arms

and narrowed his eyes on him. "Not exactly."

Cait enjoyed the frigid exchange and the firm set of RT's jaw.

Alt laughed. "What does that mean, Mr. Tanner?"

Rook stepped in. "Would you mind if I asked where you were, Mr. Alt, during the time of the shooting?"

Cait remembered Alt wasn't present in the green room when she explained the shooting incident to the actors, but now she was anxious to hear his answer.

Alt frowned. "Are you accusing me of something?"

Rook smiled. "Not at all. I'm sure you understand I need to know where everyone was when the shooting occurred. That's all. If you saw something, I'd like to know."

"Oh. Sorry." He walked to the door. "I was admiring the meditation garden. If you'll excuse me, I'll get back to the theaters." He looked at Cait. "Maybe next time you'll allow me to see the rest of the house."

In your dreams, Cait thought.

RT and Detective Rook left soon after Alt. When RT didn't return by eight, Cait took a Lean Cuisine dinner from the freezer. She removed the cellophane wrap and popped it into the microwave. While her dinner went from rock solid to steaming hot, she did something she seldom did—she drank alone. The chardonnay grapes came from the Bening Estate and gave her a sense of pride. Niki watched as she sipped her wine.

As her dinner heated, she tapped the Pandora app on her phone and listened to Jim Croce. Within moments, however, she shut the music off again. The last thing she needed was to get poignant over a relationship that couldn't possibly go anywhere. After dinner, she took Niki upstairs.

CHAPTER 16

Cait was up at six Saturday morning and downstairs by six-thirty. She let Niki out while she prepared coffee. The sun penetrated through the stained glass window over the sink, spreading jeweled tones of gold, purple, and green across the kitchen. She thought about the guy behind the AK-47 and how RT and Detective Rook planned to trap him, while she waited for her coffee to percolate. The possibility of her stalker being among a crowd of four hundred was daunting.

When her coffee was ready, she picked up her gun and went outside. Beads of moisture covered the roses that cascaded from hanging pots on either side of the door. With temperatures already in the low seventies, it could still be in the high eighties by seven that evening, but once the sun dipped below the horizon and the ocean breeze reached inland, the audience in the outdoor Elizabethan theater would need a jacket.

She slipped her sunglasses on and scanned the yard before settling on the bench beneath the cascading pepper tree in the meditation garden. Velcro jumped into her lap when Niki ran into the garden, making Cait almost spill her coffee. She'd never had a pet until now, and she wondered if there was a territorial issue between them.

As she sipped her coffee, Kenneth Alt's face crossed her mind, spoiling her moment of solitude in the garden. Her dad used to say there were more bumps on life's road than rainbows, but that those bumps would make her stronger. Alt was one of those bumps. He was a veteran actor who had been in the business a long time, so why would he come to Livermore to see a smaller version of *Hamlet* when he was going to direct the same play at Oregon's famous festival? She felt RT's immediate dislike of Alt was understandable, but she was grateful Detective Rook had been there to calm the waters before that situation got out of hand. She forced Alt from her mind and concentrated again on Wally Dillon and the people who would be attending the plays that evening. *Would Wally dare attempt anything with the police and a few hundred people here?*

Velcro jumped down and scampered off with Niki in pursuit.

She finished her coffee and reluctantly returned to the house, a place that would become a prison if Rook and RT got their way. Her cell rang as she poured cereal into a bowl. Her heart skipped a beat when she saw RT's number. "Good morning."

"Okay if I come over?"

"Sure."

"See you in a few."

When she opened the door, Niki bounced into the kitchen ahead of RT. Cait leaned over and stroked the dog's smooth chocolate coat.

"I knew you and Niki would bond." RT set a large bag of dog food on the counter and a white sack. "Last night's bagels."

"Help yourself to coffee."

"Thanks. My coffee pot bit the dust." He took two bagels from the bag, slit them, and dropped them in the toaster. As he poured coffee into a mug, he said, "I've been thinking about that guy Alt. I don't trust him, and you shouldn't either until you know why he's here. He's not even part of the casts." He pulled out a stool and sat at the counter, his eyes all business, cold and hard. "He could be the shooter."

"Alt is not my stalker or the shooter. It has to be Wally Dillon."

"You sure about that?"

The bagels popped up. Cait put them on a plate, got butter from the refrigerator, and sat next to RT. "Kenneth Alt has no connection to anything that occurred in Columbus. We were total strangers until I contacted him in Oregon about that short list for associate artistic director."

He nodded. "I know." He took a couple of swigs of coffee. "But you have to admit there's something squirrely about him, and that makes me nervous. Why do you think he's here?"

She thought for a moment. "I think he was sincere when he said he wanted to see where Tasha lived."

"Maybe he thinks Tasha left him something in her trust and he's here to claim it."

"That crossed my mind, but Stanton Lane would have told me. He drew up her trust." She buttered one half of her bagel. "Alt's jealous of Chip Fallon, our handsome and younger Hamlet. I overheard them arguing. I'll introduce you to Chip." She bit into her bagel.

"Can I see a copy of the festival's schedule?"

"Sure." She went into the office, plucked a sheet from a basket on the desk, returned to the kitchen, and handed it to him. "The actors' names are on there."

He read the schedule and then set it on the counter. "I know all about the phone hang-ups, your narrow escape on campus, and about the guy hanging around your car at the grocery store. Rook told me last night." He watched her over the rim of his coffee. "What I don't know are the details of your shooting that kid during a bank robbery. Rook said I should ask you. You need to talk about it, and I need to understand what happened."

She grimaced and swallowed the resentment that chocked her every time the incident came up. "He wasn't a kid," she said. "Hank Dillon was twenty-four." She kept the explanation of the shooting to a minimum. "Maybe Wally waited two years to come after me because he was in prison."

RT nodded, his eyes somber. "How old was Hank when he was adopted?"

"Twelve."

"What was the situation for the adoption?"

Cait explained how Wally's mother couldn't handle him and was afraid he'd be a bad influence on his younger brother. "The families knew each other from church. It wasn't the first time the Mannings had taken troubled kids into their home."

"Yet they decided to adopt Dillon. Why?"

"I don't know."

"Ever consider it might be Manning and not the younger brother who's after you?"

"Of course. He went into the police station to ask about me and brought up the possibility of racial bias. I wouldn't be surprised if that's the reason for this whole mess."

"Hmm, the old race card." Leaning close enough for Cait to smell his aftershave, he brushed a stray lock of hair from her face and then nibbled her ear.

Cait's hormones screamed.

Then he stood, breaking the spell. "Thanks for the coffee. I'll have a look around and then make a nuisance of myself at the theaters. Rook's officers should be here soon."

She took a deep breath. "Do me a favor and unlock the theaters when Ray gets here." She opened a drawer and handed him one of the remotes. "Each theater has its own remote." She told him the code for the alarms. "It's the same for both theaters. They're marked E and B, Elizabethan and Blackfriars."

"Too bad you can't control them from here. Save you a trip running back and forth."

"I asked about that, but was told they had to be separate. After Marcus called them again, he learned there's a new system—the ADT pulse system. All I need is an app for my cell phone. The house and the theaters can be linked together so I can manage and monitor each one. Rather than disrupt the festival now, I'll wait until after the festival ends this month. Them I'm getting that app."

"Hard to keep up with change." He winked, giving her a warm and fuzzy feeling.

Niki sat on his butt and watched Cait with his soft brown eyes.

Cait stared into her coffee and reflected on the brief affair they'd had before RT was recalled last month. She wondered if he remembered or had dismissed it as just another sexual encounter. She wished she could dismiss it. It seemed her feelings for RT were deeper than she thought.

Marcus arrived at nine dressed in pressed jeans, tan sport shirt, and riding boots. The mousse, she noticed, was back in his hair. "I should pay you overtime when you come in on weekends."

"You gave me a raise when you promoted me to manager. I don't expect more. I went to the ranch and brought my horse back again. I'll be discreet while I scout the property for intruders. Cops can't be here twenty-four-seven."

Marcus had slowly come out of his shell after Cait had given him more responsibility and promoted him to manager. Even though he couldn't carry a gun, he was eager to help in the search for her stalker. He appeared happier not being tied behind a desk and computer all day. After what had been a rocky start in their relationship, he had proven himself worthy of his new title. He certainly knew more about the festival than she did.

"Remember, no heroics. There's that old stall way out back if you want to keep your horse there instead of in a trailer all day." She tucked her gun at her waist, clipped her cell phone to her belt, and picked up the keychain. "I gave RT a remote so he can let Ray in when he comes. I'm going to see the Harts, and then I'll be at the theaters. RT brought bagels and there's coffee."

Niki followed Cait out the door. She found the Harts sitting at a small table set up under an awning in front of their RV.

"How's your new friend?" June asked.

"Niki's terrific." She glanced around at the area where the RV sat in an open space surrounded by a grove of trees. "Are you comfortable here? Is there anything you need?"

June and Jim exchanged glances. "No, we're fine," Jim said. "I wish you'd stop worrying about us. I'm glad we can hear the alarm at your house from here, but don't ever hesitate to call if you need help with anything. We're here for you, Cait."

"We'll take upon's the mystery of things as if we were God's spies," June said.

Cait laughed. *"King Lear?"*

"Smart girl. Are you excited about tonight? You'll get to see Chip in action."

"I'm looking forward to it. I'm going over to the theater now."

"Good. I'll join you soon," June said. "There's always something I can do to be useful."

Cait found RT at the Elizabethan coming down the stairs from the loft. "What were you doing up there?"

He brushed his hands together. "Looking for bad guys."

She smiled. "Find any?"

"Only dust."

"There's a trunk of weapons up there, probably where the halberd came from."

He raised his eyebrow. "Halberd? You forgot to tell me about that."

"Didn't Rook tell you? It was found outside the back door. You should ask Ray what weapons are kept in the trunk."

"Where's the halberd now?"

"Rook has it." She didn't know what Rook and RT talked about when they left last night, but apparently not everything about the attempted break-in.

Ray walked over. "Everything okay up there?"

RT nodded. "Could do with some cleaning."

"Not my job," Ray said and walked away.

"I want you to meet Chip Fallon," Cait said. "It's still early, but let's see if he's here."

They found Chip in the costume room, looking through racks full of medieval attire. Cait thought he looked cute in his khaki shorts and black sports shirt, his face wiped clear of yesterday's anger.

Chip turned and grinned at Cait. "There you are. Have you decided which play to see tonight? *Hamlet* or *Macbeth*?"

"*Hamlet,* of course. I'm looking forward to seeing you. Chip, I'd like you to meet Royal Tanner."

As the men shook hands, RT said, "Cait tells me you'll make a terrific Hamlet."

Chip laughed. "Thanks for the confidence, Cait." He scrutinized RT. "Are you with the police?"

"Not exactly, but I am here to look out for Cait."

Chip nodded. "Well, that's good, because I don't think whoever took that shot at her yesterday is the only danger lurking here."

Cait sensed a sudden tightness in RT's body. She suspected Chip was referring to Kenneth Alt.

RT frowned. "What do you mean?"

Niki ran into the room and sniffed at Chip's shoes.

Chip crouched and stroked the dog. "I had a chocolate lab when I was a kid. What's his name?"

"Niki," RT said. "What's this other danger you referred to?"

Chip stood and turned toward the door. "Ask Cait."

Cait nodded at RT. "I'll tell you later."

The afternoon passed without incident. Ilia and Fumié arrived at six. Ilia, his blond hair blowing across his forehead, had exchanged his jeans for dark dress slacks and a powder blue shirt. His camera dangled around his neck. Cait thought Fumié looked like an angel in her long pink flowing skirt and white lacy blouse, her guitar draped over her shoulder. Her long, windswept black hair gleamed in the sunshine. Ilia and Fumié were educated, ambitious, and apparently happy with each other and their place in life.

Cait's heartbeat kicked up a notch when she saw RT walking across the courtyard toward her. She swallowed hard. He was dressed in navy slacks and a melon shirt with the sleeves rolled up over his thick forearms. His eyes were hidden behind aviator sunglasses. A jacket was slung over his shoulder, but she knew he'd have a gun in his pocket or at his back.

"You ladies look smashing," RT said. "You clean up nicely, too, Ilia."

"Gee, thanks, boss," Ilia said.

Cait's cheeks flushed. She had taken a long time deciding what to wear. She wondered if her choice had been too obvious. It had been awhile, but she wondered if RT recognized the skirt as part of the outfit she'd worn the first night they'd spent together. Her skirt swirled around her calves, its gathered tiers in colors of merlot and black. She'd substituted the black knit top she'd worn then for a gauzy cream-colored one with a scooped neckline. She wore it unbelted to hide the gun tucked in her waistband.

She smiled. "You don't look so bad yourself," she said, wishing she could see behind his glasses.

"Maybe later we could—"

"There you are," Detective Rook interrupted. Dressed in a dark suit and ivory shirt, he introduced the man with him. "This is Sergeant McCloud. We've got five officers with us. A couple will circulate as guests. An unmarked vehicle will be on Cross Road near the bottom of the hill and another backed into the driveway across from the front entrance on Tesla. I didn't think you'd want a cruiser parked at the entrance to intimidate your guests."

"Thanks. I appreciate that," she said. "No need to advertise we have a problem." She checked out Sergeant McCloud, who hadn't spoken a word. His face wore a laced-up, tight look that matched his nondescript brown suit.

RT shook hands with McCloud.

Cait introduced Ilia and Fumié to McCloud. "Fumié's our entertainment and Ilia our photographer." She laid her hand on the dog at her side. "And this is Niki."

McCloud glanced at the dog but made no attempt to pet him.

"Well, at least everything looks like it's under control," she said.

Rook nodded. "Someone would have to crawl up here. Maybe the crowd will keep Wally away tonight. He'd be foolish to try anything."

Cait shook her head. "He's as determined as a pit bull. He's waited two years and come two thousand miles to find me. He won't be deterred by a few hundred people." In her peripheral vision, she noticed a couple with a teenage girl walking over to a picnic table in the shade of an old oak tree. Many had come early to stroll through the grounds, while others rested at tables or sat on the brick wall surrounding the courtyard.

"I guess I could start playing any time," Fumié said.

Cait noticed a lot of people coming from the parking lot where Marcus was posted. She checked her watch. "Definitely.

It's six-fifteen. In a half hour, they'll start looking for their seats. You could stroll through the crowd or sit on the wall and let people come to you."

"I'll stay close behind her," Ilia said. "Maybe even catch the bad guy on camera if he's dumb enough to come here."

As Rook and McCloud started to move away, Rook said over his shoulder, "No heroics, Ilia."

"Cait, the gift shop should be off limits until we catch this guy," RT said, as he turned to follow Rook and McCloud.

"It is." She reached for her cell to call June. "Where are you?" she asked her.

"At the Blackfriars," June said. "There's a good-looking guy in plainclothes with a bulge under his jacket hanging around."

Cait laughed. "Want me to check him out?"

"No. I got a glimpse of a gold badge at his waist when I accidentally on purpose bumped into him. They do come young these days, don't they?"

"They sure do."

Cait cut across the complex, her Glock digging into her back. She watched Fumié cradling her guitar, strolling where people congregated. A gust of wind whipped through Fumié's hair, fanning it around her face as she plucked poignant bars from songs mysterious to Cait. As her notes swelled into haunting poetic melodies, several people followed Fumié; she segued from one song to another until it was time for the seven o'clock curtain call.

Cait waited until the courtyard emptied before heading over to the Elizabethan theater. She spoke a few words with the volunteer who stood outside the door taking tickets and handing out programs, and then she went inside. She walked slowly up the side aisle, glancing down each row on her way to the back. While she waited for the play to begin, she looked out over the audience. The house was sold out. She felt a flutter of excitement and peeked at her watch: Five minutes until curtain time.

Cait worried about the heat and the inevitable evening chill at the outdoor theater. She knew the sun wouldn't set until eight-thirty, but the way the theater was situated on the hill and with ocean breezes moving in, the audience would definitely need jackets.

A uniformed officer nodded to Cait from the opposite side of the theater.

An expectant hush fell over the theater as the curtain opened. The play had begun.

Cait lost track of time as she focused on the setting—the royal castle at Elsinore—and listened as a constable revealed to Horatio that a frightening apparition was seen during his watch on a previous occasion. Just as the ghost itself entered, her attention was drawn away by a commotion below at the entrance.

Careful not to distract the audience, she slipped down the aisle. The door was cracked open. She stepped outside and quietly shut it. The volunteer she'd spoken to earlier was trying to explain to a slightly disheveled man that he couldn't take liquor into the theater.

Cait caught a strong whiff of alcohol on him. "May I help you?"

He blinked, as if trying to focus on Cait. "This lady won't let me in."

Cait wondered how he'd gotten to the theater, particularly with a bottle clutched in his hand. She'd have to speak to Rook about it. "Alcohol is not allowed in the theaters. I'd be happy to refund your money."

"Didn't think I'd need a ticket. I'm with the rodeo," he said as if that explained his presence.

"Why don't I have someone escort you to your car?" Cait asked, reaching for her cell. She stepped away from the man and called Rook. "I need someone to escort a man from the Elizabethan theater. We're at the side door."

"There's an officer in the theater. I'll call him," Rook said. "What's the problem?"

Annoyed the man had been allowed up, she said, "He's inebriated," and disconnected the call.

"I can find my own way down, thank you," the man said, tripping over his own feet.

The officer Cait had seen inside the theater came out, grabbed the man's arm before he fell, then turned his head away and wrinkled his nose.

Cait watched the officer lead the man away, then turned to the volunteer. "Sorry. I'll make sure that doesn't happen again." She walked around to the back emergency door and called Rook.

"Has the situation been taken care of?" Rook asked.

She scanned the shrubs and trees around the theater, feeling vulnerable in the dim path lights. "How the hell did a drunk with a whiskey bottle get up here? I thought you had police positioned at both entrances."

"He must have walked up."

"There's still light. He should have been seen."

"Think about it, Cait. He could have cut through the vineyard. It goes all the way down to the street on both sides of the driveway."

Embarrassed she hadn't considered the vineyard, she said, "Sorry, I never thought of that." She wondered what other ways there were up to the house and theaters as she opened the door. Inside the green room she heard soft laughter, murmurs about last-minute costume adjustments, and bottles of water being opened. She looked for Chip and saw him waiting in the wing to go on stage. She thought he made an impressive Hamlet.

He turned and smiled when he saw her.

She looked to see if Kenneth Alt was hanging around in the

back, but he was nowhere in sight. *He wouldn't buy a ticket and sit out front. So where is he?*

Mindful of being in the way as the actors hurried on and off stage, she left the theater the way she went in and reentered at the side door. The volunteer now sat inside on an aisle seat. Cait returned to her post at the back of the theater, eager to watch Chip as Hamlet, prince of Denmark.

It wasn't until act 1, scene 2, that Cait saw the young Hamlet, when Claudius asked him why he still grieved, and told him that "sustained grief is unmanly and evidence of impious stubbornness." Just as Queen Gertrude urged her son to accept his father's death and to recognize that his own bereavement was not unusual, Cait's cell vibrated in her hand.

Frustrated, she left the theater.

"The house alarm's been tripped," Marcus said over the phone.

"I don't believe this. I'm on my way."

CHAPTER 17

Cait ran toward the house, her gun at her side. When she heard someone calling her name, she glanced over her shoulder and saw Sergeant McCloud.

"Wait!" When he caught up with her, he said, "You can't go there until Detective Rook gives the okay."

"Like hell I can't," she said. "It's my house."

"Let us do our job. Please."

Cait let her gun hang at her side as she stared at him. The illumination in the courtyard revealed the concern in his eyes and the weariness in the slump of his shoulders. She knew he was right. She took a deep breath, slowly exhaled, and forced her anger to subside. "If the alarm was a trick to get me alone in the open, away from the crowd, it worked."

McCloud smiled. "Our thoughts exactly. Let's wait inside one of the theaters until we hear from Rook." Just then a voice came over McCloud's radio.

"McCloud," he answered. After a moment, he said, "Okay." He rang off and nodded. "You got your wish. Let's go."

"False alarm?" she asked hopefully.

"Don't know. Keep watch as we make our way to the house."

She checked her cell for the time. "Not long before intermission. People will stream through the doors and into the courtyard. June's in the Blackfriars theater. I should let her know what's happened."

"I'll call the officer and have him keep everyone inside," Mc-

135

Cloud said.

June answered in a whisper. Cait explained about the alarm and relayed McCloud's warning.

"There's no intermission so no reason for anyone to leave, but I'll find Fumié and Ilia and tell them what's going on," June said.

"Thanks." Cait tucked her phone away and crossed the courtyard with McCloud, their guns drawn and tracking every shadow. The sergeant opened the squeaky gate, sending chills through Cait's body as usual. As they approached the house, she had a new worry. Niki. She'd left him alone in the house. Was he frightened? She visualized the dog shivering and hovering under the piano, the only solid piece of furniture. When they walked in, Niki jumped up on Cait like they were old buddies. She set her gun on the counter and wrapped her arms around the dog's neck, relieved he was okay.

"Can you believe the jerk smashed a window?" Marcus said, eyes wide open. "I was here and shut the alarm off right away."

Rook ran his hand over his thinning hair. "This guy is like a damn snake, slithering into a hidey-hole."

Cait had never seen Rook angry enough that his face turned red. *When I was a cop, I promised to protect and serve. That oath never leaves you, even if you depart the force, but sometimes, like now, it's a hard pledge to keep. I could kill Wally Dillon.*

Just as he informed Cait that RT and the officers were searching the grounds, he was interrupted by a voice from his radio. "Anything?" he responded. He paused, frowned. "Yeah." Rook glanced at Cait. "Do you want to go back and see the rest of the play?"

She hesitated. "Yes."

"You'll need an escort." He cocked his eyebrow at McCloud.

"I'll take her," McCloud said.

"Show me the broken window first," she said.

"Don't worry about it, we'll board it up," Rook said. "Nothing in the gift shop was damaged."

"I could get my horse and scout out the property," Marcus said.

Cait sympathized with Marcus's eagerness to help, but it was almost dark, and he wasn't armed.

Rook shook his head. "I don't want you or your horse stumbling about in the dark or frightening the guests."

"Tomorrow, then, when it's light," Marcus said. "I'd like to find evidence to nail the bastard to the wall."

A smile crossed Rook's face. "That would be helpful."

Cait stroked Niki's head and then followed McCloud and Rook out the door.

"Found blood on shards of glass. He must have used his fist to break the window," Rook said.

"That idiot has got to be Wally Dillon," Cait said. "Maybe DNA will prove it."

Sergeant McCloud and Cait stood at the rear of the Elizabethan theater in time to watch act 3, scene 4. Polonius, the king of Denmark's chief counselor, was instructing the queen to be firm with her son, but when Hamlet, aka Chip Fallon, entered the queen's chamber, Polonius hid.

Cait sneaked glances at McCloud to see how he was reacting to the play. It wasn't until Hamlet drew his rapier and killed Polonius that she got her answer. The sergeant jerked upright, his attention riveted on the stage. Then when the ghost appeared and expressed concern for Gertrude, the sergeant's attention waned.

McCloud whispered at Cait's ear. "You get this stuff?"

She smiled. "*Hamlet* is the ultimate ghost story. You gotta love it. Want to go backstage to meet Hamlet?"

He nodded. "Better than standing here like statues."

They slipped down the aisle and out the exit. Cait laughed at the relief on McCloud's face when they were outside. "You didn't like it, did you?"

"I saw the play with my wife. I didn't understand it then and I don't now, but she loves Shakespeare. So for the sake of our marriage, I take her to Ashland whenever she wants to go."

The motion sensors lit as they circled to the rear of the theater. "I inherited this place from Tasha Bening, my aunt, who was a Shakespearean actor at the OSF. She modeled this festival after the one in Ashland, but on a much smaller scale."

McCloud held the door for her. "Rook told me about your aunt. He also said you'd been a cop and that it was difficult for you to take orders from us." He glanced at her with a smile, then turned to search the yard around them with his hand rested on his gun. "Should we go in?"

She nodded. The atmosphere in the green room was quiet except for voices on the mounted screen keyed to the action on stage. A few actors stood and watched while others waited in the wings for their cue. A rush of staccato words, like bullets, interrupted the room. McCloud's head shot around as he looked for the cause of the disturbance.

Then Cait saw Chip Fallon and Kenneth Alt in each other's faces off to the side of the room.

"McCloud, over there," Cait said.

Hands clenched at his sides, Alt said, "You botched it!"

Chip backed away from Alt. "Get out of my face, Alt. Go sit in a corner. I'm due on stage."

"We're not finished," Alt said.

"Oh, yes you are, Alt!" Cait said. "You have a choice. Leave now, or this officer will escort you out." She pointed to the door.

Chip and Alt turned to stare at her. Relief spread over Chip's face. Alt's face turned red. "Cait—"

"Now!"

"Told you he was dangerous," Chip said.

"What's his problem?"

"It's obvious. He wants me to mess up so he can take over." He smirked at Alt's receding back. "That's not going to happen."

"I don't believe this," she said. "It's quite a coup to direct *Hamlet* at the OSF. Why would he come here?"

CHAPTER 18

The rest of Saturday evening passed without incident. The broken window in the gift shop was boarded up with a thick sheet of plywood when Cait returned. After the guests left, the theaters were locked and alarmed for the night. Two cruisers patrolled the road below the estate. RT and Cait were alone in the kitchen with Niki.

Awkwardness overcame Cait after RT's long absence. She grabbed a towel and wiped the granite counters until he took the towel from her. He took her hand and led her into the front room. He switched on the small stained glass lamp on the grand piano, pulled out the bench, and drew her down beside him.

RT flexed his fingers and struck a chord. "Music is therapeutic, not just for the heart but for the whole being. Relax and let it work its magic."

She tried, until he segued into "Wind Beneath My Wings." The tune had drawn Cait and RT into their short affair, and she'd never be able to forget it or him. Sitting next to him now, even though it had been only a month since he'd been called for another assignment, the thin thread that held her feelings in check unraveled.

Caught up in her emotional turmoil, she'd been unaware RT had stopped playing until he leaned over and kissed her on the neck and then on the lips. His kisses left no doubt how much he wanted her, awakening Cait's body to a high pitch of desire.

"Let's get comfortable." He pulled her up, switched off the

lamp, and drew her up the stairs.

When they were locked in the third-floor bedroom, RT slipped her blouse over her head, pulled her skirt down, and kicked it away. "You're beautiful," he whispered in her ear. Lowering his head to kiss the valley between her breasts, he released her bra and caressed her skin. "I've thought about this every day since I left," he said, his voice husky.

A small moan rose from her throat under the sweet seduction of his hands.

It took Cait a few seconds to recognize the noise she heard as Skype. Instead of going to the desk and her computer, she reached over and touched the indentation on the pillow where RT's head had been and wished he hadn't left at dawn to return to his trailer. She blinked at the kaleidoscope of colors streaming through the stained glass windows as she dragged herself out of bed and crossed the room. She tapped a key to activate her computer. "I'm here, Shep."

"Sorry if I woke you, but there's something you should know."

Cait slipped into the chair and leaned close to the screen. "What is it?"

"It was Wally Dillon who requested that knife from the property room."

"I never doubted it."

"I read his police record. I think his mother put the wrong son up for adoption," Shep said. "A delinquent at eight years old." He held up a picture. "This is Wally Dillon."

She studied the mug shot of a light-skinned black man, with a shaved head, and a hairline scar from beneath his left eye to his jaw.

"Recognize him?" Shep asked.

"No, but if I didn't know better, I'd say he doesn't look evil."

Shep continued to hold the picture up to the screen. "Take a good look. Five-nine, one hundred sixty pounds, twenty-two years old. I'll email you a copy. His mother doesn't know where he is and hasn't seen him for a couple of weeks. Not unusual, she said, because he sometimes disappears without telling her where he's going. Consider him dangerous and armed. Was the guy hanging out by your car at the grocery store black?"

She flashed back to the incident. "African-American or Hispanic."

"What about at the college? Did you get a look at the driver?"

"It happened too fast. I'll make copies of his picture to hand out. This is the break we've been waiting for." She hesitated. "It must be Wally with the AK-47."

"Probably. The weapon's not designed for accuracy, but it can sure lay down a storm of lead." He removed the mug shot from the screen. "AK-47s are easy to get if you know where to look. He probably has connections in the Bay Area."

Niki reached his paw up on Cait's lap and whined.

Shep grinned. "You got a dog?"

Cait stroked Niki. "Yes, a beautiful chocolate lab named Niki."

"Where'd you get him?"

"RT's back," she said. "His daughter, Mindy, wanted me to have a dog to keep me company and to protect me since I live alone. Niki is six months old, and trained."

Shep leaned into the screen and wiggled his bushy eyebrows. "The SEAL? How long's he going to hang around this time?"

"He said a couple of weeks."

"Funny how he turns up every time there's a crisis."

"He stays in touch with Detective Rook, so he knew about my situation."

"I'm happy for you, Cait, as long as he's there for the right reason. I'll send Wally's mug shot. Be safe."

The screen faded.

By the time Cait had showered and dressed, Niki was panting to go out. As soon as she opened the back door, he dashed off.

Kurt Mathews, her vineyard manager, rushed over before she closed the door. "Cait, we have a situation in the vineyard."

She smiled. "I'm sure it's something you can fix."

"Not this time. You'll need to call the police."

She had a tingling feeling at the back of her neck as she followed Kurt around to the vineyard. He led her five rows down the driveway, stopped, and pointed down the row.

"What?" She took a couple of steps into the row of chardonnay vines and froze. Her cop senses screamed.

A body lay on the ground, head twisted at an odd angle. She went closer and gasped.

Chip Fallon was dead!

CHAPTER 19

Cait blinked back tears as she reached in her pocket for her cell and phoned RT. When RT got there, he looked at the body and called Detective Rook. Fortunately, Rook was in his office catching up on paperwork when RT called. Ten minutes later, Rook drove up in an unmarked car, and several police cruisers with bar lights flashing parked behind him along the side of the driveway.

"Cait, I'm sorry," Rook said when he jumped out of his car. "I notified the sheriff's department. I'll try to get more officers for surveillance until the bastard who did this is caught."

She pointed down the row where she stood. "He's down there. Blame Wally Dillon. I talked to Shep earlier. He's sending Wally's mug shot."

A van pulled up and parked. "That's the crime scene technicians," Rook said as he went over to talk to them.

Cait watched two women in police uniform step out of the van; one carried a camera and both carried what looked like black tackle boxes. Rook led them to the body.

June and Jim ran over to Cait. "What happened? We saw flashing lights."

"It's Chip . . . he's dead," Cait managed to say.

June gasped. Jim wrapped his arm around her shoulder. "Oh, my God." She glanced at the police cars. "Someone murdered him?"

Cait nodded, surprised June had jumped so quickly to that

conclusion. She watched one of the techs photograph the body and surrounding area; the other tech had pulled a pad and pen from her pocket. The narrow row made it difficult for them to move around as they juggled their equipment. They measured the body from head to toe before outlining it with orange spray paint and setting out tent cards.

Cait watched the techs methodically going over the area, collecting evidence, but never touching the body. The taking of another life never failed to shock her. She had been standing there watching the techs for what seemed a long time when Rook joined her. Distraught, Cait asked, "Why Chip? He was a nice man and a great actor."

"I think Mr. Fallon was in the wrong place at the wrong time or was killed as a warning to you," Rook said. "It could have been anyone who got in his way." He stripped off his latex gloves and shoved them into his jeans pocket.

She glanced up and saw Marcus running up the driveway.

"Cait! I was afraid something happened to you when I saw all those lights and police cars," Marcus said when he reached her. "What's going on?"

She cleared her throat. "Chip Fallon is dead."

"What? The guy who plays Hamlet? Well, shit. At least it's not you," he said. "There's a police car below on the road. The officer wasn't going to let me up until I showed my ID and said I worked here. I had to park on the side of the road."

RT walked over and put his arm around her waist. Grateful for his comfort, but feeling smothered physically and mentally, she drew away. "Shep is emailing Wally Dillon's mug shot." Her fingers flexed at her sides, anxious to get the photo but not wanting to leave the crime scene. "Wally's twenty-two, with a long rap sheet dating back to when he was eight. Shep said to consider him armed and dangerous." She uttered a feigned laugh.

"Can we eliminate Calder Manning now?" June asked.

Cait shook her head. "We can't eliminate anyone. When I told Shep about the AK-47 shooting, he said Wally has to have connections in the Bay Area."

"He could also have stayed in touch with a former cell mate," Rook said.

"Are you thinking two suspects?" June asked.

"At least," Rook said. "Wally's got help. Those hang-up calls were only the beginning."

Cait frowned. "A computer geek must have gotten both of my phone numbers for him."

"I can check your email if you'd like and make copies of the mug shot," Marcus said.

"Thanks. That would be helpful."

"I'll go to the office with you," Rook said. "I want enough copies to hand out at the station and some for the sheriff's department."

Cait noticed Kurt Mathews standing off by himself and walked up to him. "I'm sorry, Kurt, that it had to be you who found the body."

"But it's your vineyard," he said. "That sucks. I'll be back tomorrow. I came today to check the roses along the driveway and at the edges of the vineyard. Roses are susceptible to many of the same diseases as grapevines and are an excellent bellwether for problems that could hit the vineyard." He glanced over the rows of grapes. "At least the body wasn't there long."

She nodded. "See you tomorrow, Kurt." She turned when she heard a vehicle backfire as it came up the driveway. "Oh, no. Not Ray. That means the actors will soon follow."

"What the hell happened now?" Ray said as he and Jay climbed down from the truck.

Before Cait could answer, another vehicle drove up.

"That's the coroner," RT said.

146

"Rook said he'd called the sheriff's department. Maybe they were already in the area, to get here so fast." She glanced at Ray and thought his face looked drained of color. She touched his arm. "Ray, Chip is dead. I'm sorry."

Ray stared hard at her and then turned to walk away, but when two deputies opened the back of their van, he stopped to watch as they went over to talk to the techs.

Cait knew the coroner's deputies could take a long time fingerprinting, gathering body fluids, hair, and fibers, and she didn't want to hang around to watch. She'd seen it all before and didn't think it would be wise for Ray or Jay to see the process or the removal of Chip's body. "We have to talk, Ray." She glanced at RT. "You want to join us?"

"Of course. From now on, we're like two peas in the same pod. I'm not letting you out of my sight after what's happened here."

"You could be called back to work any time. Don't worry. I'll be okay."

"I'll be at the theater," Ray said. "I don't know how to deal with this, but maybe keeping busy will help." He started to walk away.

Marcus looked at Detective Rook. "I'll let them into the theater and then meet you at the house."

"Ray," Cait called after him, "We'll have to cancel the play."

"Not yet. I'll think of something."

While Rook waited at the house for Marcus, Cait and RT followed the Harts to their RV. "Tell me about Kenneth Alt," Cait said when they were inside the trailer.

June's jaw dropped. "You think *Kenneth* killed Chip?"

"I don't know, but I heard him arguing with Chip last night. Personally, I think Alt is an ass, but that doesn't mean he's capable of murder."

June looked out the RV's pop-out window as if in deep

thought. A perplexed expression crossed her face. "Unfortunately, you've only seen the nasty side of Kenneth, when he's being an arrogant bastard." She glanced back at Cait. "But a cold-blooded murderer? No way. I've known him a long time—since he and Tasha had a thing going in New York. They were lovers. Did he tell you that?"

Cait cocked her eyebrow. "No, just that they were very good friends."

June nodded. "He was younger than Tasha and terribly ambitious. He was twenty-two, she was almost thirty. Nothing, not even Tasha, could stand in his way, and she was a great force to deal with even then, believe me. Over the years, he's built a respectable reputation throughout the theater community. He would *never* in a million years jeopardize that."

"Then why is he here? Why come to this small festival in Livermore when he's going to direct *Hamlet* on the bigger stage at the Oregon Shakespeare Festival?"

June sighed. "I wish I had an answer for you, but like it or not, he's the only one here to take Chip's place."

Cait nodded. "I haven't processed that yet, but you're right. Should I come straight out and ask him?"

June shook her head. "Not yet. Give him the opportunity to offer to step in when he hears about Chip. Granted, Kenneth's ego is huge, but at the same time, he's a professional. He'll do the right thing."

"I hope so," Cait said, "because the matinee is at two o'clock."

"How soon before the actors return?" RT asked.

"Maybe they're here now," Cait said.

"The old timers never show up until just before curtain call," June said, "but that may not be the case here. Most of these actors are younger and happy to hang out. I enjoy talking to them. They respect you, Cait, for carrying out Tasha's wishes for the festival. You don't have to worry about them. Actors are independent and capable of managing for themselves quite nicely."

"Maybe, but wait until they hear about Chip. I suppose it's up to me to give them the bad news. I hope I can find the right words."

RT rose and gently touched Cait's shoulder. "I disagree. It's Ray's responsibility. He's the stage manager. He should also handle any calls from Actors' Equity."

"RT's right," June said. "Talk to Ray, and see what he thinks is best. Most actors are emotional people, so don't be surprised if they want to hear from you, too."

"Wait here," RT said, "while I check on Niki and see how Rook and Marcus are doing with Wally's mug shot."

After RT left, Cait asked, "Anyone know where to find Kenneth Alt?"

CHAPTER 20

Cait and the Harts were on their way to the theaters when someone called Cait's name. Detective Rook and Sergeant Mc-Cloud caught up and handed them copies of Wally Dillon's mug shot. "Memorize his face and make sure everyone sees this," Rook said.

Cait stared at the hairline scar zigzagging from Wally's left eye to his jaw. "Looks like he got caught on the wrong end of a blade." She folded the page into a neat square and tucked it into a pocket of her jeans. "Someone should have seen something or heard something." She glanced off in the distance but didn't find an answer.

"It was dark and late, and only the actors and a couple of crew members were left, but we may have something better," McCloud said.

She noticed McCloud had left his drab clothing and bland demeanor behind. Today he wore khakis, black sports shirt, and running shoes. "What?"

"A gum wrapper, like the one found in Ray Stoltz's truck."

She shrugged. "Prints become illegible over time, particularly on a small piece of paper."

"Not when there's a wad of gum inside the wrapper."

She grinned. "The guy's a neat freak? Go figure."

McCloud nodded. "We handed it over to an officer to take back to HQ. He'll see that it's sent to the county crime lab for

DNA. I think we have good cause to get it moved to the head of the line."

"That would be helpful. I don't think Wally's mug shot matches the guy I saw at Trader Joe's," Cait said.

"The guy you saw could be his accomplice," Rook said. "Wally probably networked and put out the word he needed an AK-47 or whatever."

Tormenting fear and anger raced down Cait's spine. "I should be so popular."

"We'll know for sure when the results of the DNA on that wad of gum are back."

"Can't be soon enough," Cait said. "I have to see Ray."

She didn't have far to look for Ray. When Cait and the Harts walked into the courtyard, they saw Ray pacing the bricks. "Where's Kenneth Alt?" he snapped.

"Calm down, Ray," Cait said. "You're the stage manager, not me. If you've misplaced one of your actors, find him."

"Alt is not one of my actors."

"Well, he is now, unless you can play Hamlet."

Ray looked to the sky, as if searching for an answer. "Good grief! This is one hell of a mess."

"Yes, it is," Cait said, "but we have to deal with it. Any suggestions where Alt might be staying?"

"How would I know? He isn't even supposed to be here."

"True, but be grateful he is. Without him, all those patrons who bought tickets for this afternoon's matinee will be disappointed," Cait said. "So let's find him."

"Wait," June said. "I overheard Kenneth telling someone about a fancy B and B in the vineyards."

"Rook should know where it is," Cait said. She pulled her phone from a pocket and called him.

"What is it?" he answered. "No more bodies, I hope."

"We need to find Kenneth Alt right away. He may be staying at a B and B. Where's the closest one?"

"The Purple Orchid Inn on Cross Road," Rook said, "but now it's a resort and spa."

"Any others?"

"White Crane Winery. Not far. It's out Greenville Road. It was a B and B, but I heard they specialize in weddings now."

"Neither sounds like something Alt would—"

"What the hell happened now?" someone yelled.

Cait turned. She never thought she'd be so happy to see Kenneth Alt, yet there he was running toward them, arms flailing as if in a panic.

"Who's that?" Rook asked over the phone.

"That would be Alt," Cait said. "He must have seen your crime scene tape, because he's freaking out. I would appreciate it if you'd come to the courtyard and tell him what happened before he has a heart attack. We need him healthy so he can take over for Chip."

His face flushed, Alt said, "That yellow tape could only mean one thing. Whatever happened, I had nothing to do with it."

Cait rolled her eyes. *I hope you didn't.* "Calm down, Kenneth. Detective Rook will be here in a minute."

"Was someone shot?"

She reflected on the earlier gunshot, but was saved from replying when Jim said, "Here comes Detective Rook."

Alt rushed to meet Rook. "What's happened now?"

"One of your colleagues was murdered," Rook bluntly said.

Alt looked at Cait, his face ashen. "Who?"

"Chip Fallon."

"Oh, my God!" Alt staggered and grabbed hold of the gate for support. He stumbled over to the brick wall around the courtyard and sat on the edge. "You're wrong. It can't be Chip." He bowed his head. "I talked to him last night. I apologized for being an ass."

"You accused him of messing up his role," Cait said.

His head jerked up. "You don't think I killed him, do you?"

"Hold on," Rook said. "No one is accusing you of anything. But I have to ask what you and Fallon talked about. You may have been the last person to see him alive. Except for the killer."

"Alive, yes," Alt said. "We always argued, but he was alive when we parted. He wanted to know why I was here."

"What did you tell him?" Rook asked.

"That it was none of his business."

"Well, it's my business now," Rook said, "so tell me."

His eye flicked on Cait. "It's personal."

Warning bells went off in her head. *Personal? He's here because of me?*

"Where are you staying?" Rook asked.

"The Hilton, other side of the freeway."

"I hope you aren't planning on leaving town," Cait said. "Without *Hamlet,* there's no matinee," she said as she checked the time on her cell, "which starts in four hours. Will you take Chip's place?" *So much for subtlety.*

Alt dropped his head into his hands. When he looked up again, he nodded. "Of course. I've played the part enough times to do it in my sleep."

Relieved, Cait let out her breath. "Thank you, Kenneth. I appreciate how difficult it will be for you."

June went over to Alt and laid her hand on his shoulder. "Kenneth, I don't think you killed Chip, but you can understand how the constant arguing between the two of you makes you appear suspect."

Alt nodded and stared down at his folded hands. "This is terrible. I admit I was jealous of Chip, his age, his looks. I know he was a good actor, maybe even a great one." His eyes pleaded for understanding. "I didn't kill him. You have to believe me."

"I totally understand the age thing, Kenneth," June said, "but that's no excuse to yell at and belittle your colleague and make the rest of us uncomfortable."

Cait shook her head as if she hadn't heard right. *Did Alt just admit he was jealous of Chip?* She didn't believe he killed Chip. He didn't have the backbone. She looked at Detective Rook. "Could you remove the crime tape before it turns people away? They've paid good money to come here to be entertained, not be part of a murder scene."

Rook nodded. "I'll see to it." He stared hard at Alt. "We're not done. Don't leave town."

"How was Chip murdered?"

Rook hesitated. "He was strangled."

"Strangled with what?" Cait asked.

"A bolo tie."

Cait gasped. She flashed on the drunken rodeo guy who tried to get in the Elizabethan theater. *Was it possible he'd returned after the police escorted him out?*

CHAPTER 21

The more Cait thought about the rodeo guy, the more she was convinced he didn't murder Chip, but she'd also thought it wasn't possible she had a stalker. "Did anyone get the drunken rodeo guy's name?"

Rook shook his head. "No. He left peacefully."

"Maybe you should track him down."

"There's a slim chance he'll attend the mixer at the rodeo grounds on Wednesday," Rook said, "but it would be like looking for that proverbial needle in a haystack. Our best use of the officers' time is here, where we know who we're looking for."

"You're right," she admitted.

"Look, Wally Dillon could have gone into Baughman's or Dom's western outfitters and bought a shoestring necktie as a souvenir," Rook said.

"Have you taken Wally's picture to the stores to see if they recognize him? If not, I'll do it."

"We just got his picture, Cait. We're not miracle workers. That's on my long list of things to do," Rook said.

"I have to check the costumes," Alt said. "Chip and I are about the same size, so there shouldn't be a problem. Don't worry, Detective, I'm not going to disappear. I want to know who murdered Chip as much as you do."

Something nagged at Cait until she finally pulled it out. "Was Chip in costume when he was killed? I didn't notice what he was wearing."

Rook rubbed the back of his neck. "No, jeans and T-shirt."

"If Chip was wearing his own clothes, he meant to leave. If he rented a car, he would've gone to the parking lot, not the vineyard. And if he carpooled with another actor, wouldn't that person look for Chip when he didn't show?" Cait asked.

"Jim and I saw Chip after the guests left," June said. "That was some time after ten. He said he was staying in one of Tasha's leased apartments in town and was waiting for his ride."

"So he decided to take a stroll through the vineyard where he couldn't be seen?" Cait asked.

"He did appear to be upset," Jim said, "but when I asked if he was okay, he said he'd had another argument with Alt and needed to walk off his frustrations. That's the last we saw of him."

All eyes turned on Alt.

He held his hands up. "No, no, no. I did not kill Chip. There's no way you're pinning this on me." He spun around and stalked off.

Cait hadn't spent as much time as she would have liked with the actors from *Macbeth* and was torn over which play to attend, but it was important to see Kenneth as Hamlet. Her instinct told her he was innocent of murder, but would he leave, afraid no one would believe him? She reached into her pocket for Wally's mug shot. His face was seared into her mind, along with his brother Hank's, but she wanted another look. Eyes are the mirrors of the soul. If she came face to face with Wally, as she had Hank, she wanted to compare the brothers.

"Why are you staring at that mug shot?" June asked.

Cait shoved it back in her pocket. "I was thinking about Calder Manning."

"Why?"

"He might know if Wally has contacts in California."

"Maybe your detective friend in Columbus should call him," Jim said. "Someone supplied Dillon with guns, maybe a local or someone from over the hill in the central valley like Detective Rook suggested."

Fatigue weighed heavily on Cait, leaving her feeling older than thirty-five. Everyone thought she was strong because she'd been in law enforcement. "Manning's probably out of the country, but it's worth a try. I'll ask Shep."

Niki bounded through the gate followed by RT. She studied RT's body language. When she was working, she'd paid close attention to nonverbal communication, body posture, gestures, facial expressions, and eye movements, and she continued to do so today. People sent and interpreted signals subconsciously. When she'd met her husband, she'd dismissed all the signals that screamed at her to "keep walking," but because he was a police chaplain, she'd dismissed them as nerves. How wrong she'd been.

RT's eyes were hidden behind dark sunglasses. He walked straight and tall, a Navy SEAL trained to mask his feelings. But she caught the raised eyebrow and slight hitch at the corners of his mouth. Was that a wink behind the opaque glasses? Her body hummed as she flashed to last night in her bedroom.

Niki jumped up on Cait, begging for attention. She kneeled and wrapped her arms around his neck, comforted by the warmth of his fur.

RT offered a treat to the dog. "You gotta carry treats in your pocket, Cait."

She saw Detective Rook and a couple of officers coming toward her. The officers were probably in their mid-twenties, pumped and eager to work with a homicide detective. All wore belts carrying guns, batons, and handcuffs. Rook, in jeans, wore his service weapon in a shoulder holster visible underneath his opened jacket.

"Sergeant McCloud and other officers are combing the grounds, as far back as the cave," Rook said. "These officers will split up, walk through the theaters, hike down the hill to Cross Road, and come back up the driveway in front. Everyone has copies of Wally's mug shot."

Voices from the direction of the Elizabethan theater caught Cait's attention. She saw Ray, his arms flailing in the air. He looked intense, his eyes darkly focused on her as he ran.

Oh, no. This can't be good news, Cait thought as she looked at Ray.

CHAPTER 22

Ray jabbed his finger at the Elizabethan theater. "Who is going to tell them their friend is dead?"

"Remember," June whispered to Cait, "actors are tough and ego driven but supportive of their own when it gets right down to it. It's the same with stage managers. Give Ray room to vent his frustrations, and he'll be all right."

Cait looked at Ray's flushed face and then at the actors walking into the theaters and drew a deep breath. "It's your responsibility as stage manager to tell them what happened, but I'll do it if you're not comfortable with making the announcement. I hope they'll stay. Kenneth Alt has agreed to step in and fill the role of Hamlet."

Ray kept his eyes on the actors. "They'll stay if I ask them to. Nobody wants to let you down, Cait, but I'm not sure I should ask them to stay. When will it end? What would you do in their shoes?"

Frustration gnawed at her. "I'm carrying a lot of guilt over this, Ray. I don't like it, but it is what it is. Try putting yourself in my shoes. What would you do?" Their raised voices caught the actors' attention. "The performances are sold out. Please don't shut me down."

"Their lives are at stake," he said.

"They have contracts," Cait said.

"So do I," he said, "but contracts can be broken."

"Cait—" RT cut in.

She cut him off. "This is my battle."

"Then you might remember that while you're standing here exposed, Wally could have you lined up in the crosshairs of his AK-47 again."

She'd neglected her own safety while she worried over the actors. She glanced at those standing outside both theaters with confusion etched on their faces. "How do you want to handle this, Ray?"

Ray's shoulders slumped. "June, please ask everyone to congregate in the green room."

June nodded and hurried off.

Cait followed Ray to the Elizabethan. She trusted him to do the right thing while she was doing everything possible to keep the festival going. There was no other choice.

Jim remained outside the theater with Niki to guard the door. Once everyone had gathered in the room, Cait stood off to the side to collect her thoughts in case Ray called on her.

Ray took his time, his gaze canvassing the room of expectant faces. "I have sad news. We've lost a friend. Chip Fallon is dead. He was murdered last night."

After an initial frozen silence, the room filled with the sounds of people gasping and sobbing.

His blunt pronouncement stunned Cait, even though she knew what was coming. Her eyes misted. She wanted to curl up in a corner and go to sleep, then wake up and hear Chip telling her it had all been a joke. The warmth of RT's arm around her shoulder comforted her and helped her collect herself should Ray ask her to speak.

Ray glanced at Cait and cleared his throat. "We have a decision to make. Should we close the show?"

Cait saw Kenneth Alt across the room, head bowed. She worried that under the circumstances, he wasn't strong enough to step into Chip's place, that he'd be overwhelmed with guilt because of their constant arguing. She looked at the distraught faces in the room but couldn't help but wonder which one of them was supposed to have carpooled with Chip last night. No one exhibited signs of guilt, only shock at the loss of their friend.

The first question came from Paula, who played Hamlet's mother. She coughed a couple of times and then said, "We can't have a show without Hamlet."

Alt looked up.

Ray nodded. "True." He hesitated. "But we're fortunate Kenneth Alt is here. We all know he's a seasoned and respected actor. He's played the role of Hamlet numerous times. He's agreed to take over the role if we decide to continue." His gaze swept the room as he waited for their response.

Despite the undertones of surprise in the room, Paula rose from her seat on the sofa and went over to Alt. "Kenneth, how do you feel about it? Would you be able to after . . ." she faltered, her voice shaking.

Kenneth impressed Cait when he took Paula's hands in his. "I'll do it if you want me to."

Paula nodded. "We'd all be happy if you would be our Hamlet."

Cait wondered if she'd misjudged him. She still wanted to know his real reason for coming here. Maybe the time had come to ask.

An hour before the matinee, Rook, McCloud, and the officers did a thorough search of both theaters but found no one lurking about. RT took Niki with him to check the house before he'd let Cait go upstairs to change her clothes.

Cait showered and dressed in white slacks, pink silk camisole with matching blouse, and white sandals. When she went downstairs, she felt heat rise in her cheeks as the desire in RT's eyes drew her to him.

He grinned. "You look damned edible."

RT escorted Cait to the Blackfriars theater and then had a few words with the officer stationed at the door. He whispered to Cait, "I have to go. When you're ready to leave, this officer will escort you to the Elizabethan." He gently touched her hand and then left. Annoyed to be passed from one person to the next, her instincts were to run out the door and take her chances on her own. Instead, she found a seat againt the wall to watch the reaction of the audience and how they responded to being so close to the stage. Her gun was tucked beneath her blouse and rubbed against the wooden chair when she shifted in her seat, reminding her to pay more attention to her situation than the play.

One of Shakespeare's most thoughtful plays, *Macbeth* was fueled by the occult, battle scenes, and lusty passion. Part mystery, part action, and part drama, it was one of Cait's favorite plays. Performed on the small stage with only two chairs, two goblets, and the crown, the play focused on the psychology of the characters with the crown as a central image to the play. She admired the simplicity and elegance of the costumes and tried to visualize Tasha dressed in a costume like the one worn by Betsy Ryder, the current Lady Macbeth.

She rose, walked to the back, and whispered to the officer, "I'll be okay. I'm armed," and slipped out before he could respond. She tracked her gun over the courtyard as she kept her eyes on the surroundings. She listened for sudden movements, footsteps, or nervous birds taking flight.

When she reached the outdoor theater, she tucked her gun back under her blouse and joined June inside at the rear of the theater.

"How's he doing?" Cait whispered.

"Kenneth is a pro." June pointed to the other side of the theater where Detective Rook stood with a uniformed officer.

"Looks like our detective's enjoying the play."

"Or keeping his eyes on Kenneth in case he decides to run."

June shook her head. "Not going to happen. Kenneth's innocent."

Cait hoped so, but *someone* had murdered Chip.

Act 5, scene 1, began with Hamlet and Horatio entering the stage, then pausing to listen to the first gravedigger sing snatches of a ballad as he digs in the earth. Cait watched Kenneth for signs of inability to respond to the situation as he filled the role of Hamlet, but she saw nothing abnormal until the gravedigger tossed up a skull and then dashed it to the ground.

Alt stood frozen long enough for the audience to start buzzing. Cait silently urged him on. Finally, he began musing upon death as the great leveler of all people. Hamlet questioned the gravedigger and learned the skull was that of the king's jester, who died twenty-three years ago.

Cait hadn't realized she'd been holding her breath until June nudged her. "Let's go backstage."

Cait followed June down the aisle and out the door, where they ran into RT.

"Niki's missing," RT said.

CHAPTER 23

Cait stopped in her tracks trying to control her emotions. "Niki could be anywhere. This is a big playground." *Or did Wally lure him away?*

"When did you last see him?" Jim asked.

"In the vineyard," RT said. "I was looking for evidence at the murder scene. It's not like him to run off or not come when I call him. If you see him, let me know."

June laughed. "Here comes Niki now."

Niki raced through the gate, skidding to a stop in front of RT, a black cloth hanging from his mouth.

RT took the cloth from Niki's clutches. "What have you found?" He held up what appeared to be a T-shirt.

Cait looked at the shirt, then reached out and turned it to the front. She dropped it and wiped her hands together as if to dislodge grime.

RT frowned. "You recognize it?"

"See the screen print? That's Hank Dillon, Wally's brother. There's even a gold chain around his neck."

"But where did it come from?" June asked.

"From Wally," Cait said. "I'd like to rub his face in it."

RT grunted. "I hope you get a chance."

Feet pounded across the courtyard. "Hey, there you are, you dumb dog." Ilia clutched his camera to keep it from bouncing against his chest.

A uniformed officer ran after him yelling, "Stop!"

Cait waved her arm in the air. "It's Ilia."

The officer stopped. "He's a stranger to me." He wiped his brow with the sleeve of his shirt, a smile tugging at his lips. "Anyone else I should know about so I don't shoot him or her?"

"Yeah," Ilia said. "A girl. Fumié. Asian, beautiful, and . . ." He flushed with embarrassment.

The officer smiled. "Got it."

"Your new dog's a thief, Cait," Ilia said. "He stole that shirt from the cave."

"I'm glad he did. You were photographing those pictographs?"

"You and Marcus said I could."

Marcus ran up to them. "What's going on?" He looked at the T-shirt and turned his nose up. "Where did that dirty rag come from?"

"It's a T-shirt," Cait said. "Niki found Wally's hiding place."

Cait and June went backstage to wait for a chance to speak with Kenneth. "Now I know where RT went when he left me at the Blackfriars. I could have helped him search the vineyard," Cait said. "You'd think I'm a novice at this business."

"He cares about you, Cait," June said, as Alt exited the stage.

"I'm a perfectionist. I never flub my lines," Alt said when he saw them. "It was seeing that skull . . ."

"You recovered nicely, Kenneth," June said to comfort him.

"You were great," Cait said.

"But substandard." He turned away. "Excuse me. I need a few minutes before going back on."

"I guess he doesn't need our encouragement." Cait watched Alt disappear into one of the dressing rooms.

"I never thought for a second Ray would force you to close the theaters," June said. "He just likes to prolong the agony and keep you guessing."

"I'm glad you're right," Cait said. "Bless Tasha for scheduling the plays only once a month, except for *Macbeth,* which is also playing next Saturday."

"Here comes Kenneth."

Cait watched Alt leave the dressing room, adjust the sleeves on his costume, and check the monitor. He brushed past them and was back in character. "I don't know why he's here, but I'm sure glad he is."

"I've known Kenneth almost as long as Tasha. When he's committed to something, he sticks to it, except in personal relationships. So why is he here and not in Ashland?" Her eyes sparkled. "Unless—"

"Unless he thinks Tasha left him something?" Cait asked. "She didn't. I asked Stanton Lane—he drew up her trust." She peeked around the curtain. "Kenneth doesn't need me here." She backed away. "Let me know when the play's about to end."

"Where are you going?"

"To find Rook and RT."

"Call them."

Cait wanted to search for Wally, too, now that she knew what he looked like.

"Cait, don't go out there. Why are you being so stubborn?"

"I'm trained for this. There aren't enough officers. I'll be careful."

The moment she stepped outside, a rush of voices reached her. *Macbeth* had ended at the Blackfriars theater. She set off at a trot and wove through the crowd. When she spotted an officer outside the Blackfriars she went over to him. "Any word from Detective Rook?"

"He'll be here in a second. He has new information."

CHAPTER 24

Cait saw Rook walking fast, his radio to his ear.

"Seal it up and bring everything back," he said into the radio.

"What else was found in the cave?" Cait asked when he turned his radio off.

"Ammo for an AK-47."

She narrowed her eyes on Rook. "Anything else?"

"Ammo for a thirty-eight S and W Special."

Cait held her breath, her mind spinning. "The Smith and Wesson probably belongs to Wally's accomplice. Anything else?"

"Paper cups from Peet's coffee. We'll have the lab check for DNA."

She nodded. "How do you suppose he found the cave way out there?"

"Luck? Desperation? Who knows?"

"Put a rush on the DNA. I could be dead before the sun goes down." She shielded her eyes. "What about the DNA on that wad of gum you sent to the lab?"

"Still waiting," Rook said. "Takes longer than fingerprints."

"Anything on that cowboy at the fairgrounds?"

Rook shook his head. "He's not our guy, Cait."

"I know you're right, but don't you want to know who he is?"

"There is one more thing," he said. "The cave smelled of marijuana."

"He's smoking pot in the cave?"

★　★　★　★　★

Cait hadn't realized how loud she'd spoken until a few heads turned to stare at her. Her cheeks burned with embarrassment. She spotted June standing on the sidelines in conversation with Alt and headed that way, until Ray stepped in front of her. She jumped back.

A shorter, stocky officer forced his way between Ray and Cait.

Ray glared at the officer. "Hey!"

"What's your name?" the officer asked.

Ray stared at the officer, not intimidated by the uniform, badge, or the gun the officer's hand rested on. "Ask her. She knows who I am. I want to talk to her, not hurt her."

"Ray, ease up before he arrests you," she said. She read the officer's nametag. "It's okay, Officer Hurley. I want to talk with him, too . . . in private." She grabbed Ray's sleeve and pulled him out of the sun and under the nearest tree.

"You sure have a way with men," Ray said.

"Oh, hush. Thanks for letting the shows continue. I know it wasn't an easy decision, but this has been a difficult time for everyone." She saw Kenneth Alt weaving his way over, hesitate when he saw Ray, and then veer off in another direction. "I'm sure Wally's still out there watching, but hopefully next month we won't have to worry about him." She waited for his reaction, but he remained silent.

She drew a deep breath and continued. "Ray, when I was a police officer, I shot and killed a bank robber. If I hadn't, he would have killed another officer. I was protecting my people like you're protecting yours. I understand. It's who we are." She inhaled deeply. "That bank robber's brother is Wally Dillon, the face on the mug shot we've been showing around. Now do you understand why he's here?"

Ray pulled a handkerchief from a pocket and wiped his

forehead. "You could have told me sooner."

"I hoped the problem would end and not escalate."

He shuffled his feet and looked into the distance. "Everyone has some crisis in their life. I have some stuff troubling me, but nothing like yours. I'm sorry if I let it interfere with my work here. I owe where I am today in this crazy business to Tasha, the Grand Lady of Shakespeare." He blinked, pursed his lips, and cleared his throat.

Cait wanted to reach out to Ray but knew he would reject any display of comfort. She waited to give him time to collect himself.

He smiled. "I can be an ugly SOB. When we're together, it's like striking a match. Sparks fly, tempers flare. But I like that you don't take guff from anyone. We're passionate about our work. At least I can apologize when I'm wrong. Sorry, Cait."

She raised her eyebrows. "So does this mean you'll be back next weekend for *Macbeth*?"

"Sure, but don't expect any miracles."

She grinned. "I always do."

He nodded. "So we're good?"

Cait looked around but no one was paying attention to them. "Something still bothers me. When your truck was broken into, you went ballistic. You wouldn't talk about it. Does this problem still exist? Anything I can help with?"

Ray grimaced. "When your crew is clicking on all cylinders and everyone is working together, it's a good feeling. I knew my mood interfered with work, but . . ." He shook his head. "Like most stage managers, I have visions of climbing the ladder. I like what I'm doing and I'm damn good at it. Been a stage manager for fifteen years. Now I'd like an opportunity to direct."

Whoa, everyone wants to direct. She couldn't visualize Ray doing anything but being a stage manager. He'd worked his way up and earned respect from everyone. She waited to see if there was more to his explanation.

Ray stared at her. "What?"

She shrugged. "What are you holding back?"

He paced in front of her. "You don't mince words. I was offered a job directing a damn good play. Before the contract was signed, the offer was pulled because I was already committed."

"Committed to what, Ray?"

"To Tasha and her Shakespeare festival."

Cait's mouth opened, but she couldn't find the words to console Ray.

"Now you know all of it. Go mingle," he said, "before everyone leaves."

Chapter 25

Officer Hurley stayed close to Cait while she smiled and mingled with the theater crowd in the courtyard. When the actors finally dispersed, they returned to the theaters to change and pack. Cait checked the time—slightly after five. With the sun comfortably warm and a cool breeze drifting across the hills, Cait tried to relax. The plays were over and the actors were safe, but Wally was still an issue. She didn't know what she would do if he hadn't been captured by the time the *Macbeth* actors returned next Saturday.

Alt, still in costume, walked over to Cait. "I'm not leaving town yet."

Cait noticed Rook, Hurley, and RT watching. "Why not?" She realized how rude that sounded, and added, "What about your commitment in Oregon?"

He frowned. "There's time to see the rest of the house."

"The upper floors are my living quarters."

The sun settled on the red in Alt's graying hair. "Can we talk about that in private?"

Cait stepped back from Alt. "Come on, Kenneth. What's with you and this sudden interest in the house? You thinking of buying it?"

"I told you. I'm interested in the house where Tasha lived before she died."

She stepped back out of the sun and stared at him, trying to read his mind. "Now it's my home."

I wouldn't mind showing him the upstairs if I knew why he was so adamant about it. As far as I know, there's nothing up there of any great value.

"If you came here because you think Tasha left you something in her trust, I assure you she didn't, but if you don't believe me I'll give you her attorney's phone number, and you can ask him yourself."

Alt blinked; his cheeks reddened. RT walked up to Cait. "Everything okay?"

Cait sensed Alt had been on the verge of admitting why he was interested in the house, but clammed up in RT's presence. She struggled to keep her focus on Alt and not on RT. She knew Tasha and Kenneth had been lovers when they were in New York. *Had he given Tasha something he wanted returned? Like an expensive piece of jewelry?*

"Cait?" RT said, prompting her.

"Kenneth, come by tomorrow and we'll talk about it. Right now, I have a lot on my mind. The actors haven't left yet, and I'm uneasy standing out here while Wally Dillon is still out there waiting to kill me."

Alt nodded. "Sorry. Tomorrow then." He turned away.

"Kenneth? You were a terrific Hamlet. Thank you. Without you the theater would have closed."

He glanced back at her and nodded. "Glad I could help."

"Strange guy," RT said after Alt left. "I'm particular about who I allow into my place. You should be, too. Any idea why he's determined to see the house?"

Sometimes she forgot RT was a SEAL and not just the hunky guy who sent her endorphins spinning out of control. Like now, when he touched her hand.

"Not yet, but if he doesn't tell me tomorrow, he's not going past the first floor."

"Was Kenneth still pressuring you about the house?" June

asked when she joined them. She pulled pearl clips from her hair and let it fall to her shoulders.

"Yes. He's coming over tomorrow."

"He can be stubborn. What a relief the weekend's over. Now we can concentrate on Wally without worrying about the actors. I'd like to shoot him and take him out of his misery and ours."

"June!" Cait admonished, but secretly agreed. "We want him alive to talk."

June raised her eyebrows. "What! Can the Devil speak truth?"

Hurley cracked a smile.

Rook laughed.

"Macbeth," June said.

RT shook his head. "Where'd Ray go?"

"He's packing his equipment. Which reminds me, I haven't seen much of Jay," Cait said.

"He's around," RT said, "keeping his eye on the costumes and wigs."

Niki flopped across Cait's foot. She hoped he wouldn't whine when RT left for San Diego without him. She reached in her pocket and gave him a treat.

"Okay to search the theaters?" Rook asked.

"I don't see why not," Cait said. "You won't bother the actors. They'll be gone soon."

"Maybe Dillon takes Sundays off, but I don't want to overlook anything before you lock up," Rook said.

"Don't count on it," RT said, his eyes sweeping the grounds.

"Hey!" someone yelled.

Cait turned and saw Marcus on horseback.

"It's a good time to ride," he said. "The plays are over and most of the people are gone. No one but us should be here, but if I see someone who doesn't belong here I'll call." He galloped off again without waiting for a response.

Rook shook his head. "Good-looking horse."

Cait watched until Marcus was out of sight. "I want to say goodbye to the actors. Some will return in July, but others I might never see again."

"I'll go with you," June said.

"Hey!"

What now? Cait turned to see Ilia, his expensive camera posed to take their picture.

"Keep walking. Try to ignore me," Ilia said. "Act natural. Laugh. Talk. Whatever."

When they reached the door of the Elizabethan, Ilia yelled, "Look over there!"

Her head snapped around at the sharpness of his voice. He pointed toward the trees and aimed his camera in that direction. "A reflection from behind that oak tree!"

Cait saw it too and grabbed June and pulled her behind a large planter. Heart racing, she peered out. RT, Rook, and Jim Hart drew their guns as they darted between shrubs and trees in the direction Ilia pointed. "Ilia, stay back!"

Officer Hurley had drawn his gun, and he ran after the others.

Niki barked and chased after them.

Where's Marcus? What if he runs into Wally?

Cait spotted Ilia darting in and out of shrubs, his camera held high. She pulled her gun free as she got to her feet, her adrenaline raging. "June, go inside. There could be more than Wally out there."

June started to argue, then gave up. "Are you sure someone was behind the tree? I didn't see anyone and there's been no shooting."

"I saw what Ilia did—the sun reflecting off metal. Now please, go. Tell Ray to keep everyone inside. With a little luck, maybe we can end this today." *If that were true, why are my instincts screaming?*

CHAPTER 26

Monday morning, the futile search for Wally deeply concerned Cait. She'd insisted someone check the cave in case Wally doubled back to get the S&W and ammo left there. When they looked, the cave was still sealed. Once again, cruisers were positioned on the road below her house. Unless Wally Dillon was caught soon, Cait worried the local media would descend on her like vultures, demanding to know what the police were doing to catch him. The attention could keep people from attending the festival for the rest of the summer.

Cait turned the shower on as hot as she could stand it. Kenneth Alt was another concern. When he came today, he would expect to see the upstairs. She barely knew him but disliked his pompous, overbearing attitude. But if he found what he was looking for, he could return to Oregon and she'd never have to see him again. She lingered in the shower until her skin turned pink. As soon as she stepped out of the shower, she thought she heard her cell phone ringing. She grabbed her robe from the back of the door and hurried into the bedroom.

"Hello," she answered, scrambling into her robe.

"It's Shep."

She knew him well enough to know this was not a leisurely call. "What's wrong?"

"Can't I call just to see if you're okay?"

"Of course you can." She sat on the edge of the bed.

"Everything under control?"

"I wish. Thanks for Wally's mug shot. It's been distributed, and none too soon. Chip Fallon, an actor, was found murdered yesterday morning in the vineyard, and I'm positive Wally's responsible."

"Christ, Cait," Shep said. "I'm sorry."

She pulled the robe tighter, her hand cold as she clutched the phone. "He was strangled with a bolo tie, one of those with a small slider gem."

"Interesting choice."

"The rodeo's in town," she said. "I'm told they're available in local stores." She told him about the drunken man who tried to enter the theater Saturday night. "I thought maybe he returned to retaliate because I kicked him out, but the police didn't agree and didn't get his name."

"You didn't have this much action when you were a cop."

"Yeah, well, I guess that's right." She looked out the window and stared at the valley below. "Rook has officers looking for Wally Dillon. Wally's mug shot will help."

"Hope so."

She wiped drops of water from her forehead with the sleeve of her robe. "I've been in California two months and haven't left Livermore. I want to get him so I can shop in San Francisco, go to Fisherman's Wharf, and ride a cable car before I'm too old to enjoy it."

"I'll take you to all those places when this is over. I'd like to get some golf in at Pebble Beach."

"You'd do that for me?"

"Yes, but not when your SEAL is around. Is he the jealous type?"

She laughed. "I'm not sure what type RT is." She'd never been much for the macho type, having worked with too many of them, but RT was different.

She told him about Niki finding the T-shirt and ammo in the cave.

He chuckled. "I thought it was sealed."

"Not permanently. Ilia's been photographing pictographs on the walls. He wants to use them in his next book." Movement in the driveway caught her attention. She stared down at the lone figure, then relaxed when she recognized Kurt Mathews's truck and remembered that he'd said he'd be back Monday.

"Cait, Calder Manning is headed to California."

Cait turned her back to the windows. "That's why you called?"

"Yes. At least that's what he said when he stopped by the station this morning. He wanted to talk to someone in the investigative subdivision. The commander referred him to me."

She wiped her dripping hair from her face. "I thought he might be here already."

"Why would you think that?"

"Wally is not working alone. Shep, he has guns, and don't forget the knife. He couldn't bring them on a plane."

"Maybe he drove to California."

She frowned. "Or hitchhiked. What are a couple of extra days on the road? If you get a chance, would you call Wally's mother and ask if they have family connections in California?"

"I'll make time."

"What did Manning want?"

"To talk about you and to let us know you were in danger and that he thought he could help."

"Really? How would he know I'm in danger?"

"A couple of weeks ago, Wally showed up at the Mannings' and asked about you. Mrs. Manning gave him your name but didn't know where you were living."

"Officer-involved shootings are always on the news. Wally would have seen my name on TV unless he was in jail."

"Your name was withheld because of threats. Didn't you know that?"

She sighed. "Oh . . . I forgot."

Shep continued. "Wally frightened Mrs. Manning and Calder's three-year-old daughter she was caring for. After he left, she tried to contact Calder, but he couldn't be reached. He didn't learn of Wally's visit until he returned to the States."

"You didn't give Manning my address did you?"

"You need to ask? Of course not. The commander did give him your cell number, but not until he did a background check on Manning. York kept him waiting a long time."

She smiled, knowing how long York could keep someone waiting. "Why come here? Why not just call?"

"He thinks he can convince Wally to drop this vendetta against you and get him to go home."

"There aren't any signs of Wally giving up." She didn't think for a second talking to Wally would help. He'd already shown his determination to hunt her down and kill her, even with police on the premises. "Shep, it's not being stalked that concerns me the most, it's about how experienced Wally appears to be. I'm not so sure about his partner."

"He's not a stranger to the criminal justice system."

"They start young these days. How will I recognize Manning? He's in camouflage on the Web."

"Six-two, one-ninety, sandy hair, hazel eyes, and a fresh scar above his right eyebrow. He was calm, cool, and collected, and even more handsome than me."

Cait laughed. "Wow, that's saying something."

"He thought he could hop a flight to California. Let me know when he calls."

"I will." She hesitated. "Did you believe him? His reason for coming here?"

"Commander York seemed to."

"Is that a yes?"

"I'm looking into it, Cait. I'll let you know what I find. How's your SEAL?"

"Sticking close," she said. "He wanted to move into the house, but I don't think that's a good idea. So he's staying in his trailer and Niki is with me." She glanced at the dog curled nearby.

"Interesting arrangement," Shep said. "I'll wait for your call. You be safe."

Cait dressed and dried her hair. *How can Manning find Wally if the police can't? Or does he already know where he is?*

RT motioned to the wall clock when Cait walked into the kitchen. "Sleep in?"

She shook her head. "Shep called." She went over to the coffee pot and filled a mug to the brim. "Do you remember who Calder Manning is? His parents adopted Wally's brother, Hank. He claims he's coming here to talk Wally into going home and leaving me alone."

"An honorable decision, if that's his real motive."

Cait looked at him over the rim of her coffee mug. "You don't believe him?"

"I didn't say that. I'll decide after I meet him."

Cait filled Niki's bowls, then sat on a stool at the counter nursing her coffee. She told RT the rest of her conversation with Shep.

RT frowned. "Let's hope your friend learns something useful from Manning's mother."

"If not, what are you going to do?" Marcus said, coming in from the office.

"Good question, Marcus," RT said.

"I grew up here," Marcus said. "I can ask around. Someone must know something, must have seen something."

"Or heard rumors," she said. "Thanks, Marcus." Cait stood. "Would anyone like breakfast?"

"You never eat breakfast," Marcus said, "except toast or cereal."

"I'm hungry. I need energy to deal with Kenneth Alt when he comes."

"Sit down. I'll fix it," RT said.

She smiled. "I love a man who can cook."

RT smirked, wiggled his eyebrows, and made her blush. "So when can we expect Manning?" RT asked as he took eggs and bacon from the fridge.

She sat, happy to be waited on. "He's supposed to call. He doesn't know where I live." When her cell vibrated in her pocket, she glanced at the display. "Good morning, Kenneth."

RT turned and rolled his eyes.

"When is a good time to come over?" Kenneth asked.

"How about eleven?"

"I'll be there. Good bye."

"I thought you were through with him," RT said.

Marcus dropped bread into the toaster. "He's not so bad, once you figure out if he's for real or putting on an act."

Cait laughed. "He's a stuffed shirt who likes to assert his authority."

The smell of frying bacon made her stomach growl. Soon they were hunched over their plates, too hungry to talk.

"We could make a deal," RT said, wiggling his eyebrows again, "about me cooking."

Cait caught the look that made her tingle all over. No doubt what was on his mind. Her cell rang again. "Maybe Kenneth changed his mind." Disappointed, she answered. "Good morning, Detective."

"I hear Calder Manning's on his way out here."

"You talked to Shep."

"He called. I'm okay with it as long as Manning doesn't interfere with the police. Let me know when you hear from him. I'll try to come out. In the meantime, I'm sending a couple of officers, so don't shoot them. They'll be in plainclothes and have been instructed to knock on your door so you'll know they're there. Ask Marcus to find busy work for them to do so they'll look like they have a reason for being there."

"Cops always do things not in their job description. I'll let everyone know they're coming."

When the officers arrived and introduced themselves, RT took them to meet June and Jim. Marcus settled behind his computer in his office.

Kenneth Alt rang the doorbell at exactly eleven. He appeared uncomfortable when Cait pressed him again for a reason to tour the house.

"I'm looking for a picture."

Okay, that narrows the hunt down. "A photo of what?"

"A painting. When Tasha and I were in New York, a lady friend of mine, a struggling artist, copied pictures of famous artists for a living and sold them cheap. When she met Tasha, she asked if I thought Tasha would let her paint her. I said no, because I didn't think there was a chance in hell Tasha would pose for her or anyone else. Not only did she value her privacy, it would embarrass her." Kenneth stood in the middle of the front room, his gaze sweeping the walls hung with Shakespearean reproductions. "It's not here," he said with a dismissive wave at the walls.

"Let me guess," Cait said. "Tasha surprised you and said yes. And now you think that painting is in this house."

He blushed. "It took a month for my friend to finish the painting." He pursed his lips. "Little did I know the artist painted me in the background."

"Really? How did you feel about that?"

"I didn't mind. I'm like a gray silhouette off to the side of Tasha."

"And now you want the painting as a souvenir?"

He slid his hands into his pants pocket. "Yes. I would like to have it."

"Didn't you ask Tasha for it?"

He frowned. "Tasha and I . . . well, we had a history together."

Cait sensed there was more to this so-called history than a memory of an affair that took place thirty years ago. "Is this struggling artist friend of yours now famous and her paintings are selling for lots of money?"

Crimson crept up his neck. "Yes, but that's not why—"

"Right," Cait said. "We'll go upstairs, but first I need to speak with Marcus." She wondered how close Kenneth and Tasha had been when they were struggling actors in New York. *Were they actually lovers like June said?* She stuck her head in the office door. "Marcus, I'm taking Kenneth Alt upstairs to look for a painting. It shouldn't take long."

Marcus glanced up with a questionable look and shrugged his shoulders. "Okay."

"Follow me, Kenneth." She climbed the stairs to the second floor, anxious to get it over with. The room had walls lined from floor to ceiling with bookshelves stuffed with books, a leather sofa and footstool, a small TV, and more books stacked on an end table and on the floor. She followed him around the room and watched him peek in the tiny kitchen, bathroom, and guest bedroom. "If your painting isn't on this floor, it's not in the house. The top floor is my bedroom, not open for your scrutiny, but I can say there aren't any paintings on the walls."

Kenneth walked into the bedroom. Cait watched, thinking he looked like a pricked balloon with all the air going out with disappointment.

Hope faded from his eyes. "It's not here. Maybe a quick look upstairs—"

She shook her head. "Sorry."

He turned to leave. His head snapped around. "There!" he pointed.

Cait jumped and bumped into the corner of the bed.

"I knew it had to be here!" He clapped his hands together. "Oh, my God."

A twelve-by-fifteen watercolor hung on the wall over an old cedar chest. Cait had never noticed it because it was unframed, and the pale paint faded into the floral wallpaper.

He smiled, apparently not minding the condition of the painting. He reached his hand out, then hesitated. "May I take it down?"

"Of course." Cait thought paintings were meant to provoke, but this one didn't do anything for her. "After it was painted, why didn't you ask Tasha if you could have it?"

He removed the painting from the wall and held it reverently. "I couldn't." The look on his face told Cait how much he cared for Tasha, but was he holding hands with the past or was he here for another reason? "She was so beautiful, so brilliant an actress. I never felt I measured up to her talent."

Speechless, Cait stared hard at Kenneth. *Is that why he left New York and Tasha?*

His hands gripped the sides of the canvas. "I didn't know she was pregnant when I left the city. She should have told me."

Pregnant? Was he saying he fathered Tasha's baby?

Oh. My. God.

CHAPTER 27

Cait's mind raced like a rat in a maze as she recalled the letter Tasha had written to her brother, Cait's dad. She was pregnant and said her baby's father wasn't in the picture. *Does Kenneth think I'm that baby? Is that why he's here? Not because of Chip Fallon? Not for the painting? Was it all a ruse to get to know me?*

"Cait? What's wrong?" Alt asked. "If the painting is important to you . . . well, at least I'll know where it is. Or I could pay you for it."

Cait inhaled deeply as she watched deep affection wash over his face as he stared at the painting. *He doesn't see me as his child; he only has eyes for Tasha.* Relief spread through her like wildfire. "I might consider lending it to you. I never noticed it because I spend so little time on this floor." She held her hand out for a closer look at the painting.

He handed it to her.

She studied Tasha's face, trying to compare it to the old photo RT's mother had given her. The photo had been taken when Tasha was still in New York City, about the time the painting was done. The paint appeared grainy and settled into the texture of the paper. Cait turned the painting over and noticed a scrap of paper taped to the back—*Face in Motion.*

She turned the painting back to the front. "Interesting title. Who named it? The artist?"

He pulled a handkerchief from his pocket and wiped his forehead. "I did. Tasha's vibrant face fascinated me. So alive."

Cait looked at Kenneth with renewed interest. Under all that pompous, overbearing demeanor lived a romantic. She'd misjudged him. As a crime analyst, she'd been known for her razor-sharp analysis of people. She'd trained hard and worked hard, but since moving to California her skills had slipped.

"I wish you'd known Tasha," he said.

"Me, too." *How different my life would be if I had known her.* She continued to study Tasha's face and the gray shadow of Kenneth lurking in the background. "I like the silhouette of you. It adds interest. Is the squiggle at the bottom the artist's signature?"

He nodded. "R for Raven."

"Why isn't the painting framed?"

"It was, before it was stolen."

"Why would someone steal it and then return it without the frame? Any idea who the thief was?"

He scoffed. "We assumed an ex-boyfriend of Tasha's and that he had a change of heart and brought it back a month later."

Ex-boyfriend? "How'd he know about the painting?"

"He knew Raven and saw it in her studio. He wanted to buy it, but Tasha refused."

Cait wanted to know more about the ex-boyfriend, but she had to decide what to do with the painting. Lend it to Kenneth? Hang it back on the wall?

"Cait? Are you up here?" a familiar voice called.

"In the bedroom, Marcus." She peeked out the door and saw him. He had a worried look on his face. "We found what Kenneth was looking for."

Marcus glanced at the painting Cait held. "Looks like Tasha."

"It is. Did you know it was here?"

He shook his head. "I built the bookcases in the sitting room, but I had no reason to come in the bedroom."

"Kenneth would like to have it," she said. "What do you

think?" Knowing how Marcus felt about Tasha, she thought he might want it. That would present another dilemma.

He shrugged. "Up to you. It's not a good likeness of her."

Cait smiled. "At least you're honest."

"Tasha was twenty-nine when this was painted," Kenneth said. "For me, the painting is personal."

Marcus's head snapped up. "How personal?"

Kenneth smirked. "None of your business. Cait, what's your decision? Will you sell it to me?"

"I'll think it over and let you know." She rehung the painting on the wall. *Another dang complication.*

"I don't think you should let him have the painting," Marcus said after Kenneth left and they were in the kitchen.

RT walked in from the office, accompanied by the two police officers. "What painting?"

"A watercolor of Tasha painted when she was in New York," Cait said. "Kenneth wants it."

"Show it to me before you let it go," RT said. "We've just come from the cave. I hope Ilia got all the pictures he needs, because it's sealed now. I assume the car with Oregon plates in the parking lot belongs to Alt. Unless Wally's a phantom, he's nowhere around here."

"Then I'll run into town," she said. "The cupboards are bare."

"I'll take you later," RT said.

"You know I have a gun."

"Come on, Cait. As soon as we catch this jackass, you can go to the moon alone if you want. Just not now."

When RT and the officers left, her cell rang. Shep's name appeared on the display. "What's up?"

"I found out Calder Manning is on his way there."

"He didn't waste time."

"He'll call you. He doesn't have your address, so don't worry about him showing up on your doorstep. Got more background on him you might be interested in. He wrote his dissertation on medieval history. As a grad student, part of his training was teaching undergrads, but it didn't take him long to decide he didn't like the rigidity of the academic lifestyle. He thought he was better suited to be a reporter."

"So he's smart."

"I wanted you to know about his interest in medieval history. Maybe he's in love with Shakespeare."

"I wonder what he knows about halberds."

"You might get a chance to ask him. He racked up his share of near misses in Afghanistan and Libya. Almost forgot the cardinal rule of war reportage: don't die. Might account for the scar above his eyebrow. I wonder about this sudden interest in Wally."

"Could be as simple as saving him from the same fate as Hank," Cait said.

"You don't believe that, do you?"

"I can always hope."

"Just in case, make sure your Navy boy's around when Manning gets there. Call me when you hear from Manning. Be safe."

"Are you expecting trouble from this guy Manning?" Marcus asked when she finished the call.

"I always expect trouble, particularly with Wally here." The sooner she could get back to running a festival and her viticulture class at the local college, the happier she'd be.

"I can go to the store for you," Marcus said.

Cait grinned. "Great! I'll add chocolate and coffee to the list." *More caffeine. Just what don't I need. What I do need is time away from here, like a visit to the ranch.*

CHAPTER 28

Between Kenneth Alt and the police hanging around, Cait valued what little time she had alone. With the house empty and quiet, the afternoon stretched before her. She'd vowed not to return to the ranch until Wally was captured, but she missed Bo and his family and decided time in the country was exactly what she needed.

She called June and asked if she'd like to go to the ranch with her.

"I'd love to. Jim's with RT and the officers. He said something about checking the lighting at the theaters. I'll be right over."

Cait waited until June and Niki were settled in her car before calling RT. "I'm going to the ranch. June and Niki are with me."

"Be sure to take your gun."

"You don't think I'd leave home without it, do you? Back in a couple of hours."

"Call when you get there and when you're ready to leave," he said, "and keep your eyes on the mirrors. I know you feel your wings have been clipped, but when this is over we'll do something fun to celebrate. Just the two of us."

She tingled with anticipation of spending time alone with RT as she drove down the driveway and onto the road. She looked forward to seeing Bo's engaging ten-year-old, wheelchair-bound daughter who had risen above her difficulties. Cait's problems couldn't compare to the bright future Joy lost out on after a disastrous fall from her horse during a riding competition.

Traffic was light, except for a string of yellow-jacketed bicyclists on Mines Road pumping hard toward Del Valle Regional Park. Ilia said Livermore was a biker's paradise and that they came from all over the Bay Area to ride the miles of challenging hills.

She checked the mirrors one last time before turning into the entrance to the ranch, then she relaxed and looked out the open window at the pristine white fences, cerulean blue sky, and pungent eucalyptus trees.

June sat up straight and stuck her head out the window. "No wonder you love it here. Oh, look at the beautiful horses!"

Cait drove slowly to keep the dust down and so June could admire the scenery. When she pulled up to the front of the barn, Bo came around the side with a rake in his hand. She turned the engine off. "That's Bo." When she opened the door, Niki leaped out and sprinted off.

Bo tipped his Stetson back and smiled. "This is a nice surprise. And you got a dog."

Cait grinned. "His name is Niki. He's a gift from RT's daughter."

"Handsome dog," Bo said. "Lots of playmates for him here." He looked at the shorts she was wearing. "Doesn't look like you came to ride."

"Not today. Bo, this is June Hart. June and her husband, Jim, retired and came to help me with the festival. She and Tasha go way back to when they were aspiring actresses in New York."

Bo and June shook hands. "Cait didn't exaggerate when she called this place a bit of heaven," June said. She raised her hand to shade her eyes. "Did she tell you Hilton and I were related by marriage? He was my husband's cousin. I introduced Tasha and Hilton, but it took years before she'd agree to marry him.

She thought marriage would interfere with her career."

Bo laughed. "So I've heard."

"Oh, dear," June said. "I was shameless getting them hooked up, but I persevered because I knew they were perfect for each other."

"How about a tour?"

"I'd love it."

"Let's cut through the barn to avoid a mess I've made trying to patch a cement wall. We'll go up to the house first so you can meet the family."

The empty stalls smelled of fresh straw. Hilton's saddle still hung on a hook next to Faro's stall.

"Do you ride?" Bo asked June.

"I used to, but I doubt I could get my leg over a horse now."

"I didn't know you rode," Cait said.

June laughed. "Like Hilton, I grew up with horses."

"The next time you and Cait come out, we'll go for a ride," Bo said. "Don't forget to wear jeans and close-toed shoes."

As they exited the barn, Bo asked, "Lots of people attending the plays?"

"Every performance is sold out."

"Cait's a natural-born businesswoman," June said. "She's even got the cantankerous stage manager wrapped around her little finger." She gasped. "Oh, look at that." Her eyes were riveted on the log house ahead of them.

"Wait until you see the inside," Cait said.

"Hilton built it," Bo said. "We're lucky to live here."

"Indeed you are." June lagged behind while Cait and Bo crossed the bridge over the dry creek. "You may have to force me to leave." She followed them up to the porch.

"Cait!" Joy squealed. She sat on the piano bench, her wheelchair off to the side.

Cait leaned down and hugged her.

Joy beamed. "Are you going to ride?"

"Oh, sorry, honey. Not today. But I brought someone to meet you." Cait introduced June.

June smiled and took Joy's offered hand. "What a pretty name."

"June used to be an actress, like Tasha," Cait said.

"Did you know Hilton? This used to be his house."

"I did." June told her how she introduced Tasha and Hilton.

Bo's wife, Khandi, walked into the room and Cait introduced her to June.

Cait's cell rang. RT's name popped up on the screen.

"RT," she answered, "we're at the ranch."

"Anyone tail you?"

"No."

"Say hello to the Tucks for me. Call before you leave."

"Everything okay?" Bo asked.

Cait nodded. "There's a situation at the house."

"You can't leave yet," Joy said, her black curls bobbing about her head.

"Not until June's had a chance to see the ranch and meet Faro," Cait said. "Next time I might get up my nerve to ride again. How about that?"

Joy grinned. "Maybe I can ride with you. Okay, Daddy?"

"I think that can be arranged."

"June rides," Cait said.

Joy grinned. "Yes! How about tomorrow?"

"Probably not, but soon. I promise." Cait hugged her.

"I'll be right back, Joy," Khandi said and followed them outside.

When they stepped off the porch, Khandi took Cait's hand. "What's wrong?"

Cait glanced across the fields at the horses grazing behind the white fence and at Niki running with Bo's dogs. "Someone is stalking me. His name is Wally Dillon. I told Bo about it the last time I was here, but I didn't want to involve your family."

Bo nodded. "I told her why you carried a gun. By that bulge beneath your shirt, I assume nothing's changed."

"No. Wally's here to kill me." She bowed her head as she talked about Hank Dillon. "I became a cop to help people, but you do what you have to do when another officer's life is in jeopardy. I shot Hank Dillon before he killed another officer. His brother, Wally, is looking for revenge."

"Oh, Cait," Khandi said. "I'm sorry."

"Can't blame yourself for doing your job," Bo said. "It could eat away at you if you allow it."

"I got over it. I was duty bound and did what I had to do. I would do it again under the same circumstances." She smiled. "An officer is alive because of me. That's a good feeling."

"I think you should tell them about Chip," June said.

Bo nudged his Stetson higher on his head with his knuckle. "Chip?"

"Chip Fallon, an actor," Cait said. "He played the role of Hamlet. He was murdered in the vineyard Saturday night."

Khandi's hand flew to her mouth. "Oh, no!"

Bo stopped in his tracks. "Another tragedy. Did you find him?"

"No. Kurt Mathews did. He manages the vineyard."

June filled in the details and explained that the police had been there every day.

"How can we help?" Khandi asked.

"I don't want to involve your family, but I would love to spend a little time here at the ranch whenever I can get away."

"That's a given, Cait," Khandi said. "Come any time."

What is it about the ranch that turns me into a marshmallow and stirs my emotions? "I appreciate that. While we're here, I'd like June to see Faro."

"Sure thing," Bo said.

Niki and Bo's golden retrievers romped nearby, scattering a flock of ducks while a pair of llamas munched on grass.

Hilton's chestnut quarter horse edged closer to the fence. As they approached, he extended his long, sleek neck.

"How you doing, son?" Bo asked as he held his hand out and offered Faro a butter mint.

"This was Hilton's horse?" June asked.

Bo nodded. "This is Faro."

Faro ignored June's hand when she tried to stroke him. Bo handed her a mint. "Try this."

Quick as lightning, the mint disappeared from her hand.

They spent a few minutes talking about Faro, then crossed to another pasture where Bo's horse, Cash, grazed. The black Morgan trotted to the fence, his movements free, straight, and well balanced. He nudged Bo's hand, looking for a treat.

"He's gorgeous," June said.

They spent a few minutes with Bo's horse before Cait asked, "Bo, can June see where you do surgery?"

"Sure." He dug into his jeans pocket and removed a ring of keys.

"I should get back to the house," Khandi said. "Nice meeting you, June. I hope you'll come again."

After Khandi left, Bo took Cait and June to his lab. He unlocked the door and flipped a switch. The bright fluorescent lights flooded the large sterile room.

As she had the first time she'd seen Bo's lab, Cait blinked to adjust to the sharp glare off the stainless steel counters, sinks, shelves, cupboards, and refrigerator. The room was spotless, with white walls, white tile flooring, and stainless steel drains. Hoses hung from trolleys.

June complimented Bo on his sterile lab, then Cait said it was time they leave. Bo locked up while Cait called Niki. The dog ignored her but not Bo's sharp whistle. Cait held the door open for Niki.

"Bring Niki again," Bo said.

"I'll do that. Thanks for letting us spend a little time with you." She removed her gun from her waist and set it in the compartment between the seats, then settled behind the wheel. She waved to Bo, backed her car around, and drove down the lane.

"That's a nice family," June said.

"You bet." She checked the mirrors after pulling out onto the road. A warm breeze floated through the open windows. They drove in silence, the shimmer of rising heat glaring on the pavement. Traffic picked up on Tesla, and a pickup appeared in the rearview mirror, closing in on her. With the sun to her back, she blinked a couple of times as she narrowed her eyes on the mirror. She gripped the wheel harder. The driver of the pickup stayed close behind until just before the stop sign at Greenville Road, when he swerved sharply and passed on her left and ran through the intersection without stopping. With her eyes riveted on the pickup, she almost sailed through the stop sign and had to brake hard.

Up ahead, the pickup had pulled off the road.

"June, get on the floor."

"Do you think that's Wally in the pickup?"

"Yes. Hang on." Cait brought her gun to her lap, right hand clutched around it, and with foot to the pedal accelerated through the intersection and passed the pickup. "Got a partial plate: four-XQC-four."

A short distance ahead, she braked hard to avoid hitting a family of turkeys ambling across the road. She slapped the wheel. "Damn!"

The pickup caught up, swerved hard to Cait's left, and roared past, leaving more exhaust fumes in its wake. His brake lights lit up when the driver slammed on the brakes, smack in the middle of the road.

Cait hit the brakes. "What the—"

A loud pop.

The windshield cracked like a spider's web, leaving a bullet hole through the middle.

Niki barked; the sudden stop tossed him against the back of Cait's seat.

Cait watched the pickup take off and disappear from sight. After the air cleared, she expected to see a mess of turkeys on the road, but they'd escaped.

The neat twist of curls on top of June's head tumbled down. "I think someone tried to kill us!"

CHAPTER 29

Shaken, Cait stared at the cracked windshield. "Thank God for safety glass. Are you all right?"

Her voice quivering, June said, "I think so. That pickup came at us like a bat out of hell."

Cait reached back to stroke Niki as he tried to crawl between the front seats. He was shaking but didn't appear to be hurt. She leaned over the wheel and poked her finger through the hole in the windshield. "I wonder where the bullet went." She ran her hand over the leather seat. "No damage in here that I can see. Let's get out of here before he decides to come back and try again." She checked for traffic, then lightly tapped the gas pedal to avoid jarring shards of glass from the windshield.

"Maybe we should call RT," June said, "in case that pickup is parked ahead. Can you see okay to drive?"

"Well enough. We don't have far to go. They wouldn't have caught up to me if not for those turkeys." She glanced at June. "I'm still glad we went to the ranch. Are you?"

"Absolutely. 'Pleasure and action make the hours seem short.' "

"What?"

"*Othello.* Think about it."

"Oh." When she turned into the driveway, she struggled to see out the cracked windshield so she wouldn't clip the char-donnay or cabernet vines or run over the red roses bordering the edges. RT stood in front of the house, arms crossed as he talked with the police officers. He turned and stared as she drove past, his face registering shock. He ran after her, but she continued until she pulled up in front of the garage and cut the engine. RT yanked her door open.

The officers caught up and stared at her car.

Niki barked, his front paws up on the back of Cait's seat.

"What the hell happened?" RT demanded.

"We were shot at. We're not hurt, but I want to find the bullet that ruined my windshield." She reached to unbuckle her seatbelt but it wouldn't budge. She pulled harder. "What's wrong with this thing?"

RT let Niki out. "Jesus, Cait, if I didn't know better I'd think you liked being in the crosshairs of a crazy killer. Maybe now you'll stay home until he's captured."

RT's disapproval upset her; that she deserved it only made it worse. She quit wrestling with the seatbelt. "Shut up and get me out of here. I'm glad I went to the ranch." She tugged again on her seatbelt. "What's wrong with it?"

June released her belt to help Cait. "Maybe it's the angle." She pushed the release button. "It's damaged." She tugged until the buckle opened.

"This is a new car. It can't be damaged," she said as she climbed out of the car.

RT slid in. "The buckle's dented." Then, pointing at a depression in the buckle, he said, "It looks like this buckle took the bullet instead of you."

Cait stared at the buckle RT held up.

"I told you to call before you left the ranch. Better yet, you should have stayed home," he said as he backed out of the car.

She glared at him and then walked away. *I hate it when he's right.*

"Got it!" June said.

Cait swung around.

June held her hand up, a smile spreading across her face. "The bullet! I found it in the gearshift well."

"Let me see." RT held his hand out.

" 'This all lies within the will of God.' *Henry V,* in case anyone cares." She dropped the bullet in RT's hand.

"Well, what do you know," RT said. He turned the bullet over in his hand. "Came from a thirty-eight S and W Special, same as was found in the cave." He showed it to Cait.

"Detective Rook's coming if he can get away," one of the officers said as he slipped his cell into his pocket.

Cait glanced at the bullet and then handed it to the officer. "Have a look at the buckle."

While one officer examined the bullet, the other officer slid inside the car. Using his hands, he gauged the angle and distance from the bullet hole to where it struck the buckle. He wrote measurements on a pad before he backed out of the car. He looked at Cait with his thumb and forefinger separated an inch. "That's how close you came to being shot in the hip. He had to have been hanging out the window to shoot at that angle."

She remembered her gun was still in the car and reached in to get it. "Someone had his head out on the passenger side. It's a big pickup with big tires."

Jim Hart came around from the back of the garage. He stopped and stared at the fractured windshield. "I thought you left here to escape trouble."

"That was our intention," Cait said. "Change your mind yet about coming here to retire, Jim?"

June smiled and wrapped her arm through Jim's. "Well, you know how it is with the best-laid plans of mice and men. Life needs some zing to keep it interesting."

Cait noticed RT sweating from either the hot afternoon sun or anger. Struck with a pang of guilt, she wanted to take his hand and reassure him she was okay.

"Marcus can arrange to have your windshield replaced," RT said.

She stooped to run her hands over Niki, looking for signs of injury. "I'm sorry, Niki." She glanced at RT. "Any treats in your pocket?"

He shook his head. "Let's go in."

Marcus stood in the doorway, looking as if he was about to leave. "I heard the car. Something wrong?"

"Isn't there always?" RT responded.

Marcus held the door open for them. "What happened?"

"My windshield is cracked," Cait said. "Would you please call the insurance company and arrange to have it replaced?"

Marcus frowned. "It's a new car."

"Better tell him," RT said.

She rubbed the back of her neck. "The window is shattered because someone shot at us."

His face pale as parchment, Marcus said, "I'll take care of it. I want to look at the damage first." He turned to the officers. "You're not doing a very good job protecting her."

"They're doing their job," RT snapped.

"Marcus," Cait said, "it happened. We'll deal with it."

Worry lines etched in his brow, Marcus said, "I hope no one leaves me anything in their will."

The afternoon dragged on into the dinner hour, and Cait became more exhausted with each tick of the clock. She'd explained what happened too often, almost in a robotic state. When Detective Rook arrived, she repeated the story again. She wanted to go upstairs with Niki and crawl into bed with a romantic suspense novel. Instead, she asked the officers to stay for dinner, but they declined, saying they had other obligations. Rook called the station and made arrangements for a couple of officers looking for overtime to be there by nine in the morning.

Rook passed on the beer RT offered while June grilled pork chops Marcus had bought at the grocery store. They sat at the counter and talked about how to capture Wally Dillon and what to do with Calder Manning when he arrived.

"I hope this is over before RT leaves," Marcus said.

Cait's eyes locked on RT. She'd fallen back into the pattern of having him around again. Being part of one of the best special forces units in the world, he could be called up at a moment's notice—something she didn't like to think about. With the exception of those storybook incidents played out on television, their operations against terrorists were shrouded in secrecy, as were RT's.

RT smiled and rested his hand on Cait's knee.

The light touch of his hand caused a heat wave to flash through her.

"RT," Marcus said, "how long's your leave?"

RT cleared his throat and took a quick swallow from his glass of water. "Supposed to be a couple of weeks."

Rook pushed his plate away. "The Navy doesn't run on our schedule." His cell rang; he answered, listened. "Twenty minutes," he said and slipped off his stool. "Sorry to eat and run, Cait. Thanks for dinner." He shook RT's hand. "Don't leave without letting me know."

Cait walked Rook to the front door. "It must be hard being a cop's wife, with the hours you keep."

Rook laughed. "My wife goes with the flow, one day at a time, until I retire. You were a cop. How'd your husband handle it?"

"Not well. He was a police chaplain. He should have understood." She opened the door and Rook stepped out onto the porch.

"From one cop to another, keep your gun loaded."

She nodded and locked the door after him.

Jim and June returned to their RV. Marcus left after he called the insurance company about her windshield. Cait and RT were suddenly alone. She cleared the dishes and RT put them in the dishwasher.

"I'm spending the night here," RT said, "and every night until Wally is in handcuffs."

"That's not necessary. The house is alarmed and I've got Niki."

RT grabbed hold of Cait's arms. "This is not negotiable. I'll sleep upstairs in the guest bedroom."

Like that's going to help me sleep, she thought, with one staircase separating them. She wasn't made of stone. She wanted him in her bed.

"So," he said. "Ready to go up?"

"Don't you need things from your trailer? Toothbrush, pajamas . . ."

He grinned. "Never wear pajamas. And the guest bathroom's equipped with everything I'll need. I checked."

"You planned this?"

"Navy's motto—be prepared."

She wondered what else he prepared for.

He wound a lock of her hair around his finger. "Don't worry, Cait. There's a lock on your bedroom door."

He turned the lights out. "Lead the way."

When they reached the second floor, she hesitated. Her hand shook with anticipation as she reached in her pocket for the key. RT took it from her, unlocked the door, and returned the key.

"Want me to come up and tuck you in?"

Yes, her mind screamed. Still, she hesitated.

RT grabbed her around the waist and kissed her hard and released her. "Adults don't play games. Good night, Cait."

Stunned, she stared at his back. *What just happened?*

CHAPTER 30

It took Cait awhile to get to sleep with RT one floor below. It was a restless sleep with a returning dream, similar to one she'd had when she moved into the house. She was in an open convertible heading south on Coastal Highway 1 with Roger, her deceased husband. Low-flying shorebirds and gulls glided in and out along the blue Pacific. Instead of being on their honeymoon, like in the first dream, they were headed to Carmel to attend a funeral.

A fog bank of new faces drifted overhead—Chip Fallon, Kenneth Alt, and Hank Dillon. The car missed a curve on the road and plummeted over the side toward the sea.

Cait screamed and shot up in bed. Her chest pounded; tears spilled down her cheeks.

Niki leaped on top of her, licking her face.

She hugged him and squeezed her eyes shut against the vision of falling into the ocean. She didn't believe dreams were messages from Beyond any more than she believed in coincidences, but what did the dream mean?

Someone banged on the door.

"Cait, open the damn door!"

She stumbled out of the bed. "Coming."

She unlocked the door and almost fell into RT. He caught her and held her tight against his warm body. "Jesus, Cait! I heard you scream and thought someone crawled in the window and attacked you." He held her away and stared hard into her face. "It scared the hell out of me."

Cait felt tremors in RT's hands as he held her and saw tears well in his eyes. It shook her to the core to see this big, tough SEAL with his emotions transparent. She wrapped her arms around his neck. Her body reacted like a match to gas. She couldn't hold back any longer. "RT, please . . ."

RT loosened Cait's hold on him and took a step up, closed the door, and locked it. She felt his heart beating as he swept her up in his arms and carried her up the rest of the way.

When he laid her down on the bed, she realized RT wasn't wearing pajamas.

Cait awoke at dawn to an empty bed, except for Niki sprawled at the foot. Filtered sunlight drifted across the room. She stretched and forced herself to get up and in the shower. She left her hair to dry naturally and dressed in shorts and T-shirt, then stood at the window for a few moments to admire the golden hills, cloudless blue sky, and the sun shimmering over the vineyard. She turned away and picked up her keys, cell, and gun. "Come on, Niki."

The kitchen smelled of toast and coffee. Detective Rook and two officers in jeans and sport shirts stood in the middle of the room talking with RT and Marcus.

"What's going on?"

"These officers saw a pickup parked on Cross Road," Rook said, "and a couple of guys climbing on the hill."

"They saw us," one of the officers said, "and took off running. We chased them, but they had a head start and we lost them."

Cait felt the hairs at the back of her neck prickle. "What did they look like?"

"Too far away to tell, but we traced the California plate to a John LeBow."

Cait shook her head. "The name means nothing to me. What about the pickup?"

"Ford, black, big tires," Rook said. "Sound like the pickup you saw yesterday?"

She nodded.

"We had it towed," Detective Rook said, "but they'll find new wheels. They haven't finished what they came here to do." He raised an eyebrow. "We'll get them. The longer they're here, the more desperate they'll be. Desperate people make mistakes." He introduced the officers. "Perough and Vanicheque will hang around for awhile. I got catching up to do at the station, but I'll be in touch."

"Cait's expecting Calder Manning sometime," RT said. "Let's not confuse him with Wally Dillon and his pal."

"Shep probed deeper into Manning's background," Cait said. "Manning wrote a dissertation on medieval history. Co-incidence?"

"Wonder if he knows a halberd from a hammer," Rook said.

"It crossed my mind," Cait said.

"I hope Manning can convince Wally to turn himself in. I'd like nothing more than to slap cuffs on him and arrest him for Chip Fallon's murder and the attempts on you, Cait."

A knock at the door drew their attention.

RT opened it.

"Hi," Fumié said as she stepped inside and looked at the officers. "Why are the police here?"

Cait smiled. Fumié was like a breath of fresh air in pink shorts and white T-shirt. "You know Detective Rook. Officers Perough and Vanicheque will be here awhile."

"Does it have anything to do with the guy I saw in the vineyard?"

The officers and Rook exchanged glances. "What's he look like?" Rook asked.

"I don't know, but he wasn't working, and there's no truck in the driveway like the one Kurt Mathews drives. He saw me staring at him."

"Stay here." Rook and the officers ran out the door.

RT pulled his gun and checked the chamber as gunfire erupted outside.

"Down!" RT shouted.

Cait and Fumié scrambled under the counter and Marcus ducked into his office.

CHAPTER 31

When Marcus came back in the kitchen, he gasped: "What happened?"

Cait stood and shook her head. "We don't know yet." She grabbed her gun off the counter and hurried to the front of the house.

"Cait—" RT said.

"I'm going to look out the window."

"Jesus," RT muttered, slamming the back door as he went out.

"We're lucky RT and the officers are here," Fumié said.

Cait peeked around the window frame and swept her gaze across the vineyard, but the shooting had stopped. Minutes passed while they waited for the police to return. "They're coming back," she said, disappointed they were alone.

"Where's RT?" she asked when they came in.

"He'll be here. He wanted to look in the vineyard," Rook said.

"Who was doing the shooting?"

"The guy in the vineyard started it. The officers returned fire," Rook said.

Rook pulled out his ringing cell. "Find anything?"

Cait watched Rook's expression as he listened to the caller.

"On my way." Rook smiled. "RT found a trail of blood."

Cait's heart lurched. "That should slow Wally down."

"Sounds like he got tangled in the wires and mangled one of

the grapevines."

"Serves him right," Cait said.

Rook and the officers left and Marcus returned to his office.

Cait filled two coffee mugs and set one on the counter in front of Fumié. "Be right back." She went into the office, where Niki was sprawled out in a patch of sunlight while Marcus attacked his keyboard.

"It sucks. I should have found the bastard when I was riding yesterday. I know this property. I wanted to find him and turn him over to the police."

Cait's heart went out to Marcus, but she didn't know how to console him. Even the cave he loved was sealed after the police learned Wally had hidden in there. Marcus had protected the cave and the pictographs covering the walls since he was a kid growing up on the property. "She leaned on the edge of the desk as an idea took hold. "You're a computer whiz. You can help by Googling John LeBow, the owner of that pickup Detective Rook mentioned. See if you can find where he works and if he has family in town."

Marcus looked up and nodded. "And maybe find a connection to Wally."

"Exactly," Cait said. "Most cops aren't as computer savvy as you. While you're doing that, they can search for Wally."

Marcus rubbed his chin. "That's a kick, me helping the police."

Cait grinned and held the palm of her hand out for a high-five.

Fumié was looking through the glossy magazine insert in the local *Independent* newspaper Cait seldom had time to read. She showed Cait an article about the rodeo. "You should go sometime."

"Maybe next year."

"I have something to tell you." Fumié's black eyes glistened, her long black hair silky and shiny. "Remember the lady who called and asked me to sing at her winery?"

"Of course."

"I've had more offers, even for a wedding reception at Ravenswood."

"Congratulations. But I'm not surprised. You're talented."

"Thanks. Since you introduced me to people from the wineries and the city chamber at the tea, I've been asked to entertain at the Harvest Wine Celebration in the fall and the Holiday in the Vineyards at Christmas."

"Fumié, that's terrific. Aren't you excited?"

She nodded. "Sure, but I also received a letter from the park ranger school in Santa Rosa. They're holding a place for me, but they want to know now if I plan to start in the fall. I haven't answered it yet."

"How far is Santa Rosa? Maybe you could do both—the wedding and festival and go to school."

"A couple of hours."

"Being a park ranger is your dream. When does the class start?"

"Middle of August. Classes go to mid-November."

"There you go," Cait said. "If this is what you want to do, then don't toss the opportunity away. How is your mother doing?"

"She's in remission. My parents are urging me to go to Santa Rosa."

"Three months isn't long," Cait said. "Then you can apply for a job wherever you want."

"I know," Fumié said. "So it's okay with you?"

Cait was momentarily at a loss for words. "Of course, but it's not up to me. It's your decision." Cait set her coffee mug on the counter. "I'm going to ask Marcus to come up with a plan to build the gift shop in the theater complex. You might like to help until you leave. We don't have a license to sell alcohol, but I want a place where people can picnic and shop for souvenirs."

Fumié grinned. "I have a plan in mind. I told Tasha about it."

"You're way ahead of me. Talk it over with Marcus." Cait opened the door for Niki.

"Going somewhere?" RT stood on the step.

"Niki wants out."

"Got something to show you." He reached into his jeans pocket and pulled out a paper clipping and handed it to her.

Curious, she unfolded it and stared at the grainy picture of her taken before she shot Hank Dillon. Exasperation crackled through her. "Where did you get this?"

"That's you, isn't it?"

The article was wrinkled, but she couldn't deny it was her in uniform with her gun positioned to shoot. "Yes."

"I found it in the vineyard. Wally must have dropped it when he got caught in the wires."

"Someone sent it to the *Columbus Dispatch.* I was too busy to notice a reporter. My department kept my name out of the paper as long as they could."

"Not unusual."

"No, it isn't. I was on leave during the investigation." She returned the clipping to him. "That shooting is why I'm in the position I'm in now."

RT tucked the paper in his shirt pocket. "Hang in there. We'll get him."

She'd believe it when it happened. In the meantime, she was working on a new angle. *What if the reporter who took that picture was Calder Manning?*

CHAPTER 32

Later that afternoon, Cait grabbed treats for Niki and hurried upstairs to her bedroom to call Shep. Disappointed when she got his voice mail, she left a message. While she waited for him to call back, she sat on the chaise and thought back to the tragic event that led to her shooting Hank Dillon and his connection to Calder Manning's family.

Two years is a long time to wait to avenge the killing of a relative. Was it possible Wally and Calder Manning formed an alliance against me? How well did they know each other? Would Manning sacrifice his career and family for Wally Dillon?

Cait went to the desk and opened her laptop, logged onto the newspaper's archives, and searched for the bank robbery; the date was embedded in her mind. Soon she was staring at the same grainy picture RT had shown her. She scanned the article but the reporter's name wasn't mentioned.

She heard the Skype beep and tapped a key. "I'm here, Shep."

"Sorry I missed your call. Any word from Calder Manning?"

"No. I was checking the paper's archives for that picture taken of me during the bank robbery. The reporter's name wasn't mentioned. Do you think you can find out who it was?"

"I have a contact at the paper. I'll ask her and let you know. Is it important?"

"Could be. RT found a copy of the picture in the vineyard. Wally Dillon or his partner must have dropped it when they ran from the police."

"You think the reporter was Calder Manning?"

"I think there's a good chance it is. Maybe that's why he's coming here. I'd like to know if he was out of the country during the bank robbery before I ask him. Maybe you could find that out, too?"

"Manning's mother said he was in Afghanistan."

"Parents are notorious for protecting their children."

"Good point. I'll make a few calls when we hang up. If it was Manning, I'll have another chat with his mother."

"Thanks," she said.

He smiled. "I like to keep my ex-partner happy." He raised his hand. "Back soon."

Cait watched Shep fade. He had more contacts than a phonebook. If anyone could find the answers, it would be Shep.

Her cell rang. She hoped it wasn't Calder Manning. She wanted to hear back from Shep before talking to Manning. Relieved to see Marcus's name, she said, "What's up?"

"The guy's here to install your new windshield. Do you want to talk to him or do you want me to handle it?"

"Did you check his ID?"

"He's legit."

"Okay, I'll be there in a minute." She found her keys, grabbed an old hoodie from the back of the chair, and pulled it on over her shorts and shirt. Then she slipped her gun into one of the pockets. "Come on, Niki."

She glanced at the wall clock in the kitchen on her way out. It was nearly four o'clock. Niki followed her and then chased Velcro, who'd been lapping water from a bowl on the back step. She went around to the front where Marcus hovered near the serviceman as he removed the cracked windshield from her Saab.

The man glanced up as Cait approached. The look he gave her made her wish she'd changed from shorts to an old pair of baggy jeans and a man's shirt.

"This is Cait," Marcus said. "The Saab is hers."

Cait read the name on the man's shirt—Jarvis—and then looked at the white panel truck in front of the garage. The company logo was too faded to read.

The man nodded at the damaged windshield. "Someone take a shot at you?"

"It was a rock."

"Oh. Won't take long to fix, then it'll be good as new." He turned back to his work.

Cait rolled her eyes at Marcus. "Have you seen RT?" She watched the man go to his truck, take a tool from the side door, and walk back.

"Yeah, he said he wanted to see Jim. Something about that painting on the second floor."

She frowned. "That's where you'll find me, at the RV." She gave Jarvis one last glance before she walked away. She gripped the gun in her pocket and cut across the front of the house. The vineyard was a constant reminder of what happened to Chip. Niki shot around the corner and stayed close to her. She knocked on the Fleetwood door. "Anyone in there?" She retrieved a treat from her pocket for Niki. "Stay."

Jim swung the door open. "We're here having strawberry pie." He held his hand out and helped her up into the RV.

Her eyes locked on RT sitting in the booth eating pie.

"RT was going to take pie back for you and Marcus," June said, "but you can have yours now. Do you want it smothered with whipped cream?"

Cait licked her lips. "Yum. It might sweeten my mood." A corner of her lips curled when she noticed whipped cream on RT's lips, then she tried to dismiss the lustful thought running through her mind. She slid into the leatherette booth across from him. "The guy's here to replace my windshield."

"I know. Where's your gun?"

"In my pocket."

June set a slice of pie covered with whipped cream in front of Cait. "I keep telling you she never leaves home without it, RT."

Jim set a steaming cup of coffee in front of Cait before sitting down. "We were discussing that painting upstairs in the guest bedroom."

She looked at RT. "I thought you hadn't seen it."

"I spent the night there, remember?" He nudged her foot under the table.

Cait felt her face flush as she took a forkful of pie. "The painting's titled *Face in Motion*."

Jim smiled. "I know. I was in the art recovery business many years. RT asked me to look up the artist."

"Wasn't easy with only the initial R," RT said.

"R for Raven," Cait said. "At least that's what Kenneth said."

Jim nodded. "He's right. Hope you don't mind that RT invited me to see it while you and June were at the ranch. Did Kenneth say how much he thought the painting was worth?"

Cait thought back to her conversation with Kenneth. "No, only that it was probably worth even more today."

"I couldn't put a price on it, but don't be too quick to hand it over to Kenneth."

She set her fork on the plate. "Make a guess. Hundreds? Thousands?"

"Who knows? It's worth what a buyer is willing to pay. If Kenneth knows the artist, maybe he should call her."

Cait sat back in her seat. "I don't even like the painting."

"Well," June said, "I'd like to think it's valuable to Kenneth because it's of Tasha."

Cait agreed. She remembered how emotional Kenneth was when he saw the painting.

"Earlier paintings often are more valuable than later ones

after the artist becomes famous," Jim said.

"What did you tell Kenneth?" RT asked.

"I said I'd think about it, but I was stalling because I didn't want to give in too fast." *And I'm not sure the painting is the real reason he's here.* "It's Kenneth's silhouette behind Tasha. Were they really lovers, June?"

"Oh, yes, a long time ago, in New York when they were up-and-coming actors. They were like a pair of star-crossed lovers. I don't think Kenneth ever got over her, and maybe that's why he's never married."

RT wiggled his eyebrows. "How sweet—like Romeo and Juliet."

Cait laughed, not expecting a Shakespearean comment from him.

June giggled. "Ah, a romantic amongst us." She winked at Cait.

Cait's cell beeped. She glanced at the screen. "Shep. What did you find?"

"The picture in the *Dispatch* came from a cell phone and was forwarded anonymously with a text message saying it was taken at the time of the bank robbery. Sorry, that's all I was able to find out."

Disappointed but not surprised, she said, "The paper doesn't check their sources before publishing pictures?"

"Exactly what I asked my contact," Shep said. "Same old, same old. Reporters and papers hustling to meet deadlines and be the first to get their stories published."

Cait sighed. "I'll ask Manning."

"Tread lightly until you get to know him," Shep said.

She set her cell on the table. "You gotta love high tech."

RT was on his cell with Detective Rook when Cait left the trailer. Niki lay sprawled in the sun at the foot of the step. She slipped her hand in her hoodie pocket and gripped the gun. She noticed the repairman and his white panel truck had left; she was starting to go inside the garage to look at her new windshield when Niki growled.

"Hello," an unfamiliar voice said.

Cait swung around. She raised her hand to shield her eyes from the sun and stared at the tall man standing a little too close for comfort. His erect stance and reflective wraparound shades suggested a military background. "Who are you?"

"Calder Manning. You must be Cait."

"I was told you would call."

His voice smooth as scotch, he said, "I apologize, Cait, for not calling, but since it's late in the day I hoped you wouldn't mind if I stopped by just to introduce myself." He removed his glasses and extended his hand.

Cait slid her hand from her gun and shook his. "How did you know where to find me?" The shock of seeing him subsided and she gave him a long, hard look. He was at least six-two, tan, with a runner's slim build, sandy hair, hazel eyes, and dressed in a Tommy Bahama deep shrimp–colored shirt over khaki slacks. He wore a simple gold necklace and cross that probably cost more than her month's salary as a crime analyst. In the only picture she'd seen of him, he was in army fatigues and a helmet.

He grinned. "I hope I pass inspection. I have a feeling you did your homework and checked me out on the Web when you heard I was coming to see you. You know I'm a war correspondent. That might explain how I have the sources to locate almost anyone."

There was a warm likeability about him, a charisma that would have women bidding for his attention. She didn't trust him.

"I'm here to help," he said.

Of course you are, she thought. *Or on a fool's errand?* "What makes you think I need your help? What advantage do you have that the police don't?"

A voice ripped through the air. "Put your arms up and turn around!"

Cait spun to see RT with his gun directed on Manning.

Manning slowly raised his arms high in the air. "I'm not armed."

"Who are you?" RT demanded.

Manning smiled. "Calder Manning. Cait was expecting me."

"Drop your ID on the ground and step away."

"No problem." Manning reached into a back pocket, pulled out his wallet, and leaned down to put it to the ground.

Damn, I didn't even ask for his ID.

"Cait," RT said, "check his ID."

How does RT know I didn't already ask to see it? She picked up the wallet and was relieved to see several credit cards with Manning's name imprinted on them, including his Ohio driver's license and a glossy card identifying him as a war correspondent. She nodded. "He's Calder Manning." She handed the wallet to Manning.

"Caution's always a good thing," Manning said.

RT lowered his gun. "You were told to call first."

Manning repeated what he'd told Cait. "I don't like to waste time on trivialities."

"You've taken a lot for granted," RT said.

He shrugged. "Sometimes that's all you have, but this time I knew before I came what I was looking for."

The standoff between RT and Calder Manning amused her. *Manning reeks of confidence. I hope this doesn't become a war of another kind.*

CHAPTER 33

"I don't like it," RT said after Calder Manning left.

Cait didn't like it, either. That Manning showed up without calling as instructed left her with even more questions about him. "I'll let Rook know he's here."

RT nodded, his eyes glued to the driveway and the tail end of Manning's white Toyota rental. Rather than inviting Manning into the house, Cait suggested he return in the morning at ten. As genial as Manning had been, she didn't like his arrogance, as if he alone could set her world straight and solve her problems.

"I thought you were still with the Harts."

"I left after Rook and I talked. Good thing, too."

"Your gun didn't intimidate Manning. He looked amused."

RT tucked his gun away. "He won't feel that way long." He leaned over and scratched behind Niki's ears.

Niki didn't need encouragement. He jumped at RT's legs, begging for a treat.

"Maybe you should call Rook while I call Shep before he hops a plane out here."

RT reached in his pocket for a treat for Niki. "You and that detective friend of yours have a thing going?"

Is it possible RT's jealous of Shep? "He's just an old friend from work. You know that."

"If he comes here, we should have a party. Get to know one another."

This side of RT secretly pleased her. "Royal Tanner, I do

believe you're jealous."

His head shot up. His blue eyes bore into hers as he stepped close enough for her to smell strawberries on his breath. "I am *not* the jealous type." He pulled her against him, kissed her hard, and released her. "Ain't so."

Cait smiled. *Liar.*

RT's cell buzzed. He unclipped it from his belt and glanced at the display. His demeanor froze. "Tanner."

Fear crept up Cait's spine as she watched RT's jaw tighten and his body stiffen, signs she recognized. She knew this was the dreaded call—RT summoned to another secret mission. It couldn't have come at a worse time.

"Yes, sir." RT closed his cell, looking as if it had bitten him.

Cait said, "You have to leave already?"

He nodded and gathered her in his arms. "Sometimes I hate this job."

"What happened to the two-week furlough?"

"Nothing's cast in cement."

Velcro crept over and stood next to Niki and Cait as if aware something was wrong.

"Call Shep," RT said. "Ask him to come. You two can party together."

"Oh, shut up," she mumbled into his chest.

Ilia's yellow VW bug rolled up the driveway. He parked in front of the house and he and Fumié jumped out. They hesitated when they saw Cait and RT clinging to each other.

Cait and RT stepped apart.

"Something's up and it doesn't look good," Fumié said.

"I have to leave," RT said.

"Now?" Ilia asked, as if RT's leaving was imprudent.

RT nodded.

"Who decides when to call you back? The Navy? The CIA?" Ilia asked.

RT shook his head.

Marcus cut across the front of the house with a plate of strawberry pie smothered in whipped cream in his hand. "Jim wants to see you, RT." He looked at Fumié and Ilia. "What are you two doing here?"

"We're going to the movies," Ilia said, "and thought Cait and RT might want to come with us. But now . . ."

Marcus looked at Cait and RT. "Did I miss something?"

"RT has to leave," Ilia said.

Marcus almost dropped his pie. "Well, that stinks."

"Couldn't have said it better," RT said. "Calder Manning was just here. If I'd known I had to leave, I would have sat him down and had a hard talk with him. Now it's too late. I'll be gone by daybreak."

"What the hell? He didn't call?" Marcus asked.

"No," Cait said. "He'll return at ten in the morning."

Marcus blinked and ran one hand over his spiked hair. "How did he know where to find you?"

"Contacts." Cait reached into her pocket for her phone. "Shep will be upset Manning didn't call."

"I'll call Rook." RT walked away with his phone to his ear.

Cait watched him go. *I want tonight to be memorable for both of us.*

The evening was somber when RT returned to sit with Cait and the Harts at the kitchen counter. Fumié and Ilia had left for the movies, and Marcus went to visit his mother at a nursing home in Tracy. Cait and June prepared dinner.

RT didn't bring up Shep's name again, but Cait sensed he hadn't forgotten him. Shep offered to fly out when she told him RT was leaving, but she convinced him that Rook had promised extra officers for the weekend.

"What time do you leave, RT?" June asked.

"Early." He set his glass on the counter with a clink. "There's a slight chance I can convince my boss how urgent the situation is here. If not . . ." He shook his head and refilled his wine glass.

Hope flared briefly for Cait. But she didn't like this depressed side of RT. "Don't jeopardize your career. Think about Mindy. Your daughter needs you. We'll be waiting when you get back. Rook will have officers—"

RT's dark eyes snapped. "Don't be naive. You were a cop. There are never enough police for a situation like this." He hesitated. "I should have asked Rook about bringing in one of Livermore's K-nine dogs."

"Maybe he should first check with the sheriff's department, but I'll ask him," Cait said.

"Any idea where you'll be going?" Jim asked.

"No, only that it's in my area of expertise, whatever the hell that means." RT finished his wine and stood. "Should I open another bottle?"

"Not for me." Jim rose. "Back to the computer. Maybe Raven will want to buy back her painting and make you rich, Cait."

"I don't think it's money that interests Kenneth Alt," she said. "It's personal."

"Because Alt and Tasha had an affair," RT interjected.

Cait didn't want to get into it now, not with RT leaving in the morning.

"I'll go with Jim," June said. She gathered the plates and took them to the sink.

Jim held his hand out to RT. "If I don't see you before you leave, be safe, and try not to worry about what's going on here. Everything will work out. It usually does."

Cait closed the door behind the Harts and turned to see RT at the desk in the office. "What are you doing?"

"Leaving a note for Marcus."

She watched him write, fold the note, and slip it in an envelope. He propped it against the computer.

"I'm going to my trailer for a few things."

"You don't have to stay here. I'll be fine with Niki."

"I'm spending the night in the house." He walked past her and into the kitchen. "I'll leave the Hummer and trailer in the parking lot, if that's okay." He paused at the door and looked at her.

Confused, she wondered why he sounded angry. "Of course it's okay."

He opened the door. "Rook's taking me to the airport."

Stunned, Cait stared at the closed door. *What just happened?*

Cait waited for RT to return, but after awhile she went upstairs. The bedroom felt hot and stuffy. She opened the windows that weren't sealed shut. Night had fallen. She sat on the windowsill and looked at the stars, the moon and their light caressing the vineyard.

She tried to think about her dad and not about RT's leaving. He'd been a history professor at Ohio State, and when she was ready to leave home for college, he told her the true self is always in motion, like music, a river of life, and how self-appreciation leads to healthy self-esteem, a positive self-image, and a sense of dignity. And when she divorced, he said it again.

What words of wisdom would her dad offer her now? How did she really feel about RT? Is it possible he'd already left to avoid saying goodbye? She stepped away from the window, stripped out of her jeans and T-shirt—the shirt was stained with strawberry juice—and tossed them in a heap on the floor to be washed later. She took pink silk lounging pajamas from a drawer, and as she dressed, she heard music so soft she had to strain to hear. Drawn to the stairs, she listened, then continued barefoot to the second floor. When the music intensified, she recognized the powerful music from *Phantom of the Opera* and wondered if music was how RT released his frustrations.

Cait continued down until she saw a soft glow from the lamp on the piano. She tiptoed down a few more steps until she saw RT over the banister, then she sat on one of the steps to watch and listen. His fingers flew over the keys as he segued from one song to another.

Cait silently mouthed the words from *Yentl,* an older movie she'd discovered they both loved. RT segued into "Evergreen," another favorite of hers, tightening her chest from the passion it evoked.

She closed her eyes and swayed to the music. *Why did he choose that particular song?*

Without missing a beat, RT said, "You'd be more comfortable down here beside me."

Her eyes snapped open. "How did you know I was here?"

RT smiled up at her, his hands over the keys. "I know you and how you think. Don't always agree with you, but you have to admit ours is an interesting relationship. Ever think about it and wonder where it will go?"

I try not to. "I wonder where you'll go when you leave and if I'll see you again."

He chuckled. "And our relationship?"

She eased up off the step and leaned over the banister. "Do we have a relationship?"

RT continued to play, his eyes raised to hers. "We have a connection."

"Tasha."

He nodded and stood. "Yes, but it's up to us what we do about it. I've been thinking a lot about our situation. Any suggestions?"

Oh, yeah. "One." She dangled her ring of keys over the banister.

RT grinned. "Love the way your mind works."

CHAPTER 34

RT left at the crack of dawn. In the wee hours before she'd fallen asleep, he whispered, "See you later." Now, sitting in the meditation garden with a cup of tea, her gun in a pocket of her jeans and Niki curled at her feet, Cait experienced emptiness not unlike how she'd felt when her parents' plane went down in the sea five years ago. When had RT become so important in her life? How had he managed, in such a short time, to tear down the walls she'd erected after the split from her husband?

Her thoughts were broken by a thunderous noise from the front of the house. Niki jumped up, ran circles around her, and barked. "What the hell . . . ?" She set her cup on the bench and started running, almost colliding with Marcus as he came out the door.

"What was that? Sounded like loud explosions," he said.

Cait reached for her gun as she ran and was followed by Marcus and Niki. "Damned if I know, but someone's going to pay for disturbing the peace this early in the morning."

Jim and June Hart staggered up the path across the driveway looking as if they'd just gotten out of bed.

Cait glared at the man in front of her, who wore a leather jacket, jeans, and helmet and who had arrived on a huge, noisy, red motorcycle. "Shut that thing off!" Her hand tightened on the gun she held by her leg. "What were you thinking?"

The man shut down the engine, pushed the kickstand down, and then stepped off and removed his helmet. "Morning, Cait.

Sorry about the noise."

Stunned, Cait stared at Calder Manning. Yesterday, he'd driven a white Toyota. Today, it was this loud, red monster of a bike.

"You probably woke half of Livermore with that *thing*," she said. She couldn't help but notice his ease of getting off the bike, as if he was used to riding one that big.

He grinned. "This *thing* is a Ducati sport bike. If you'd like, I'll give you the thrill ride of your life, but first I suggest you leave your gun behind. Might cause unwanted attention."

Taken aback at seeing Manning on a bike instead of driving his rental, she'd almost forgotten about the gun and tucked it away. "I've had enough thrills in my life. What happened to the rental you were driving yesterday?"

"Parked it at a friend's house. Not as much fun as the bike."

This guy is full of surprises. "You have friends in Livermore?"

He grinned. "I have friends all over the world, even in this valley." He adjusted his helmet under his arm, then removed the gloves he'd been wearing and tucked them inside the helmet. "You know how I make my living." He walked over to her.

I'd like to cram that boyish grin down his throat. But inwardly, she admired his good looks and confidence. The Harts subtly positioned themselves on either side of Manning, like a couple of sentries, but he ignored them, which irritated Cait.

Neither Manning nor the motorcycle intimidated Marcus. "I assume you have a watch and cell phone. Come back at ten when you were expected."

Way to go, Marcus. Cait stepped in and introduced them. "Marcus Singer is my manager."

Manning hooked his sunglasses on his jacket pocket and offered his hand to Marcus. When Marcus ignored him, Manning glanced at his watch. "It's eight twenty-two. Not early for most people." He looked at the Harts and smiled. "Do you work for Cait, too?"

"No," Cait snapped. "They're friends."

"We're here to help with the Shakespeare festival," Jim said. "Are you going to take Wally Dillon back to Ohio before he ends up like his brother Hank?"

Cait suppressed a grin. *Yeah, Jim, you tell him.*

"That's partly my intention, of course," Manning said, "but we have to find him first, don't we? Or have you already located him?"

"Not yet," Cait said, "but we will. You got another reason for coming here?"

A fleeting frown crossed his face. "Only time will tell."

His evasion irritated her. "What makes you think you can find Wally when the police can't?"

"Because I know him."

"I thought it was his brother, Hank, you knew. It *was* Hank your parents adopted, wasn't it?"

He hesitated, then shrugged. "Know one Dillon, know the other."

"Really? One's a bank robber, the other a murderer. I guess you could say they chose the same destructive path."

Manning smiled, showing his pearly whites. "The brothers were close, if not by age."

"Four years isn't much," she said. "If I recall, Wally was eight and Hank twelve when he was adopted. Were you happy with the adoption?" She hoped to unhinge him with unanticipated questions—by the flicker of anger in his eyes, she knew she had.

Manning snapped, "Once a cop, always a cop."

Cait hoped she'd never lose the training she'd received at the academy and on the job. "It's in my blood. Was that knife you gave Hank a souvenir from Afghanistan? Wally tried to use it to break into my house."

Manning laughed. "I don't remember ever being interrogated under such pristine conditions or by such a beautiful woman." The sun sparkled off the gold cross around his neck. "I'm usually holed up somewhere in Afghanistan or Iraq. Have we become enemies already, Cait?"

A wave of guilt swept over her, but she couldn't help badgering Manning. RT would have had a quick comeback for him. She felt a vibration in her jeans pocket, pulled out her cell, and glanced at the screen. "Excuse me," she said. "I have to take this." She stepped away, but kept her eye on him. "Manning's here. It's been a rocky start," she told Rook.

"He's early," Rook said.

"He is, and he didn't call first." She glanced at the bike, silently thinking it might be fun to ride if RT was the driver. "You need to see what he's driving."

"I'm leaving the station now. A couple of plainclothes won't be far behind. Have Marcus give them something to do at the theaters for cover."

"That can be arranged." She slid her phone back in her pocket. "Okay, Manning. Let's go inside. It's getting hot." *In more ways than one.*

"Okay if I leave the bike here?"

"Sure. We're looking for a murderer, not a thief."

As soon as they stepped in the kitchen, June turned on Manning. "I swear on Shakespeare's head if you don't keep your promise and find Wally, you'll have me to deal with. I may be old, but I've the mind of a construction worker." Jim gasped, then clamped his hand over his mouth to keep from laughing. "Cait's been through hell. Fix the problem or go home and take Wally with you." She glared at him with her hands on her hips, then settled on a barstool.

Cait covered her mouth with her hand to suppress her laughter.

Marcus giggled.

"Christ on a broomstick," June said. "I hate when people get away with murder."

Speechless, Manning stared at June.

Cait cleared her throat. "You'll get used to her. She's a dramatic actress like my Aunt Tasha before someone murdered her."

Manning cocked his eyebrow. "Your aunt was murdered?"

"That's how I happened to inherit this place."

Manning slid his hands in his pockets. "Sounds like this house brings bad luck to its tenants."

She looked at Marcus for his reaction, since he'd grown up here. "People, not houses, are responsible for the environment."

Manning's face suddenly looked taut as piano wire. "You're entitled to your opinion."

"Sit down, Mr. Manning, and relax. Detective Rook will be here soon. Coffee?"

Manning nodded. "Please. Black. And call me Calder."

"I'll be in the office," Marcus said.

"I'll help you, Cait," June said. She whispered as she poured coffee into mugs. "I should have held my tongue. He'll think I'm old *and* crazy."

"I love you the way you are." Cait carried their coffee to the counter and pulled out a stool and sat next to Manning.

Someone tapped on the back door.

June opened it. Fumié stood on the step with a notebook in her hand. "Hi."

Wearing cutoff jeans and a yellow tank top, Cait thought Fumié looked like a Barbie doll with her hair pulled back in a ponytail. "Marcus is expecting me. I've drawn sketches for your new gift shop." She looked at Manning. "Am I interrupting?"

"No, come in," Cait said. She closed the door and introduced Manning.

"Beautiful girl," Manning said, his eyes lingering on Fumié as she went into the office. "Anyone else I should meet?"

"Only Detective Rook."

"Where's your friend from yesterday, the one who was ready to shoot me if I blinked?"

"He's unavailable." She didn't detect a bulge under his jacket, but she wanted to know if he was armed. "Did the friend who lent you the motorcycle also provide you with a gun?"

"Why would you think that?"

The doorbell rang.

"That should be Detective Rook. I'll be back."

Rook stood on the porch and cocked his head at the motorcycle. "He drove that beast all the way from Ohio?"

Cait laughed. "No. You're not a motorcycle fan?"

"Sure, but that's some bike. Expensive, too."

"Manning has a rental car. The bike belongs to a friend of his in the valley. He's in the kitchen." Cait introduced them and then hung back to observe their reaction to each other.

"Let's hear your plan, Mr. Manning. Do you know where Wally Dillon is?" Rook asked. "I assume you have one or you wouldn't have come all this way."

"Of course," Manning said. "I don't know where he is, but he knows I'm in town."

"What? You didn't tell me you talked to him," Cait said.

"It never came up."

What the hell? She couldn't believe his nonchalant attitude about a life-and-death situation. She saw Rook's ears turn pink.

Rook shook his head. "Have you seen Wally since you've been here?"

Cait saw a hard look in Manning's eyes, as if he were weighing his answer.

"No," Manning said. "He wouldn't tell me where he's staying."

"Apparently he has friends here, and money. What's he planning to do?" Rook asked.

"I assume he means to kill Cait." Manning held his hands up. "Hey, don't blame me. I'm just the messenger. Don't get me wrong. I intend to find him and end this."

Fuming, Cait said, "Oh great! He's already killed an innocent person, one of my actors." She struggled to stifle her anger. "What's motivating you? What do you have to gain by coming here?"

Marcus stuck his head out the door. "Found something on John LeBow."

Manning's head snapped around.

"LeBow is Wally Dillon's cousin."

"Good work, Marcus," Rook said. "LeBow has a criminal record but no outstanding warrants. He's the registered owner of that pickup we towed."

She nodded. "I asked Marcus to investigate LeBow. Now we know where Wally got the guns and who his partner is." Cait turned to Manning. "Do you know John LeBow?"

"The name's familiar," Manning admitted, "but I don't know him and I didn't know he was their cousin. What does he have to do with anything that's happened?"

Cait sneered. "You mean besides providing Wally with a truck, firearms, and ammunition?"

"Why don't you start by telling us why you went to the Columbus police station to inquire about the officer who shot Hank Dillon," Rook said. "Then tell us about your phone conversations with Wally. After that, I'll think about letting you in on our investigation, but you are not to interfere with the police. Is that clear?"

Manning nodded, but Cait wasn't convinced Manning agreed with anything.

Chapter 35

Cait wanted to ask Manning if he was the anonymous reporter who took her picture outside the bank and sent it to the *Columbus Dispatch,* but she decided to wait for the right moment. She thought about the officers posing as maintenance workers, but, like Rook, she wasn't ready to let Manning in on who they were until she knew more about him. Marcus instantly disliked Manning.

"How about giving me a tour?" Manning asked.

She nodded. "Wait outside while I talk to Marcus. I'll only be a minute."

"Take your time."

When the door closed behind Manning, Cait turned to Rook. "The officers are here, right?"

"Yes. They came in an unmarked car."

"Good." She peeked in the office. "Marcus, would you let the officers in the theaters and find something for them to do? Maybe maintenance inspectors? Then I'll bring Manning out for a tour."

"Okay, but I don't trust him. Fumié can wait here," he said.

"I'll hang around awhile," Rook said.

Cait found Manning in the meditation garden with a gun in his hand.

"I hope you're not planning on shooting anyone," she said.

Manning tucked his gun under his jacket. "Just checking it." He slipped his mirrored sunglasses on. "Don't you check yours?"

"Why would you ask that?"

"I wondered how you felt after you shot Hank."

She froze then retorted curtly, "I saved an officer's life!"

"What's your problem, Manning?" Rook asked when he crossed to the garden.

Cait held her hand up. This was her battle. "I value life, especially the lives of my fellow officers. It was Hank Dillon's or the police officer's—easy decision."

Manning switched on his boyish charm, a smile tugging at his lips. "Sorry. That was insensitive and out of line. Let's see the theaters."

Cait waited. "Who told you about the theaters?"

Manning turned. "Some cop I met from your old department. He said you'd inherited a couple of Shakespearean theaters and a vineyard."

Cait let it go, but she planned to ask Shep how much Chuck Levy, the retired cop who'd crossed paths with Manning in a bar, had disclosed about her inheritance. As far as she knew, the vineyard was all that came up in their conversation. *Maybe Wally told him.*

Manning pointed to a small sign at the edge of the meditation garden. "What's this about?"

"My aunt liked to meditate every morning." She glanced at the marble dolphin, bench, and crimson roses the size of peonies. "I try to do the same."

" 'O fearful meditation! where, alack, shall Time's best jewel from Time's chest lie hid? Or what strong hand can hold his swift foot back? Or who his spoil of beauty can forbid?' Are you a fan of Shakespeare, Mr. Manning?" June asked as she walked into the garden.

Cait couldn't remember the sonnet, but loved the look of surprise on Manning's face.

"If you're trying to embarrass me," he said, "you've succeeded."

"I meant no harm, but since you're the one with a gun," June said, "I'll hold my tongue."

"Let's take a walk," Cait said, as she tried not to smile.

"You must feel vulnerable outside the house," Manning said. "You're an easy target."

"We're armed, even you," Rook said. "You might remind Wally about that when you see him. Did you go to that particular police station in Columbus because you knew that's where Cait worked?"

"Yes."

"Columbus is a large city," Rook said. "Lots of precincts."

"I must have heard about it on TV."

"You had TV in Afghanistan? Your mother said you were out of the country at the time of the bank robbery," Rook said. "Is that true?"

His eyes narrowed. "You talked to my mother?"

Rook shrugged.

"We live on opposite sides of town. I'd just returned after a long stint in Afghanistan and was tired."

Rook nodded. "The work you do is admirable. But I'm curious. You're gone so much, how did you get close to Hank? Why was it important to know the officer involved in the shooting?"

"Wouldn't you want to know in that situation?"

They had reached the trellised gate to the theater complex. Cait rested her hand on it but didn't open it. "Are you the anonymous journalist who sent my picture to the newspaper?" She could tell by the direction of a person's gaze if they were constructing or remembering information but wished she'd waited to ask, because Manning was wearing mirrored glasses.

The sun reflected on the gold cross at the opened neck of his shirt, his tanned skin glistened in the warm sun. He smiled.

"Busted. You got me."

His admission surprised her. "Why anonymously?"

"I didn't want to get involved any further than that."

"And yet you're here now. What changed your mind?"

"Wally."

Jim had been silent up until now, but Manning's attitude finally got to him. "Cut the crap! No one dragged you into that police station. No one dragged you to that bar where you just happened to meet a retired police officer who'd had enough alcohol to loosen his lips to a stranger."

Way to go, Jim. Couldn't have said it better myself.

"Wally contacted you?" Rook asked.

Angry creases appeared around Manning's mouth, and he ripped his glasses off. "Why am I under the microscope? Do you want my help with Wally or not? If not, just say so because I have assignments waiting for me. I work hard at a job I love, helping to defend our country by supporting the troops in every branch of the service I come in contact with. I write about their stories, their fears, and their hopes for the future. Sometimes even their prayers." He shifted his feet. "I'm good at what I do, but it keeps me out of the country seventy-five to eighty percent of the time." He hesitated. "Yeah, Wally called. He loved his brother."

"Doesn't leave much time for your daughter," Cait said. "And coming here cuts into it even more."

Manning hung his glasses on his shirt pocket. "How do you know about my daughter?"

"I have an inquiring mind." Cait smiled.

He nodded. "*Touché.* I have questions of my own for Wally. I don't need to know where he's hiding, but I'll catch him as soon as he shows his face. And the same goes for his cousin, LeBow."

"I thought you didn't know LeBow?"

"I don't need to know him to understand someone who supplies felons with guns."

"So you know LeBow and Wally have records," Rook said.

Manning shrugged.

"You sound confident you can find Wally and bring him to justice," Cait said.

Manning smiled. "That's about it."

Prove it. Cait couldn't put her finger on what bothered her about Manning. He was too smooth, too confident, and too good-looking to be believable. She never went for classically handsome guys. She preferred RT's rugged good looks. She opened the gate and was surprised to see Fumié with Marcus. They were on their hands and knees with pencils and a ball of string. Fumié stood and gestured for them to come over as a single gunshot split the air.

Cait and Rook simultaneously yelled, "Get down!"

Everyone dove to the ground.

Cait twisted her body around and reached for the gun at her back. Rook crouched, gun in hand.

Two officers ran out of the Elizabethan theater with their guns drawn.

Cait glanced around and saw Niki slithering toward her on his belly. When he reached her, he covered her face with kisses. She ran her free hand over his head and whispered "Good boy, Niki."

"Cait!" someone called.

She looked up and saw June and Jim peering over the brick wall. Jim gripped his gun while June raised her hand to indicate they were okay. Cait waited a few moments, and when there wasn't any more firing, she got to her feet and stood beside Rook, who was up and motioning to his officers.

"Shot fired from over there," Rook yelled, pointing to the trees and shrubs across the courtyard. "Spread out." The officers took off running, dodging behind the tall vegetation.

"I don't get it," Cait said. "Why didn't he shoot me when he had the chance?"

"He's playing with you." Rook glanced around. "Let's ask Manning."

Cait turned but didn't see him. "Manning?"

"Over here." Manning stepped through the gate, his gun in one hand, cell phone in the other.

Cait thought it strange that he'd gone back through the gate. "Were you talking to Wally?"

"Yes, he called with a message for you."

Surprised, she said, "What?"

"To remind you how vulnerable you are and that he can shoot you any time."

"Hell, I know that," she said.

"I never said it would be easy."

"You haven't said much of anything." She watched Rook with his phone to his ear.

"I think Wally wants to give up," Manning said.

"Could have fooled me."

"Let's look in the theater," Rook said.

Marcus and Fumié waited behind the bushes. She waved, indicating they were okay.

"That gunshot hit the trellis," June said. "Ripped right through the roses." She looked at Manning. "I saw you run the other way through the gate. Maybe you were Wally's target instead of Cait."

"You're mistaken," Manning said, "He wouldn't shoot me. He knows better—" His lips snapped shut.

"Better than what?" Cait asked.

"He knows better than to cross me. I've helped him financially since his brother was killed."

Sounds like a reasonable explanation unless the money went to buy guns to kill me.

Fumié and Marcus ran over to Cait. "I saw him," Fumié said, "but Marcus grabbed my arm and wouldn't let me follow him."

"Did he look like the mug shot of Wally?" Cait asked.

"I couldn't tell."

"What was he wearing?"

"Oh, gosh, Cait. I only got a quick look before he saw me, then I ducked back."

Cait caught her breath. "He saw you watching him?"

"Oh, yeah."

"Don't ever try to follow someone like that," Rook said. "You could get in serious trouble." He turned to Cait. "I want to make sure he didn't circle back and go inside the theater."

Cait walked with Manning. "I thought you didn't know how to get in touch with Wally. How do you get money to him?"

"I leave it with his mother." He smiled at Cait. "How are your cop instincts?"

"Wait and see."

"Why? Don't trust me?"

"I've just met you, Mr. Manning."

If I find you're here under false pretenses, I'll take you down and make sure you never see your daughter for a long time.

CHAPTER 36

Manning's been pleasant and anxious to help. He has an honorable job. He has a daughter. So why don't I trust him?

"Know much about Shakespeare?" Cait asked as they walked.

Manning smiled. "O Romeo, Romeo, where art thou Romeo?"

Cait smiled and shook her head but didn't comment on his misquote. "Everyone knows that."

He looked heavenward, as if picking words from the sky. "O my love, my wife, Death that hath sucked the honey of thy breath."

Surprised, she kept her eyes on him and the cell he still held. *Okay, so he knows a little Shakespeare. Most people do.*

Rook scowled. "Are you two going to stand all day quoting Shakespeare?" He held the door to the theater open.

Cait, Rook, and the Harts went inside, but Manning hesitated and turned back to the courtyard. "You coming?" she asked.

"I'll catch up," he said.

June asked, "What's he up to?"

"I wish I knew, but he might be expecting another call from Wally." She followed him.

Manning turned. "I assume those two guys running out of the theater with guns were cops. Any more of them around?"

"Not that I know of," Cait said. "Why?"

"I don't like surprises."

"That makes two of us. Are you coming inside?"

With a last glance at the courtyard, he said, "Lead the way."

Rook stood inside by the stairs. "I'm going to have a look in the loft." He took the stairs to the stage two at a time and ducked behind the curtain.

"Waste of time to look for Wally in here," Manning said.

"Why? He's been in here before. He stole a medieval weapon and was stupid enough to leave evidence behind."

A dark look crossed Manning's face. "Maybe it was his cousin, LeBow."

June rolled her eyes. "See you around."

"Manning and I will be in the back." Cait started up the stairs.

Manning stepped into the green room behind Cait. "I always wanted to know what it looked like behind the curtains." He strolled around the room, pausing to scan handwritten notes on white boards and flipping through sheets clipped to a large ring hung on the wall.

Cait wanted to remind him they were there to look for Wally but swallowed her words.

He stuck his head around a doorway. "What's this room?"

"Wig and makeup." She flipped on the lights. The makeup tables had been cleared and cleaned; their mirrors sparkled beneath the overhead lights. A couple of Styrofoam heads had been left out on one of the tables.

Manning picked one up. "Where are the wigs?"

"Stored so they won't get dusty when they're not in use. Sometimes the actors bring their own."

He turned to Cait. "Why store them now? Doesn't the festival run all summer?"

"It runs the first weekend of each month, May through September."

He flashed her a smile. "That leaves you a lot of spare time. What do you do during the off weeks?" He set the Styrofoam head back on the table.

Look for bad guys. "I wasn't born to this. I have to learn how to run the festival and how to maintain the vineyard."

"All by yourself?"

"I have someone to manage the vineyard."

"Does Mr. Tanner stay with you?"

Her guard shot up. "Why would you think that?"

"I couldn't miss seeing the Hummer and trailer in the parking lot. They don't appear to belong to anyone else."

She wanted to deny they belonged to RT because it was none of his business, but decided it would be better if Manning thought RT might show any time. "They belong to RT."

"He's a cop?"

"No, just a good friend." She opened the closets. Bins filled with bags of cotton balls, boxes of tissues, packaged cosmetics, and hair accessories were stacked against one wall. A half dozen Styrofoam heads were lined up on a shelf. Cait closed the doors. "Let's move on."

The closets in the costume room were filled with large white cloth bags hanging from a long metal rod that extended from one end of each closet to the other. The bags held everything from Victorian dresses to warrior costumes. One included some of Tasha's gowns Cait had donated when she cleaned out the wardrobes in the master bedroom. All of the bags were zipped up and hung a foot off the floor. Cait didn't think it possible anyone could hide inside them, but gave each a firm shake. Satisfied Wally wasn't hanging out in the closet, she closed the doors, then turned and bumped into Manning, who was practically breathing down her neck.

He grabbed her arms to steady her. "Sorry."

She stepped back, perturbed at the amusement in his eyes. "Closets are clear."

"I still don't understand why you don't keep the wigs on the heads. Wouldn't it be easier than going up and down the stairs all the time?"

Why the interest in wigs? "Because that's how Tasha did it. They're also cleaned and dressed in the loft."

She walked out in time to see Detective Rook brushing at smudges of dirt on his slacks and then wiping his hands on a handkerchief.

"It's a waste of time looking for Wally here," Manning told Rook.

"We won't know unless we look, will we?" Rook said. "Do you have something better to do?"

"As a matter of fact, yes." He glanced at Cait. "Will you have dinner with me tonight?"

Cait fumbled for an excuse not to go out with Manning. "Sorry. I'm busy."

Manning smiled. "Another time." He turned and walked out.

"That was odd," June said.

Jim shook his head. "I wonder what he's up to."

Cait turned to Rook. "You should have someone follow him. He must know where Wally is staying."

Cait recognized Perough and Vanicheque as they returned to the theater after searching the vineyard for the man Fumié saw hiding.

"No luck," Perough said. "But we found this." He pulled a slip of paper from his pocket and handed it to Rook.

Rook stared at the paper and sighed. A grim look crossed his face.

"Think he might be staying there?" Perough asked.

"Worth checking," Rook said.

"Where?" Marcus asked.

Rook hesitated. "Pagan Alley."

"In Livermore? Never heard of it," Marcus said. "Sounds like vampire territory."

"Close enough," Rook said. "It's the back end of an abandoned lot."

"I know of it," Fumié said.

Rook looked up. "It's not the type of place you would be familiar with."

Fumié smiled. "I don't know if anyone lives there. It's a converted garage. I think it's a place where people go to hook up, you know, for drugs and stuff. It's weird."

She caught Rook's attention. "Care to share how you know about this infamous alley?"

Fumié shot a glance at Cait. "It's no secret I want to be a park ranger. Because I know how to shoot and have a black belt, my friends wanted to see if I was too scared to go to the Alley. So I did . . . on a dare."

How far would this girl go to prove she could take care of herself? "Where did you find the paper?" Cait asked the officers.

"Down the hill in some bushes," Perough said.

"Then it wasn't Manning's," Cait said with a sigh of relief. "He was with me."

Rook pulled a small pad from a back pocket of his trousers and wrote a note. "It's a lead. I'll look into it." He glanced up at Fumié. "When did you go to Pagan Alley? Was it at night?"

"I was in high school," she said. "It was five years ago, and yes, it was at night."

Rook slipped his notepad away. "It's gotten worse since then. I think we're done here." He looked at the officers. "Better check the Blackfriars, see if anything's been disturbed. I'll see you back to the house."

"I'll open it for them," Marcus said.

Rook nodded. "Thanks."

Marcus and Rook had a contentious history; it pleased Cait when Rook acknowledged Marcus. "And thanks for offering to build a gift shop. I can't wait to have it out of the house."

Marcus nodded and pulled his ring of keys from his pocket.

"Manning might still be here," Cait said. "I haven't heard the motorcycle, unless he walked it down the driveway."

"If he's here," Rook said, "I'll ask him about Pagan Alley."

"He did say he has friends in the Bay Area," Cait reminded him. "If this place has the reputation you're suggesting and if Wally is staying there, Manning had to know about it."

"I agree. The Alley's an open secret. We keep an eye on it."

"There isn't a town on earth," Jim said, "that doesn't have at least one seedy place. It's like a magnet for the lowlife."

"Even in the art world," June said. She took hold of Jim's hand. "Right?"

Jim smiled and nodded. "Recovering stolen art isn't as intriguing as people think. Sometimes the search takes you to the deepest, darkest, most secretive holes on earth."

"That's why I'm happy you're retired and we're here," June said.

"Let's see if Manning's still around," Rook said.

Cait was glad to leave. Empty theaters were cold and sad without the actors, the excitement of rehearsals, and complaints about rips in costumes. Outside, the warmth of the sun and the trill of meadowlarks cheered her. *This could be paradise if danger wasn't lurking behind every tree or shrub.*

CHAPTER 37

June was right. The bullet had gone through the rose vine, ripping flowers from their branches on the trellis. Niki jumped on Cait in quivering anticipation of a treat. She offered him one as her cell rang. She didn't want to take the call from Alt, but answered it anyway.

"Kenneth, I didn't expect to hear from you so soon."

"I'm anxious to know your intentions for the painting," he said.

"I've been busy and haven't had time to think about it."

"I'm sorry to bother you, but I'm willing to offer a reasonable amount of money to own that painting."

"Kenneth, please don't rush me. Someone is taking shots at me daily. I can't think straight right now about the painting, but I will call with my decision soon. Be patient."

A sixth sense caused her to look across the yard to the parking lot. She squinted to see Manning standing in front of RT's trailer. That explained why she hadn't heard the motorcycle. She held her cell away from her ear. "Rook." When he turned, she pointed. "There's your chance to ask Manning about Pagan Alley."

She brought the phone back up to her ear. "Kenneth, I have to go. We'll talk about this later."

"Of course," he said. "Be careful. It would be terrible if anything happened to you just after we've met."

Was that a threat?

"See you later," June said. "I've had enough of Manning."

"I don't blame you." Cait followed Rook.

Manning turned as Cait and Rook approached.

"Mr. Tanner has good taste," Manning said as he admired the vintage Airstream. "What does he do for a living?"

"He travels. I thought you were leaving."

"I couldn't resist a closer look at the trailer. What do you know about it?"

"Just that it's a nineteen-seventy Airstream." Cait wished she had her sunglasses. The sun reflected from Manning's gold necklace and shimmered off the silver trailer.

"Maybe he'll let me see the inside sometime." Manning peered over the top of his sunglasses at Cait. "Unless you happen to have a key and would let me in."

She thought about the keys RT left with Ilia in case of an emergency. "Sorry."

Manning shrugged. "Never hurts to ask."

"Ever hear of Pagan Alley?" Rook asked.

Manning's eyes were unreadable behind his mirrored sunglasses, but his lips were pressed tightly together, and his body was suddenly taut as a bowstring.

Cait swallowed a smile. *Rook caught Manning off guard.*

Manning seemed to make a conscious effort to relax. He reached down his right leg as if to adjust the hem of his jeans on top of his boot. "How would I know? Is it in Livermore?"

Cait wondered if he had a knife strapped to his ankle or inside his boot to go along with the gun he'd blatantly revealed earlier. Just looking at his leather jacket made her hot, but he didn't appear to be sweating despite the ninety-degree temperature.

Rook removed his sunglasses from his shirt pocket and slipped them on. "Yes. I thought Wally might have mentioned it."

Manning shook his head. "He doesn't make a habit of calling me, Detective. When he does, it's usually about money. Is this place important?"

"Could be," Rook said. "You were leaving. We won't keep you."

But Manning shifted his feet, as if unsure what to do. "Cait, walk with me. Maybe you'll change your mind about letting me take you for a ride while I still have use of the Ducati. I'll give you a few minutes to decide." He walked away.

She looked at Rook. "This won't take long. Might even be interesting to hear him try to convince me why I should risk my neck."

Rook's scowl told her he didn't like her going off alone with Manning. After a short distance, she glanced back and saw Rook with his phone to his ear and his eyes riveted on her. She knew Rook to be cautious, weighing each decision before acting. He reminded her of Shep. By contrast, she was impatient and far more outspoken than either of them.

Manning waited for Cait by the motorcycle in front of the house. Cait sensed he had something more on his mind than a motorcycle ride with her.

"I'll be honest, Cait. There is another reason I'm here."

Well, duh. "Did you lie to Detective Church?"

"No, I just didn't tell him everything." A warm breeze tossed Manning's sandy hair around the top rim of his glasses. When he removed them, his eyes flicked past her. "It's hard getting you alone."

"This is as alone as we can be considering the circumstances. What's on your mind?"

He shook his hair back, replaced his glasses, and shifted his feet. "I'll be blunt. Was race a factor in shooting Hank Dillon?" He held his hand up before she could respond. "Let me finish. I see a lot of discrimination in my line of work . . . in the war zones. Like it or not, it's there. I write about it."

Cait tried not to sound as startled as she felt. To accuse her of racism was absurd. "*My* line of work was on the streets of Columbus! I wrote about that. You're accusing me of killing Hank because he was black? That's absurd. Black, red, yellow . . . color never entered into my decision. Then or ever. You were there; you took my picture. Hank Dillon was a split second from pulling that trigger and killing a police officer. I couldn't allow that to happen." Her head pounded; she had to dig deep for her next breath. "Why don't you hop on that fancy bike and leave? It's obvious you're here under false pretenses. Not for Wally, but because of who you think I am." She turned away.

He grabbed her arm. "Shit. The racial possibility's been eating at me for a long time and I had to get it out. Don't go. Please."

Cait yanked her arm back and glared at him. "You asked before if I trusted you. You haven't given me a reason to."

A corner of his lips curled. "And maybe you shouldn't, until I prove I am here for the right reason."

Manning muddled her mind, just like her ex-husband, a police chaplain, used to do. Roger Pepper toyed with her to keep her guessing and off balance. At the same time she'd worked hard at her job as a cop and as a crime analyst, she'd fluttered like a flag in the wind in her personal life. Without Shep, her friend and mentor, she would have cracked under the pressure of having shot and killed a human being. Not something to be proud of, but it had been necessary to save another's life.

Manning raised his leg over the seat of the motorcycle. "See you in the morning?"

Cait nodded. What choice did she have? She needed him, her only link to Wally.

He grabbed his helmet, pulled it on, then keyed the ignition.

The engine purred to life without the thunderous noise when he'd arrived.

Manning reached for the throttle, turned the bike around, then gunned the engine and shot down the driveway.

Cait watched until he'd disappeared. *"Out of my sight! Thou dost infect my eyes." Great. Now I'm quoting Shakespeare.*

Cait got as far as the garage when she heard an engine coming up the driveway. *Is Manning coming back?* Then she recognized Stanton Lane's orange Land Rover and went over to greet him after he parked his car.

"Are you lost?" she asked.

Lane smiled and held his hand out to her. "No. I had to check on the house across the road and wanted to see you before I went home. How are you?"

The diamond in Lane's Masonic signet ring winked at Cait as he reached to shake her hand. Tasha's lawyer, an aficionado of cartoon suspenders, wore Bugs Bunny today. "That depends on how much time you have, Mr. Lane. There are things regarding the house I'd like to talk with you about, but it's not urgent."

"You still can't call me Stan."

"Afraid not," she said. "Doesn't feel right." She squinted at the sun. "Would you like to come in out of the heat? I can offer you iced tea."

"I'd like that." He removed his jacket and tossed it in the car. As they walked, he said, "I know this estate doesn't have financial concerns, so what troubles you?"

As they went around the house, they ran into Rook and the two officers, Perough and Vanicheque.

"I'm glad you didn't give in and go on a joy ride with Manning," Rook said.

Cait rolled her eyes. "That would never happen. Detective Rook, you remember Stanton Lane." She introduced the officers. "Would you care to join us for a cold drink?"

Inside, Cait pulled stools out for everyone, then went to the refrigerator and took frosted glasses from the freezer.

"Are you in trouble?" Lane asked. "Obviously something's wrong, or these officers wouldn't be here. Does it have anything to do with the motorcycle that flew out of here as if hot on a mission?"

Interesting question. She poured the iced tea and sat down. She kept her story about the bank robbery short, but thought Lane deserved to know should anything happen to her. When she finished, she desired something stronger than tea.

Lane's face pinked. Cait wasn't sure whether it was from anger or the heat.

"You were doing your job," Lane said. "Maybe it took him two years to trace you because he was in prison. I'm partly responsible because I coerced you into coming here."

"I'm a big girl. It was my decision to accept my inheritance."

He stared into his tea. "Who is Manning?"

Cait looked at Rook. "Maybe you should tell him."

Rook took a long drink from his glass. "Calder Manning's parents adopted Hank Dillon when he was twelve." His short explanation took only a couple of minutes. "You just missed him."

"The maniac on the bike," Lane said. "Can he help?"

"That remains to be seen," Cait said.

The officers slid off their stools. "Thanks for the tea. We should be going."

"Hold on." Rook looked at Cait. "What do you want to do about Marcus and Fumié?"

"Do you think they'll be okay outside while they work on their sketches?"

"I doubt Wally would give them a second look." He looked at the officers. "How are your carpentry skills?"

"Good enough to impress even you," Perough said.

Rook smiled. "Offer to help them. Marcus can give you tools. Before you do that, split up and check the vineyard and that hill behind the theaters. I need to get back to the station." He stood. "Nice to see you again, Lane."

Lane got to his feet. "I wish it were under different circumstances."

Cait walked Rook and the officers to the door, then turned back to Lane. In light of her problems, he had taken in the situation more calmly than she expected.

"Good thing you've got a security system," he said. "Any word from Royal Tanner?"

Lane asking about RT surprised her, since theirs hadn't been a friendly acquaintance. "He was here recently but was called back to duty. He left his Hummer and trailer here because he had to leave in a hurry. He brought me a dog. A chocolate lab named Niki."

"Wonderful! Everyone should have a pet. I used to have a couple of schnauzers."

"June and Jim Hart, a retired couple, are here now living in their RV. She and Tasha were good friends. Maybe Tasha mentioned her to you. I'd like you to meet them."

"Another time. I'm happy you have someone else living up here."

Cait decided to tell Lane about her plans for the house. "Marcus and Fumié have come up with plans for a gift shop near the theaters. I'll be glad to have it out of the house. That will leave room for my own office and a combination glass shop and workshop." His smile encouraged her to continue. "I'll need furniture for the rooms."

Lane snapped his suspenders and smiled. "Not a problem. Let me know when you're ready to go shopping. This should have been done long ago. Have the bills sent to me."

Relieved, she said, "Thank you."

Cait walked him outside and watched as he backed his car around and drove off. Telling Lane about Chip Fallon had been difficult, but she thought he should know. If anything happened to her, Lane needed to know why and who was responsible.

CHAPTER 38

After Stanton Lane left, Cait refilled her glass and went upstairs. When she called Shep, he was unavailable, so she left a message. She turned the desk lamp on and settled in with her laptop to check her email. A red light flashed on the landline. Everyone she knew called on her cell phone. Marcus used the landline for theater ticket sales and other property business.

She hesitated to listen to the message in case it was from Actors' Equity. *Did Ray Stoltz change his mind and call Actors' Equity to complain about the incidents that continued to plague the festival? Was Sam Cruz calling to warn her he was shutting her down?*

"Bang! Bang! You're dead!"

Click.

Cait dropped the receiver, as if bitten.

Definitely not Actors' Equity.

Her cell beeped. She replaced the receiver and shuffled through papers on the desk until she found her phone. She grabbed it, relieved to see Shep's name.

"Hey, Shep."

"You okay?"

She sipped her iced tea and sat back in the chair. "Just had a threatening call on the landline. Wally must not have enough to do."

"He has your cell and landline numbers?"

"Apparently. I can't change the landline because it's my business number. People need to call for theater reservations."

"Does Detective Rook know?"

"Not about this one. Two officers are here, but Rook had to leave. He gives me more time than he should." She set her glass aside. "Shep, Manning asked to see the theaters and said a cop told him about them. Was he referring to Chuck Levy? Do you know anything about that?"

"I read Levy's notes," Shep said. "I don't recall the theaters being mentioned, but I'll check on it. Maybe the commander told him." He hesitated. "Is there reason to keep the theaters a secret?"

"No, but I hate that he knows more about me than I do about him. And guess what? Manning's the anonymous reporter. He admitted he sent my picture to the *Dispatch* and shrugged it off as no big deal."

"He probably knew you'd find out sooner or later."

"Yeah, maybe. There was another shooting today, but the only damage was to a rose vine. He got away, but a piece of paper with an address was found. Rook's looking into it."

"Wally's playing with you."

"Of course he is. Wally also calls Manning for money. If Manning has as many contacts around the world as he claims, he should be able to find Wally."

"The police should follow Manning."

"That's what I told Rook." She rubbed the back of her neck and noticed her hair had grown. Something else she hadn't found time for. "Manning asked me to dinner, which I refused, and then accused me of racism. How bizarre is that?"

"Don't go anywhere with him."

"Are you kidding? I'd have to be desperate."

Cait stared at the computer screen and the dust motes floating in the lamplight, then checked her email. A couple were from her best friend, Samantha, asking about the festival and if she'd heard from their mutual friend in Santa Cruz. Cait didn't want to burden Sam with her problems and sent a breezy note before logging off.

Her cell beeped.

"Detective Rook," she answered. "You're going to get in trouble for devoting so much time to a case that's not in your jurisdiction. But without you, I'd probably be dead by now."

"Your case involves the LPD and the sheriff's department," Rook said. "I talked with Wally's mother."

Cait picked up a pen and reached for a tablet. "She called you? What did she want?"

"Your friend, Detective Church, told her what's going on out here, and she wanted to know how she could help."

"I just got off the phone with Shep. He didn't mention it."

"I told him I'd call you."

"Mrs. Dillon must have had a good reason to call you."

"She said Wally came into some money recently, apparently enough to get him to California," Rook said, "He wouldn't tell his mom where the money came from or why he was going to California, but she did say Wally's cousin lived somewhere in California."

Cait twirled the pen in her fingers. "I can tell you where the money came from. Manning."

"Then why does Wally blame the Mannings for Hank's death? Wally thought they adopted Hank to get him off the streets and out of a gang. Obviously, that didn't work and Wally thinks the adoption is the reason why. Remember, the two families knew each other from church."

"I don't understand. Is Wally's mom afraid he'll hurt the Mannings?"

"She's afraid he'll take his anger out on Calder Manning's three-year-old daughter."

"Oh, God." Cait shut her eyes against the painful thought of that happening. "I didn't see that coming." She opened her eyes. "Can Shep protect her?"

"He says she's safe as long as Wally's in California."

"So what have we got here, Rook? Wally and Manning are at odds with each other, while I'm in the middle accused of murder and racism?"

"In all my years in law enforcement, Wally has to be the most complicated criminal I've encountered. I think Wally and Manning have contradictory reasons for being in Livermore, neither with your best interest at heart. So be careful. Manning's a smooth operator."

"No fooling." A seed of an idea began to germinate. "This needs to end. How about using me to force Wally out into the open. Set something up."

He hesitated. "I'll have to think about that. Maybe they'll kill each other and put an end to it. I have to go."

She picked up her gun, slipped it into her pocket, and went downstairs.

Niki wasn't in the kitchen. She opened the backdoor and tripped over him sprawled on the step. Arms flailing, she fell, landing hard on the brick walk. Except for an aching hip from hitting the ground on the side where she had her gun, she wasn't hurt.

The alarm went off. Cait winced as she stood and used her modem to stop it.

Officer Vanicheque appeared, stopping short when he saw Cait. "What happened?"

June and Jim ran from the side of the house. "Cait? Are you okay?"

Embarrassed, Cait laughed. "I tripped over Niki."

"I thought he was supposed to protect you, not hurt you," Jim said, a smile on his face.

"Come inside. I want your opinion on something." Cait told them about the message left on the landline and Rook's conversation with Wally's mother. "I want this to end now, so I asked Rook to set a trap for Wally and to use me as bait. But we'll need Calder Manning's cooperation."

"I certainly would not use you to corner Wally, and I seriously doubt Detective Rook would approve," Vanicheque said. "We're here to protect you, not endanger you. I hope you won't try something on your own."

"I agree," June said. "Let the police handle it."

Cait shook her head. "Then they need to find a way to end this before Wally or someone else harms Manning's mother and daughter."

CHAPTER 39

Cait tossed and turned all night worrying about Wally Dillon and thinking of what she could do to catch him without going against Officer Vanicheque's warning or Detective Rook. Rook had become more than a police officer; she considered him a friend who had sacrificed family time by going beyond the call of duty to help her since she'd moved to Livermore.

She slipped out of bed and went through her morning ritual. While standing under the steaming shower, she thought about Calder Manning. He had his own agenda for Wally, one he refused to share with her or the police. *I wonder if he knows Wally not only blames me for Hank's death but that he also blames Manning's family.*

Niki sat on the carpet in the sun, tail thumping, while Cait dressed. When she went back in the bathroom to blow-dry her hair, she stared in the mirror at the puffy circles under her eyes and felt she'd aged since she'd inherited the estate. Her life as a cop put her in danger every day, but nothing like what she'd experienced in the past couple of months in Livermore. She slipped her cell in a pocket of her jeans and grabbed her keys and gun. "Time to go, Niki."

Downstairs, she checked his food and water bowls.

"Already taken care of," Marcus said from his office doorway.

"My God! Look at the clock—it's eight-thirty! I couldn't go to sleep last night, then when I finally did, I overslept."

"My mom used to say sleeping in was time well spent, that it cleared your head."

"Your mom is a wise woman."

He showed her a large sketchpad. "When you have time, look at what Fumié came up with for your gift shop."

Cait wasn't in the mood to look at sketches, but what she saw interested her. "An English cottage. I love it." She handed the pad back to him. "I'll leave it in your and Fumié's capable hands." She opened a box of Cheerios and took a bowl from the cupboard. "I wish Manning would call and let me know when he's coming."

"I don't expect him to." Marcus bent over to rub Niki behind his ears. "Do you honestly think he can help, or does he just want to impress us with his credentials?"

She sighed. "I don't know. Maybe a little of both." She went to the refrigerator for milk.

Someone tapped on the back door.

"No one ever uses the front door." When she opened it, Detective Rook stood on the step.

"Have you heard from Manning this morning?" he asked.

"No."

"What was he driving?"

"A white Toyota rental. Why?"

Rook pulled a slip of paper from his jacket pocket. "I went by Pagan Alley at seven-thirty. A white Toyota sedan was in front of the garage."

Cait's body tensed. "You think that's where Wally lives?"

"Who knows, but it was Manning's car."

"You drove in for a closer look?"

He cocked his eyebrow with a half smile.

"If I'd done that without backup, I would have been called in and dressed down. But then, you're a detective."

"I didn't have a warrant to go inside, or I would have called for backup. But there were plenty of trash containers to duck behind in case someone caught me snooping around."

"Where is this infamous Alley?" Marcus asked. "I grew up in Livermore and I've never heard of it."

"I'm not surprised," Rook said. "It's in a commercial district over by the airport. It's not a real alley, only a dead-end dirt lot filled with weeds and trash. Someone christened it and the name stuck. It's a garage converted into a small living quarters."

"Where dopers meet and connect," Cait said, recalling Fumié's description. "Pagan means those without a specific religion."

"That about sums it up."

"Can't believe Fumié went there," Cait said. "She's a tiny, beautiful girl, who looks as innocent as that bowl of water Niki's lapping up."

"That's her advantage," Rook said.

"But she was in high school at the time. A daredevil teen."

"Who toyed with danger," Rook said. "Turns out I know her dad. He took early retirement from Sandia Labs and became a full-time rancher. He taught Fumié how to protect herself."

Marcus brushed at imaginary dirt on his jeans. "She could still get hurt."

Cait remembered Marcus's reaction when she introduced Fumié, how he'd straightened his shirt and blushed. He liked Fumié. A lot.

"I hope no one saw you at Pagan Alley, because if Manning knew you were there, he could decide not to come back," she said. "I wouldn't miss him, but he is our only link to Wally."

"He's not going anywhere. He waited too long and came too far to give up now."

She pulled out a stool and sat. "I was awake all night thinking of how to catch Wally. I have to do something, Rook. It's not safe for the actors."

"Whatever's going on in your head won't work without police assistance."

"I'm not naive. And who said anything about not involving the police?" She reflected back to when she was a rookie cop. There'd been times when she'd been removed from a situation because she was female, but she'd fought hard and won that battle, at least in her department.

Rook shifted his feet. "You don't have to convince me. I know you're tough and confident, but this is different. You're no longer a cop."

With a glint in her eye, she asked, "Are you saying that when I turned in my shield I became nothing?"

He chuckled. "Of course not, but do you think I want your blood on my hands if Wally kills you?"

"Look," Cait said, "I've given this a lot of thought. Use me, set something up to get to Wally. War correspondents cover stories firsthand in war zones close enough to the action to provide written accounts, photos, and film footage. Even though Manning had protection, he was exposed and vulnerable. Like I am every time I step outside the house. But it's an adrenaline roller coaster for him. I just want this over with so I can get on with my life."

"I'm working on it," Rook said, "but you don't make it easy."

She rolled her eyes. "I know something is going on between Wally and Manning, like a score to settle between their families."

He hesitated. "I'll talk to Manning."

Cait smiled. "Come on, Rook, *we'll* talk to Manning. After all, I'm your bait."

Rook grunted. "So where is he?"

Cait saw June and Jim looking in the window. When she opened the door, Niki ran outside.

"You have company?" June asked.

"Only Detective Rook."

"Two cars are parked in the driveway," Jim said. "A blue one and a white one."

Rook exchanged glances with Cait. "The blue one is mine."

"Are you expecting police officers?" Cait asked.

"Yes, but they'll be in a gray car." He walked to the door. "Has to be Manning's."

"I'm coming with you." She grabbed her sunglasses from the table next to the door.

"That's Manning's, all right," Rook said when they reached the driveway.

A gray Ford pulled up and parked behind the white Toyota.

"Practically a traffic jam," Cait said.

Rook slipped his sunglasses on. "Perough and Vanicheque."

The officers wore jeans, sport shirts, and running shoes, their shields tucked out of sight. Perough nodded to Cait while Vanicheque flashed a dimpled smile.

"Manning's here," Rook said. "Let's find him."

"I don't like him wandering off and not letting me know he's here," Cait said.

"Neither do I." Rook turned to the officers. "Cait and I will start in the parking lot. He's shown interest in RT's trailer. We'll catch up with you."

Cait watched the officers leave. "I don't think he'd break into the trailer."

"Worth checking. I sure wish we had Manning's cell number."

The temperature had risen steadily; it was nine o'clock and Cait was already wishing she'd worn shorts and a sleeveless shirt instead of jeans. "I'll ask him for it."

He smiled. "Use your persuasive powers if you have to."

"Not going to happen, Rook. He'll want something in return."

Rook's cell buzzed. "Yeah," he answered. "Thanks." He clipped his phone on his belt. "Vanicheque's with Manning."

"That didn't take long."

Vanicheque and Perough stood near the courtyard talking with Manning.

"Why didn't you let Cait know you were here?" Rook asked.

Manning turned, his face flushed from the sun or anger. "I've been waiting for Wally. He said he'd come up this way. I should have known not to believe him."

"Do you mean he was going to meet you and then turn himself in to the police?" Cait asked.

Rook glanced down the hill. "Why was he coming here now?"

"I don't know. If Wally is anything, he's unpredictable, and you should believe the opposite of what he says," Manning replied.

"Maybe he doesn't trust you," Cait said.

Manning smirked and slid his hands in his pockets. "I don't trust him either. Our relationship is strained beyond repair."

Cait wanted to know if Manning was staying with Wally. "Were you with Wally last night?"

He took his hands from his pockets and cracked his knuckles. "We talked last night."

Cait cringed. The noise sounded like nails being hammered into her coffin. "In person?"

Manning wiped his glasses on his shirt and looked at Cait for a few seconds. His eyes reflected his anger. "I'll see you later." He walked away.

Cait stared at his back. *I wonder what he'll do now.*

CHAPTER 40

Manning was full of surprises, but Cait had enough. *He's not getting off that easy.* She ran after him.

"Hey, hold on, Manning. Did you promise Wally something if he turned himself in?"

He glanced at her but kept walking. "You don't know what you're talking about."

"I'm open for an explanation. You did say he called you for money. I hoped we could come up with a plan to satisfy everyone. How about a little cooperation?"

Manning stopped in his tracks. "A plan?" He laughed, a deep, gut-wrenching sound. "That only happens on TV. You should know that."

She wanted to punch him. Her blood boiled. "Who the hell do you think you are, trying to put me down?"

"Last I checked, a journalist who puts himself in danger on the front line."

"Maybe you're possessed with delusions of personal grandeur. I'm trying to understand what's going on." It felt good to let her feelings out, even if he did deserve bragging rights for working in war zones. She stepped back when she saw his balled fists.

"My business with Wally is personal. Where you come in is a separate issue." He turned away.

So he knows Wally has it in for his family? Cait went after him. She couldn't wait to kick him off her property. "So, is it Wally you're here for or me?"

Manning glanced over his shoulder. "We could talk about it sometime when you're not surrounded by the police."

She looked back and saw Rook and his officers keeping their distance. "I'll talk to Detective Rook, but from my viewpoint, our issues are related. What is Wally to you?"

He pulled a handkerchief from his trouser pocket and wiped his brow. "He's Hank's brother. He spreads blame around like butter for Hank's murder, if that makes you feel any better—his mom, my family, and you. When you shot Hank, that was the last straw."

Cait cringed. "For Wally or for you?" Now they were getting into dangerous territory, and she was glad Rook was behind her.

He glared at her. "Wally took his anger out the only way he knew how—by going after you."

"But he murdered one of my actors!" She drew a deep breath. "Either he's a poor marksman or he intentionally missed each time he took shots at me. Why would he do that?"

He smirked. "That's where I come in."

"Empty words, Manning. Where exactly do you come in?"

"In time, Cait. In time." He left her wondering where he was going, but she was so exasperated, she let him go.

Her cell beeped, and she pulled her thoughts from Manning. "Hi, Shep."

"Got a minute?"

"Sure." Rook and the officers stopped a short distance behind her.

"I read a few more articles Manning wrote, and then I went to see his mother."

"Don't get in trouble because of me."

"We're cool. The commander understands and gave me the go-ahead. When I got to Mrs. Manning's house, she showed me

265

the family album. Manning's dad was African-American. That would explain the racial comment he made to you."

Surprised she hadn't thought of that possibility, she said, "I assumed he was tan from the sun; his eyes are hazel."

"His mother's white."

"Oh." She ran to Rook and told him what Shep said.

"Ask if that had anything to do with his family adopting Hank," Rook said.

"I heard him," Shep said. "It did, but the adoption was never finalized."

"What? The adoption was never finalized?" Cait said. "I wonder why Manning didn't tell me."

"Manning's dad died before the adoption papers were signed." He paused. "Mrs. Manning said that was about the time Calder changed. She assumed it was because he'd seen too much in the war zones, but he refused to talk to her about it."

"Maybe he has PTSD," Cait said.

"Possible, but we can't dismiss the racial issue, since he's brought it up."

"I know. He was here a few minutes ago. He and Wally concocted some kind of plan, but Wally failed to show up."

"It's up to you if you want to ask Manning about the racial issue, but I'd suggest you wait and see if he brings it up first."

"You're right. Thanks."

"Now what do we do?" she asked Rook. "Twiddle our thumbs and wait for something to happen?"

"You go to the house," Rook said. "I'm going to the station. I'll see if I can set up a raid at Pagan Alley. It's time to bring SWAT in."

"That sounds good. Maybe we can end this before the actors return."

He turned to Perough and Vanicheque. "This will take awhile.

I'll let you know when it's going down. One of you should stay here in case Wally comes up that damn hill." He pulled his cell. "But if he's at the Alley, we'll get him."

She squinted from the sun. "What if Manning's there when SWAT arrives?"

"If he cooperates, there shouldn't be a problem. If he interferes, he'll be arrested. His call." He hurried off, talking on his cell.

"I'll walk back with you, Cait," Vanicheque said.

They had almost reached the house when a familiar voice yelled, "Hey! Wait up!"

Cait turned and saw Ilia running toward them, waving his arm. She hadn't seen him today, but assumed he was there to check on RT's vehicles. RT left an extra set of keys with him.

"I saw a guy running from the Elizabethan theater," he said, out of breath. "Someone needs to check it out."

Cait glanced at the theater. "I didn't hear the alarm."

"I'm telling you what I saw. How hard would it be to scale the wall around the theater?"

"Not if you're a monkey."

"Let's look," Vanicheque said. He raised his cell to his ear. "I'll let Perough know."

"I'm going with you." Cait pulled her gun from under her shirt. "Maybe Wally tricked Manning into thinking he'd meet him, while all along he intended to break in the theater."

"You may be right," Vanicheque said.

"Ilia, Marcus can let you in the house."

"No way. I'm going with you."

She reluctantly agreed.

As they ran with their guns drawn, Vanicheque grunted, "Rook's not going to like this, Cait. You should wait at the house."

"He'll get over it."

They met up with Perough, but when they checked the doors, they were still locked. "Let's split and circle around," Perough said.

"Stay with me, Ilia," Cait said. They went to the right around the back of the building, while the officers went to the left. They hadn't gone far when one of the officers yelled Cait's name.

Cait circled back around the theater and found the officers standing next to a wooden ladder propped against the wall. "Looks like you were right, Ilia." She eyed the wall and discovered the bricks weren't flush together, and some of the mortar had eroded, leaving narrow toeholds between some of the bricks. She tested the wooden ladder and went up several rungs, then reached her foot out and stuck her toe in a crevice. "That's easy. See how the bricks are staggered all the way to the top. Like a climbing wall. Plant your foot and work your way up. Wonder if it's the same on the inside."

"Maybe he turned chicken when he saw the long jump down on the other side. Open up and let's take a look," Vanicheque said.

Cait disarmed the theater. At the back of the theater, she shielded her eyes from the sun and stared up at the brick wall. "Aha. Now we know. This wall must be nine feet high, but look at how those arches are staggered across it. I wonder what Tasha was thinking when she had this wall built. Each recess has a little shelf, maybe intended for a small statue or just decoration."

"Probably not to make it easy for a burglar," Ilia said.

"Sometimes the bad guys get all the breaks. I should have paid more attention to the wall."

"Maybe Wally's been in the theater before," Perough said, "and knows his way around."

"Oh, he's been in here all right," Cait said, "and in the loft."

They went down the aisle. Vanicheque hesitated and looked

up at the stage. "Any doors behind those curtains to keep people from going in the back?"

"No."

"When the scenery changes, do the panels pull up into the ceiling?"

Cait tried to remember. "They're motor driven and slide up."

"What about the curtains? Do they come down or tuck away from the elements in the winter?" Perough asked.

"I'm told they come down, but I've only been here since April." She squinted at the rafters. "Are you thinking someone could hide up there?"

"You'd be surprised where a desperate person can squeeze into. Let's have a look," Perough said.

She gripped her gun. *"Defer no time, delays have dangerous ends." Now I sound like June, quoting Shakespeare again.*

CHAPTER 41

Cait held the curtain back for the officers, then crossed the green room and went into the costume room where empty metal racks on wheels were pushed up against a wall. During the festival, they were filled with medieval costumes. She flung the closet doors open. Styrofoam heads lined a shelf above rods filled with zippered clothes bags. The bags were squished together, as they had been when Cait showed Manning the theater. Nothing appeared disturbed, but she had no idea how many costumes were in the bags. She closed the doors. "I've no idea if anything's missing in here. I'm going up to have a look in the loft."

"What's up there?" Vanicheque asked.

"Wigs and more clothes bags of costumes, but nothing as valuable as jewels. If Wally thinks he can disguise himself by wearing a wig, he's mistaken. These actors recognize each other, and none of them are black." She crossed to the stairs.

Ilia laughed. "I think he's dumb enough to try anything."

Cait started up the open stairway. "Ilia, was everything okay with RT's vehicles? It could be a serious problem if Wally broke into either of them."

"Crap. I got distracted when I saw that guy running. I better check," he said as he left.

"Hold on, Cait." Vanicheque said. "I'll go first."

She smiled. "This is my theater, but feel free to follow." She didn't like the hot, cramped loft but wouldn't let on to the officers. She felt for the wall switch when she reached the top and flipped it on. The dim light barely reached the far corners beneath the sloping roof, and the one window only allowed a little light in.

The officers ducked as they stepped into the loft. "Kind of dark up here," Perough said.

Cait sneezed. "Not much air either. I don't know how Jay, the stage manager's brother, works up here mending the costumes and handling the wigs." She pointed to matching wooden steamer trunks with retro-style hinges beneath the window. "Some of the wigs are in there, but I don't know how many. They're kept between layers of tissue. If you'll check, I'll look at the clothes bags." She turned and bumped into a wire dress form, gasped, and nearly screamed.

Perough grabbed the form to keep it from falling.

"Are the trunks supposed to be locked?" Vanicheque asked as he lifted a lid.

"There aren't any keys that I know of." She ducked to avoid a low rafter. Three clothes bags hung on metal rods. One held Tasha's costumes that Cait had discovered when she moved into the house; there had been some in the guest bedroom and some in Tasha's wardrobe in the master bedroom. Donating them to the festival felt less disrespectful when she wanted them out of the way to make room for her own clothes. She unzipped one of the bags and shook the bunched-up costumes.

"Take a look at this," Perough said.

"What is it?"

He pointed to a stick of blue and white paper in one of the trunks. "Gum." He pulled a tissue from his pocket and picked it up. "Dentyne Ice."

"It looks like the wrapper from Ray Stoltz's truck. We have to assume a wig is missing."

"Yeah, but have you ever come up against a burglar as careless as Wally?"

Never, but I will as soon as he's caught.

Cait felt relieved to breathe fresh air after they left the theater. "Do you want to call Rook about the break-in and the gum, or should I?"

Perough looked at his watch. "He's probably at Pagan Alley with SWAT. We'll let him know when he calls."

"Fine. I'll go to the house."

"I'll go with you," Vanicheque said. "Is there a play this weekend?"

"Only *Macbeth* on Saturday at the Blackfriars. There are only four or five actors in the play, and the theater seats a hundred and forty-two." Her eyes flicked on the bushes as they walked. "I'm disappointed Wally hasn't been captured. The actors won't be safe until he is." She turned to him. "Look, I'm capable of going from here to the house. Why don't you join your partner and look for Wally?"

"I'm sure you are, but no," Vanicheque said firmly.

Marcus opened the door as if he'd been waiting for her. "Sam Cruz called." Niki tried to follow Vanicheque, but Marcus caught his collar.

"Perfect," she said. "Actors' Equity, that's all I need. Surprised he waited this long to call."

Marcus handed her a paper. "That's his number."

"Any word from Ray Stoltz?"

"Yeah. He'll be here sometime today, and the actors will arrive tomorrow." He frowned. "Did someone really break in the Elizabethan theater?"

"Yep, went over the wall. For all we know, he might have stolen a wig from the loft."

Marcus groaned. "Sure be easier to break into the Blackfriars."

"You'd think so, but I don't think any wigs are kept there."

"Maybe Wally knows you have a play this weekend and thinks he'd be safe hiding among the crowd."

"I'm not sure he's smart enough to think that far. I have to let Ray know about the wig so he can tell the actors and they can be on the lookout. I hope they kept the mug shot of Wally." She set her gun on the counter and reached in her pocket for her cell. "Can't put off calling Sam Cruz any longer."

"Ms. Pepper?" Cruz answered.

"Yes. I'm returning your call."

"Have the police caught the guy who murdered Chip Fallon? Tasha would have closed the festival until it was safe for the actors. Will there be enough police to protect them?"

Cait bit her lip to stop the torrent of words she wanted to scream at him. She glanced at Marcus and rolled her eyes. "The police are here every day looking for Wally Dillon, the suspected killer, and will be here during the festival. I'm sure Tasha would do exactly what I'm doing—taking care of business and providing security for everyone."

An ominous silence hung across the line.

"I'm sorry if I offended you, but put yourself in my place," he said.

"I appreciate your position, Mr. Cruz. I'm confident Wally will be apprehended soon."

"Let's hope so. Security will remain tight?"

"Of course. It always is."

"You'll let me know when he's caught?"

"Absolutely."

He hung up.

She turned her cell off. Frustrated, she said, "Let's have a beer."

They sat at the counter with beer and chips while Cait brooded about the lack of light in the loft. When someone knocked on the door, Marcus got up to open it.

Niki also ran to the door and barked as his tail flapped against the tile floor.

Cait drank deeply from her bottle of chilled beer.

"The police are becoming permanent fixtures around here," Ray Stoltz blustered when he walked in. "At this rate, you won't have a festival to worry about, only the vineyard."

Cait flinched. Beer sloshed in her bottle.

"Do you always enter a room like a cyclone?"

"Ha. Got your attention, didn't I? Like the police got mine. I could have been shot."

"But you weren't. I just talked with Sam Cruz. Did you call him to complain?"

Ray rubbed his chin. "Hell, no. I wouldn't do that to you. I complain a lot, but only to you because I think you like it." He pulled a handkerchief from his pants pocket and blew his nose. "When the cops stopped me, they said there was a break-in at the Elizabethan. I showed my ID and assured them I didn't hate you enough to kill you, but sometimes you do push my buttons."

"They wouldn't mistake you for Wally. He's black and about half your size." Cait liked Ray, even his crankiness. He sounded and acted gruff, but he knew the stage business and was respected by the actors. But when he pushed her too far, she pushed back. "So Ray, how many wigs are kept in those trunks in the loft? If we knew, we would know if one was missing."

Ray reached into the bag of potato chips and grabbed a handful. "Hell, I don't know. It's not like I need to keep track of them like the weapons." He ate the chips he'd taken and reached for more.

His cavalier attitude toward the wigs surprised Cait. "I hoped you could tell me so I could tell the police. Marcus, do you keep a list of everything that belongs to the festival?"

Marcus shook his head. "But it's a good idea. I'll do an inventory after this year's festival is over."

"I'd appreciate that. And, Ray, I'd like a list of anything you store here between festivals. I feel really stupid not knowing what belongs to who." She hated to spoil Ray's day, but she had to ask. "Remember that gum wrapper the police found in your truck when it was broken into?"

"Yeah. I had to buy a new hammer to replace the stolen one." He cocked his eyebrow. "Why?"

"A stick of the same gum was found among the wigs in one of the trunks."

Ray stared at her, his hand holding a chip frozen in midair. Then he slammed his hand on the counter, and the chip flew across the granite surface. "The police didn't tell me that. If it's the same SOB, he's going to buy me a new hammer."

"Calm down, Ray. You'll have a heart attack. Have another chip. The officers took the gum with them and will have the wrapper fingerprinted. It's pointless, really, because we know who it was."

"Wally Dillon?"

"Or his partner."

Someone tapped on the glass in the door. Ray opened the door for the Harts.

"Ray, you big oaf, what are you doing here?" June asked.

"It's Thursday. Haven't forgotten about *Macbeth* this weekend, have you?"

"No," she said, "but I thought you had. I expected you sooner. Are you harassing Cait again?"

"No, it's the other way around," he said, a glint in his eye when he looked at Cait. "I have to get to the theaters. Need a modem, Cait."

Cait slid off her stool. "Jim, do you have your gun?"

He nodded. "Want me to shoot Ray if he doesn't behave?"

She smiled. "Not yet. Will you go with him and open the theater? And if you see the officers, ask if one will stay with him. I wouldn't want to be sued if someone shot him."

"I don't need protecting." Ray pulled his plaid work shirt up to show off a gun that was tucked at his waist.

Everyone's carrying heat. "You got a permit to carry? Do the officers know you're armed?"

"They didn't ask, and I didn't tell."

"Is it loaded?"

He smiled.

"Don't you know it's illegal to carry a concealed weapon in California?"

Niki growled at the door.

"Damn traffic jam in here," Ray said as he opened the door.

Officer Vanicheque walked in. "Detective Rook wanted you to know Pagan Alley was a bust."

"They'd cleared out?" Cait asked.

"Coffee was still warm, so he'd just left." He glanced at Ray. "He wants in the Blackfriars. Want me to escort him?"

Cait smiled at Ray. "Sure. Jim can open the theater."

Vanicheque nodded to Ray. "Ready? Don't go Rambo on me if we run into trouble."

Cait assumed Vanicheque noticed the bulge under Ray's shirt. "Ray, is there anything you'd like to tell the officer?"

Ray's mouth opened, then closed, and he shook his head.

After the officer left with Ray and Jim, June asked, "Did I miss something?"

"Ray should let the officers know he's carrying, but I didn't want to push it."

"He'll do what's right, but only when he's ready. Have you heard from Fumié?"

Cait shook her head. "She doesn't have regular hours. Why?"

"Ilia asked about her. I think he was expecting to meet her."

"Marcus, have you talked with Fumié today?"

"No. She's probably at home. She said she wanted to call the ranger school to confirm her place in the fall class."

"We talked about that," Cait said. *It's not like Fumié to say she'd do something and then not do it.*

CHAPTER 42

"I want to call Shep on Skype. Want to come upstairs with me, June?"

"I've never been there."

"Really? I assumed . . ."

"I offered to come and be with Tasha when Hilton died, but she wanted to be alone for awhile, so I didn't push it."

Cait stopped on the second floor to guide June through the sitting room, guest bedroom, bath, and kitchenette, and then showed her the hundreds of books filling shelves that Marcus had built for Tasha. A small older television sat on a table in a corner, but Cait had been too busy to turn it on. When she had time, she preferred to read, run, or pull out her yoga mat and work out.

Cait unlocked the door to the third floor master suite. June gasped. "Oh, it's like living in a tree house." The sun bled through the three rectangular stained-glass panels at the top of each window in the bay area, casting shades of gold, red, blue, and green over the bedroom. June went to the windows and looked out over the golden hills. "I feel Tasha's presence. Maybe it's the lavender smell she loved."

"Her wardrobe still smells like lavender."

"Ignore me and make your call while I enjoy the view."

Cait went to the desk and opened her laptop. "Shep stays late to write reports. If he's there, you can meet him." She sat in the eco-friendly chair, tapped a few keystrokes, and soon Skype was up and running and Shep appeared on the screen.

"Hey, Cait," Shep said.

Cait smiled. "Someone's here I'd like you to meet." Cait introduced June to Shep.

Shep smiled. "I've heard about you, June."

June smiled. "And I've heard about you. It's so nice to meet you. I'll leave you two talk."

"Cait, does Manning know yet that you know his dad was African-American?"

"Not yet." She picked up a Chinese health ball and rotated it in the palm of her hand. "Was there any criminal activity discovered in his background check?"

"No. He wouldn't be allowed into a war zone if he'd been convicted of a serious crime. Is there reason to believe he has a record?"

"No, but he's hiding something, and that bothers me. He acts like he's doing us a favor by coming here. He's getting on my nerves."

"No one's as innocent as a newborn baby. I stole a comic book once from the corner drug store when I was a kid," he joked.

She laughed. "Shame on you. I snatched an ice cream bar once," she confessed. She glanced at June staring out the window. "Shep, someone went over the wall at the Elizabethan theater. He left a stick of gum in a trunk full of wigs."

"He wants to disguise himself, but a medieval wig would only make him stand out."

"He's not very smart. Rook and SWAT went to Pagan Alley this morning, a hangout where we thought Wally was hiding. Someone had been there but was gone when SWAT arrived. I haven't talked to Rook since then and don't know what he plans to do next, but the actors return tomorrow." She set the health ball back on its pad. "Had a call from Actors' Equity. They're losing patience with me."

"Maybe it's time I talk to Wally's mother."

She leaned closer to the screen. "Do you know where she lives?"

"I'll find her." He saluted and signed off.

"Shep reminds me of RT," June said.

Cait smiled. "I'm lucky to call them friends."

Someone knocked on the door at the foot of the stairs.

"Cait?"

Cait jumped up. "That's Marcus. Maybe the police found Wally."

"Detective Rook and Ilia are here," Marcus said when Cait opened the door.

Worry lines etched his brow and his hands ran over his spiked hair, signs she recognized that meant he was anxious. "Is something wrong?"

"They're here about Fumié."

Rook and Ilia stood in the middle of the kitchen when Cait walked in. "Vanicheque told you Pagan Alley was a bust?" Rook asked.

Cait nodded. "Does that have something to do with Fumié?"

"I hope not, but Ilia thinks she's missing. Have you heard from her?"

"Not since yesterday." Cait looked at Ilia. "What makes you think she's missing?"

"She was going to help me with my coffee table book," Ilia said. "We were supposed to meet downtown at Peet's coffee, but she didn't show." He fiddled with the camera dangling from around his neck. "That's not like her."

Cait fought the urge to assure him Fumié was okay. She was young and ambitious and had many interests. "Did you call her parents?"

He tugged at the collar of his sports shirt, as if it was too tight. "They thought she was with me."

"You tried her cell phone?" Cait said.

He nodded. "Of course. That's the first thing I did."

Now I'm worried. Her missing couldn't have anything to do with Wally. Could it? Cait looked at Rook as she felt a surge of panic racing through her body. "We'll search for her."

"It hasn't been twenty-four hours since she was last seen," Rook said.

"The hell with that, Detective," Cait said. "You know Fumié. At least look for her Jeep. It's old and could have broken down."

He hesitated. "I'll pull Vanicheque and have him cruise the area between her house and here," Rook said. "Would that satisfy you?"

Cait nodded. "It's a start."

He reached for his phone. "What's her address?"

"She lives at her family's ranch east of here," Ilia said. "I'll go with the officer and show him."

Rook nodded. "Go with Officer Vanicheque. Perough can stay here." He spoke into his phone. "We have a situation. Fumié appears to be missing."

Fumié missing? This can't be happening. The words hit Cait like the sting of a Taser. She felt as if she'd been hurled through the air and caught up in a cyclone.

"They'll find her," Marcus said after Rook and Ilia left. "Fumié's tough. She's trained in martial arts and knows how to use a gun."

Cait knew he was trying to convince himself Fumié was safe. She flashed on Chip Fallon. He was murdered for being in the wrong place at the wrong time. *Could the same have happened to Fumié?*

"I'm sure there's a logical reason for her to be out of touch," June said. "Young girls today are constantly multitasking. Isn't she leaving soon for a park ranger school? Maybe something came up about that."

"She would have told her mother," Cait said. "I blame myself if anything happened to her. I should have insisted she stay away until Wally is arrested."

"Come on, Cait," Jim said. "She's young with a mind of her own. You can't protect everyone."

She glanced at the clock. *It's almost five. What if Fumié isn't found before dark?*

Marcus made a fresh pot of coffee and set out clean mugs.

Minutes ticked off the clock.

Cait refilled Niki's bowls.

Cait's cell phone beeped. She grabbed it. "Did they find her?"

"Not yet," Rook said. "Vanicheque extended their search for Fumié's car. Ray and I will be at the Elizabethan awhile longer, and then we'll go over to the Blackfriars and catch up with Perough. We'll let you know when you can lock up."

Cait paced. "I need to help look for her. Someone can ride with me in my car."

"Wait a little longer," Rook said. "Then we'll see."

"Half an hour, then I'm out of here."

"Where do you think Manning's gone?" Jim asked.

For the past couple of hours, she'd forgotten about Manning. "Probably with Wally."

They jumped when someone knocked on the door. When Cait opened it, Rook and Perough were standing on the step.

"They found Fumié?"

Rook shook his head, his expression grim. "No. But they found her Jeep."

Cait fought her rising panic. "What about Fumié?"

"No sign of her."

Oh my God. He took her.

CHAPTER 43

"Where's Fumié's Jeep?" Cait demanded. "I want to see it."

"There's no need for you to go there," Rook said. "I'll call and let you know what we find."

"I'm going." Her hand closed on the doorknob. "Where's her Jeep?"

Rook sighed and rubbed his forehead, conceding defeat. "Behind the Dirty Dog Saloon."

Cait froze. "What? That fire trap?"

"Afraid so. Corliss saw it when she took the trash out. At least she had the sense to call it in, even if it was only to complain about it being there."

"Holy crap," Marcus said.

"That place is like a magnet for someone like Wally Dillon and his cousin." She ripped open the door. "Let's go. Marcus, please secure the theaters when Ray leaves."

The Harts stayed at the house with Marcus and Perough, while Cait rode shotgun with Detective Rook. She stared out the window at the empty stretch of road, silently urging Rook to go faster. The Dirty Dog Saloon was located in the middle of a fork in the road—the right branch went to Del Valle Reservoir, the left to Mount Hamilton above San Jose. She cringed as she recalled going to the saloon once with Ilia while seeking information about Marcus. Sitting on prime real estate, the old brick and wood saloon was small, dark, and a fire marshal's nightmare. It smelled of beer and stale cigarette smoke, and it had barely enough lighting to transform black shadows into human beings. She had a disagreement with Corliss, the owner, and prayed never to have reason to step foot on the property again. *Sometimes life has other plans for us.*

Rook pulled into the dirt lot and parked next to Vanicheque's blue unmarked vehicle. A rusted pickup, which Cait assumed belonged to Corliss, was parked off to the side. Cait flung the passenger door open before Rook killed the engine. She ran until she found Fumié's Jeep behind the building, its doors standing wide open.

"Cait!" Ilia called when he saw her.

She'd been told Fumié wasn't in the Jeep, but she approached it with trepidation.

As Cait and Rook approached, Vanicheque backed out of the Jeep holding a pair of cords and a piece of duct tape.

Cait began to understand the blind instinct that would drive someone to lash out at another human being. At this moment, she did not trust herself. She shook with rage, and it made her lightheaded. Fear for Fumié consumed her. She glanced over her shoulder at the saloon. It didn't look any better after the sun slipped below the horizon than it had when she'd been there during the daytime. "Ilia, have you talked to Corliss?"

"I tried, but she was too busy accusing me of bringing cops to the saloon to answer me when I questioned her. She didn't show any interest in Fumié. Hope I never have to see this place again."

Officer Vanicheque stared at Cait. "You know Corliss?"

"I met her when I heard Marcus hung out here," she said without going into detail. She stuck her head in the Jeep and tried to think like a cop. "Any sign of blood?"

"Negative," Vanicheque said. He reached in a pocket of his jeans and handed Rook a zippered plastic bag with a fractured cell phone. "The cell's been stomped on. No keys. No purse."

"She doesn't carry a purse," Ilia said. "She puts everything in her pockets."

Cait forced herself to think rationally. "Maybe she's walking." She looked around. "We need to find her before it gets completely dark."

"Maybe she went to the ranch," Ilia said. "She'd have to pass it along the way."

Cait frowned. "I don't know if she's ever been to the ranch. She never said. Bo or Khandi would have called me if she was there." She started to reach in her pocket for her cell. "Damn, I don't know their number."

"I could get it," Rook said, "but we're so close, let's just go there."

"I knew it! Pegged you for a cop first time I saw you," a voice boomed.

Cait turned and stared at the six-foot Hispanic woman charging toward her, hands clenched at her sides. Despite the heat, Corliss was dressed in the same raunchy clothes she wore when Cait first saw her—baggy overalls over a red plaid flannel shirt, the sleeves rolled up over heavy, hairy arms. Her cropped silver hair hadn't seen soap in ages.

"Corliss—" Cait said.

"You!" She pointed. "Get off my property!" When she stopped within a foot of Cait, Cait stepped away and rested her palm on the Glock at her back. Corliss reeked of marijuana.

"Somehow I get the feeling you don't like me," Cait said, sensing Rook and Vanicheque moving closer in case Corliss lunged at her. "Simmer down. What do you know about this Jeep and the girl it belongs to?"

"Don't know a damn thing about any girl and wouldn't tell you if I did." She shot a dark look at Rook and Vanicheque. "Cops are lousy for business."

Cait glanced around. "You won't have a business if you don't talk to us. A girl's life is at stake."

Corliss turned away. "Leave me alone and don't come back."

Rook reached under his jacket and pulled out a pair of handcuffs. "Maybe you'd prefer time in a holding cell for not cooperating with the police."

Anger flared in Corliss's eyes. "I didn't see nothin'!"

"How about your customers? Or were they too busy inhaling the atmosphere to notice what went on outside that piece of shit you call a business?" Cait said.

Ilia stepped up and calmly said, "Please, Corliss. Tell us what you saw."

She looked at him and hesitated. "Saw nothing, but maybe I heard a couple of cars. Doors slamming, a motor revving up in a hurry to get away."

Cait's heart skipped a beat. "Did you see a girl? Did she go inside the saloon?"

Corliss frowned and scratched her head.

Cait demanded, "Did you see a girl?"

Red blotted Corliss's face as her eyes shifted to Rook. She shook her head. "I had the TV on in the back."

Oh, God. "You didn't hear anyone yell for help?"

Corliss shrugged.

"We're wasting time here," Cait said. "We have to find Fumié."

Her heart in her throat, Cait rolled the passenger window down and stared hard at shadows, shrubs, and ditches as Rook drove down Mines Road. Vanicheque and Ilia remained behind to have Fumié's Jeep towed to the police station.

Rook reminded Cait, "She's trained to be a survivor."

"I wonder how long her Jeep's been there. If she's walking, we would have passed her on our way out here," Cait said.

"Not if she's scared or she ducked behind bushes when cars

passed. We're almost at the Bening ranch. Maybe she's there."

"I don't understand why anyone would abduct Fumié or why her car was left behind that saloon."

"She could have witnessed something she shouldn't have, like Chip Fallon. Whoever drove her car out here has to be a local and familiar with the saloon."

"Probably John LeBow, Wally's cousin," Cait said. "Corliss wouldn't give up his name if she knew it."

He slowed and turned in to the ranch. When he parked by the red barn, Cait jumped out and ran to the house. "The spotlights on the barn could have been a beacon of hope for Fumié if she could see them from the road." She crossed the footbridge, ran up onto the porch, and pounded on the door. Lights were on inside. Disappointed, she said, "Their car isn't here."

"If Fumié found her way here, Bo could have driven her home."

Frustrated, Cait looked through the porch windows but saw no movement inside. She paced the porch. "What should we do?"

"Call Marcus. Maybe she called the house."

"She couldn't. Her cell phone's trashed."

Rook pulled out his own cell. "I'll call Perough."

Cait's cell beeped. She reached in her pocket and grabbed it. "Bo?" She stared at Rook. "Where are you? Detective Rook and I are on your front porch."

"We're in the ER at Valley Care Medical Center with Fumié."

"Oh, my God! Bo, we've been searching for her. Is she hurt?"

"She says she's fine, but I wasn't taking any chances and insisted she be checked out," he said. "The doctor examined her. Except for a couple of bruises, she appears to be okay. Fumié will explain everything when you get here."

"We're on our way. Don't let her leave." She disconnected

the call. "Where's the hospital?"

"About twenty minutes away."

As they ran to the car, Cait said, "I hate to admit it, but it's darn convenient having the Dirty Dog Saloon on the same road as the ranch." She got in the car and strapped on her seatbelt.

Rook backed the car around. "Was that a positive thought about the saloon?"

"No, just saying. It's a rat hole and should be condemned."

"Can't argue there," he said, "but I can't help wonder if there's some connection to the saloon. It's not the most convenient place to dump a car . . . or a body, for that matter."

"Do you think Corliss was lying about not seeing Fumié?"

"No, but she is guilty of watching TV instead of the bar. Then again, what's to steal? Whiskey? Beer? But if Fumié says she went inside, I'll go back out there for another chat with Corliss."

Cait and Rook rushed into the emergency room. Rook held up his shield to the clerk behind the counter. "We're looking for Fumié Ondo. She was brought in here not long ago."

They followed the clerk's directions to a room of curtained cubicles where Bo was waiting.

Bo nodded to Rook. "The doctor wanted to call the police and report Fumié's abduction, but I told them you were on the way." He pulled a curtain aside. "Fumié, you have company."

Cait stared at Fumié, who was sitting on the side of the bed clutching a flimsy hospital gown wrapped tightly around her and looking anxious. "Are you okay?" She gave her a gentle hug when she noticed a purple bruise on her left arm.

Fumié smiled. "Better than the guy who grabbed me. Can we get out of here?"

"What about your parents? Are they here?" Rook asked.

Fumié shook her head. "I called and told them not to come,

that I was fine and wanted to talk to the police before going home. The doctor said I could leave after they finished some paperwork."

A nurse entered and handed Fumié a release form. Fumié signed the paper and the nurse said she was free to go but gave her instructions to take it easy for a day or so.

After the nurse left, Fumié said, "I'm sorry I spoiled your evening, Bo, but I'm sure glad you were home. I was getting cold in my jogging clothes."

"We're glad we were home and able to help you," Bo said.

"Did you know the ranch was on Mines Road?" Cait asked.

"Yes. Tasha used to talk about it, but I'd never been there. When I got to the saloon, I looked in but didn't see anyone, which was a relief, because that place gives me the creeps. So I decided to walk until I found the ranch. If you'll excuse me, I'd like to get dressed. I'll meet you in the lobby."

Cait and Rook left and saw Khandi and her daughter, Joy, waiting in the lobby. "Hi," Cait said. "Thanks for helping Fumié. Other than some bruises, she's okay and will be out soon."

Joy reached for Cait's hand. "Will you bring Fumié out to the ranch sometime?"

Cait saw Fumié limping toward them. "I think you can ask her yourself."

Rook pulled his phone from his pocket. "I'll be outside."

When everyone left the hospital, Rook was standing next to his car outside the door.

Bo carried Joy, but hesitated long enough for Fumié to promise to visit the ranch sometime soon.

With Fumié settled in the backseat and Cait in the front, Rook pulled out of the parking lot and onto the street. "Do you care to talk about what happened, Fumié?"

"Sure. I was jogging on Cross Road when I heard a gunshot."

"That's rural," Rook said. "Could have been a farmer shooting to scare crows from his crops or vineyard."

"I don't think so," Fumié said. "I heard voices before the gunshot. Then I was grabbed from behind and thrown to the ground. You need to take a look, Detective. I think someone was murdered."

CHAPTER 44

Cait twisted in her seat. "Fumié, did you notice anything else out of the ordinary or see anyone else on the road before you were grabbed?"

"No," Fumié said. "There was a pickup parked on the side of the road. I'd been jogging about an hour and was on my way back to my car when I saw it."

"Anyone in the pickup?" Rook asked.

"Not that I saw."

"Maybe someone thought you witnessed something," Cait said. "How many were there?"

"At least two."

"I'm sorry to keep asking," Rook said, "but what do you remember up to the time you were tied up and left in your car behind the saloon? Did you pick up on any of their conversation or an accent?"

Cait watched Fumié for signs of fatigue. She didn't want to press her too hard for information, but time was critical if they were to catch Wally and his cousin.

Fumié shifted in the backseat. "They were angry and yelled at each other. Like I said, I was on Cross Road where I often run. I was thinking I needed to get back in time to meet Ilia." Then she gasped. "Oh, no! He must have been worried when I didn't show up."

"He's with Officer Vanicheque," Cait said. "They were looking for you when they found your Jeep."

"By the way, it's being towed to the police station," Rook said. "Were you parked on Cross while you were jogging?"

"Yes, near a clump of trees. I was getting into my car when I heard the gunshot. I reached for my cell. I thought it would be cool to take a picture of a crime scene. I intended to call the police, but I didn't get a chance. I was grabbed, and he took my cell." She grinned. "I got the guy who grabbed me though, kicked him in the groin as hard as I could and slammed my palm into his face. I think I broke his nose because he was bleeding."

Way to go, Fumié. Cait watched as Fumié rubbed her wrists where they'd been bound. "Can you describe the guy?"

Fumié's brow furrowed. "Everything happened so fast, but he was stocky, dark skin, average height. He wore a baseball cap backwards. I'm sorry, that's all I remember."

"That's okay. Then what happened?"

"I kicked and screamed. Then another guy came to help the first one. He wrapped a scarf or something around my head so I couldn't see or breathe very well. He left for a few seconds, but when he returned, he tied my wrists and ankles and taped my mouth."

"How did you manage to escape?" *Fumié couldn't weigh more than a hundred pounds.*

"Easy. I grew up on a ranch. My dad taught me to shoot, ride horses, and rope cattle. I'm good with knots, and fortunately they weren't. I started working on the knots as soon as they tossed me into my Jeep."

"Why didn't they leave your car on Cross Road?" Cait asked.

"I heard them say they'd have more time to get away if my car wasn't left in plain sight on an open road. I think the guy who drove my car was familiar with the saloon, because I overheard him say the owner would never call the police about an abandoned vehicle."

"Did they hit you?" Rook asked.

Fumié hesitated. "One of them slapped me on the side of my head. My ears buzzed."

"You told this to the doctor?" Cait asked.

"Yes. She checked me out and said I'd probably have a headache for awhile."

"We're almost back," Rook said. "Maybe Vanicheque and Ilia are there."

"I remember something else," Fumié said. "The guy I hurt wore a gold chain with a cross."

Cait stared at her. "The guy who grabbed you wore a gold chain?"

"Yes. I tried to grab it when I smashed his nose."

Cait pictured the chain she'd seen Manning wear, but he was over six feet with a runner's build. Then she remembered another gold chain, the one Hank Dillon had worn at the bank robbery. It went into Evidence along with the knife. *Did Wally request Hank's necklace as well as his knife?*

"What about the other guy? The one who went to get the cords?"

Fumié shook her head. "I was too busy trying to escape to pay attention to him."

Cait faced the front as Rook pulled into the driveway. "I hope you won't have terrifying nightmares from this. You may want to talk to a doctor."

"I'll be okay. Each day is a new experience, some good, some not so good."

Rook parked in front of the house. "Vanicheque's not back yet."

Cait opened her door and then Fumié's and helped her out. She pulled her cell from her pocket and handed it to her. "Call your parents. Let them know you're here and that someone will take you home soon."

"Thanks," Fumié said.

"Let's go around back," Cait said. "I don't have my keys."

They ran into Officer Perough as they cut between the house and garage. "It's been quiet," Perough said. He looked at Fumié and smiled. "Hey. Are you okay?"

Fumié brushed her long hair from her face. "Better than the guy who grabbed me. He may limp for awhile and probably needs a nose job."

"I need to call in," Rook said. "Fumié heard a gunshot near where she was abducted."

Perough frowned. "Dispatch hasn't reported any gunshots."

"This happened near Cross Road and Tesla," Rook said. "Probably no one heard a gunshot or thought it was a backfire."

As soon as Marcus opened the door, Niki jumped up on Cait. She hugged him and rubbed behind his ears.

Marcus's eyes were glued on Fumié. "Are you okay?"

She smiled. "Yes."

"My God, Fumié." June embraced her.

Rook took out his cell phone and stepped into the hall to call Dispatch.

"Fumié, call your folks, and then we'll talk," Cait said.

There was a knock at the door. "Should be Vanicheque. He called after the tow truck left with Fumié's Jeep," Perough said as he opened it.

Ilia rushed in, followed by Vanicheque. "Where is she?"

Cait cocked her head at Fumié. "She's on the phone with her parents. You might want to take her home." Ilia's face explained a lot to Cait. His relationship with Fumié had progressed beyond friendship, at least for him. Exhausted, Cait longed for a hot shower and bed. She glanced at the large wall clock. It was almost nine but felt more like midnight.

Fumié returned Cait's phone and said, "Thanks. I told my mom I'd be home soon."

"I'll take you," Ilia said.

"I'd like that."

Rook returned. "Fumié, are you up to returning to the scene? I need to know where you stood when you heard the gunshot and the direction you think it came from. Officers are going to have a look, but it's dark without streetlights."

Eyes wide, Ilia gasped. "You saw someone get shot?"

Alarmed, Marcus asked, "Someone shot at you?"

Cait admired how calm Fumié appeared as she answered everyone's questions. "Sure, I'll go with you," Fumié said. "Or I could draw a map."

"I'll get a pad." Marcus hurried into his office. "She shouldn't go back out there." No one contradicted him. When he returned, he handed a notepad and pen to Fumié.

Fumié leaned against the counter and sketched the location, adding a few trees, shrubs, and where her Jeep was parked. Then she drew a large X. "I was standing here when I heard the gunshot." She drew an arrow. "And this points to where I'm sure it came from. A simple sketch, but that's all there is. There is a driveway on Cross Road near the corner with some old machinery in the yard. Maybe someone there heard the gunshot."

Rook ripped the sheet off the pad, folded it, and laid the pad on the counter. "You didn't mention a ranch before."

Fumié shrugged. "You can't see a house or any buildings because of the trees and bushes. Maybe it's not a house but a business."

Rook nodded. "Worth checking." He looked at Perough and Vanicheque. "A couple of officers will be here within the hour to relieve you."

"Want us back in the morning?" Vanicheque asked.

"Probably, but I'll let you know," Rook said. "Cait, officers will cruise the area and walk the property. They'll try not to disturb you, but *please* don't shoot them if you hear strange noises outside your window. I'm leaving to help search for a body."

Cait smiled as she walked Rook to the door. "Do you ever sleep?"

He smirked. "What do you think? Talk to you tomorrow."

The Harts returned to their RV soon after Rook left. Marcus took Niki out before going home. Cait offered snacks to Perough and Vanicheque while they waited for their replacements, but they refused and went outside to wait. Ilia took Fumié home.

Cait and Niki went upstairs. The long, hard day weighed heavily on her—a heaviness she couldn't ignore. And she wondered when RT would return. She skipped the shower she'd craved and crawled between the cool sheets and fell asleep.

CHAPTER 45

A faint beeping interrupted Cait's dream of gold bricks, each one about twenty-seven pounds. She wanted to know how much a brick that size would be worth, but before she found out, persistent ringing pulled her from the dream. She reached out to locate her cell on the nightstand. "Hello."

"It's Rook. Did I wake you?"

She blinked a few times, dazzled by the morning sun, trying to focus on the red numerals on the clock. Almost 8:45. "No," she said struggling not to sound sleepy.

"We found a body."

Wide awake now, Cait pulled herself up to the edge of the bed. "Where Fumié said?"

"Yes. I'll have to learn not to underestimate her."

"I never doubted for a second there was a gunshot, but I thought it might have been a rancher shooting at crows. Have you identified the body?"

"John LeBow."

Cait ran her hand through her tousled hair. "Wow. Wally's cousin."

"Yes," Rook said. "And the guy who shot up your windshield from that pickup we towed a week ago."

"That's one less bad guy to worry about. Find anything else besides the body?" *Like a gold necklace?*

"We looked, but it was too dark. Also wanted you to know Vanicheque and Perough will return. Did you hear the officers

297

during the night?"

"I doubt I'd hear a blast of dynamite up here on the third floor," she said. "You might remind Vanicheque and Perough that the actors will be here today. Will the officers be dressed in plainclothes?"

"Yes. They'll let you know when they're there." He hesitated. "Should Manning turn up, have one of the officers call me. I want to have a few words with him."

"You and me both." After they hung up, she tossed her cell on the bed and headed to the bathroom to shower. She reflected on how LeBow's death would affect Wally. *Would he give up or intensify his vendetta against her? And who was the other guy Fumié said was there?* Before she turned into a prune, she shut the water off and grabbed a thick towel from a rack.

She slipped into jeans and a white blouse, applied light makeup, fluffed her curly hair to dry it naturally, and roused Niki from his favorite place in the sun. She took everything she'd need and went downstairs. Shep called as she poured a cup of coffee.

"Cait, is Manning there?"

"No, why?"

"Good. There's something you should know before you see him. I talked to Wally's mother. She wasn't too cooperative at first."

Cait took her coffee into the front room and looked out the window. "She's used to hearing bad news about her boys. Rook also talked to her."

"I know. Mrs. Dillon wouldn't let me inside the house because I'm a cop, but she agreed to talk on the porch."

She sipped her coffee. "You must have charmed her. What did she have to say?"

"When I asked if she'd met Calder Manning, she said she met him at church and liked his family."

"I should hope so, if she let them adopt Hank."

"She saw Manning again at his dad's funeral."

"Oh. Not the best of circumstances."

"No. After some prodding, she opened up and told me Mr. Manning didn't die from natural causes. He was an innocent bystander in the wrong place at the wrong time and got caught in a line of fire during a grocery store robbery. She said Calder took it hard." He paused. "The bullet that killed Manning's dad came from a police officer's gun."

Her breath caught in her throat as she digested the news. "Now I understand Calder Manning's attitude toward me." She rubbed her aching temples.

"Yeah, and why he's there. Remember, Hank's adoption was never finalized after Mr. Manning's death."

"Unfortunate for everyone."

"I don't think not signing adoption papers changed the outcome," he said. "Mrs. Manning, in effect, adopted Hank."

"There you are." Marcus walked into the room. When he saw she was on the phone he said, "Sorry to interrupt, but the police officers are here. They want to talk to you."

Cait nodded. "Shep, Fumié was abducted yesterday while she was jogging. She's okay. She got free, but she heard a gunshot. Rook and his officers searched the area where she was abducted and found a body—John LeBow, Wally's cousin."

Cait heard Shep release a long sigh. "The body count's growing, but at least the girl wasn't hurt."

"Rook's officers are here. Thanks for the news. I'll call you later."

"Isn't that Manning in the driveway?" Marcus said.

Cait stared out the front window and watched Manning step out of his rental car. When she opened the door, she set off the alarm. Marcus quickly punched in the code while she went outside. "Where have you been?" she asked Manning.

Manning took his time going up the steps. "I didn't know I was supposed to report in and out."

Cait's eyes narrowed on the gold chain around his neck. "Nice necklace. One like it keeps turning up in unexpected places."

Manning removed his sunglasses. "What's that supposed to mean?" He looked at Marcus standing in the doorway. "He's not wearing one."

"Hank did. Does Wally wear a gold necklace?"

He frowned. "Why would you think that?"

"Because a guy fitting his description abducted Fumié yesterday. He wore a similar necklace with a cross. Know anything about that?"

His smile threw Cait off balance for a second. "As a matter of fact, I do. The necklace is a sign of brotherhood. I gave one to Hank to make him feel part of my family. Wally wears it now. As for the girl, I'm taking care of that. What happened to her shouldn't have happened."

Surprised, she said, "She could have been shot and left in a field . . . like John LeBow."

Manning's jaw clamped shut.

Officer Vanicheque appeared in the doorway next to Marcus. "Everything okay?"

"I think Mr. Manning's about to explain Fumié's abduction and John LeBow's murder," Cait said. *Or I'll pull it out of him one word at a time.*

Vanicheque stepped onto the porch as Perough walked around from the side of the house and stood at the foot of the stairs blocking Manning. "This should be interesting. Let's hear it," Vanicheque said.

Manning's eyes shifted between the two officers, and then he held his hands out in a "calm down" gesture. "Wally told me what happened when I confronted him, but he didn't hurt her."

"Did he kill John LeBow?" Perough asked.

"I don't know any John LeBow."

Frustrated, Cait said, "Sure you do. He's Wally's cousin. He and Wally have been busy taking shots at me, breaking into the theater, and murdering one of my actors. LeBow also supplied guns to Wally."

Manning shrugged. "I'll have to ask Wally about him the next time he calls."

"Cut the crap, Manning. We'll escort you to Wally's hideout," Perough said. "Where is he? Pagan Alley?"

"Look, I'll handle it. I don't trust the police any more than Wally. You guys are all trigger-happy."

Cait's thoughts flashed to Manning's dad and how he was cut down with a police officer's bullet. She chose a softer touch to get him to cooperate. "Can you bring Wally in like you promised? There's been enough tragedy, and I have a busy weekend ahead. I'd like to end this today."

Manning nodded. "I agree, but I'll bring him in my way."

She looked at Vanicheque and Perough for their reaction to Manning's cavalier attitude.

The officers exchanged glances. Vanicheque looked at his watch. "You've got twenty-four hours. If Wally's not in custody by then, we're coming after both of you."

Manning nodded and returned to his car and drove off.

Cait released a long sigh and looked at Vanicheque. "You're to call Detective Rook."

He reached in his jeans pocket for his cell.

"Whew, glad that's over. If anyone's hungry, I brought bagels," Marcus said. "Would anyone like scrambled eggs to go with them?"

"Sounds good," she said. "The way things are going, it may be the last meal I get today."

CHAPTER 46

Cait hesitated as she passed the gift shop. *If it isn't opened soon, people are going to wonder why.* Marcus posted signs saying the shop was being remodeled, but obviously it wasn't. She hadn't seen any news trucks converging on the festival since the tea in April. She seldom watched television, and the only paper she read was the local *Independent,* so she hadn't seen anything about Chip Fallon's murder. She continued to the kitchen and was about to refill her coffee when she heard a light knocking on the back door.

"Got it," Marcus said.

When he opened the door, the Harts and Ray walked in. "Look who we found wandering around like a lost puppy," June said.

"For crying out loud," Ray said, "I was walking the perimeter of the Blackfriars theater. Did you forget about *Macbeth* on Saturday?"

"Of course not, you big lug. Find any criminals? I hope you've got your gun, because you just might need it."

Cait watched their bantering with amusement.

Ray turned on Cait. "What's she's talking about?"

"Would you like coffee, Ray, while I tell you?" Cait asked.

"Got a full thermos of coffee. Just tell me and don't spare the details."

"Fumié was abducted yesterday." When he didn't react, she continued. "The good news is she's back and she's okay. The

302

bad news is, Wally's still out there."

Ray pulled his gun and checked the chamber. "I've been waiting for a chance to use this." He tucked it back under his shirt.

"There's also been another murder."

Ray rolled his eyes. "Christ almighty. Soon you'll have enough bodies to start your own damn mortuary."

June stared at Cait. "The police found a body?" She glanced around the kitchen as if to count heads.

"Detective Rook called," Cait said. "John LeBow was found last night where Fumié said she heard a gunshot."

"She'll make a darn good park ranger," June said. "So that means one bad guy down and one to go—Wally."

"Wally must be desperate," Jim said. "All the more reason to be cautious."

"Talk to the actors, Ray, as soon as they're here," Cait said. "Manning was here a little while ago. Officers Perough and Van-icheque gave him twenty-four hours to bring Wally in or they would find and arrest both of them."

Ray ran his hand over his scruffy chin. "Lord help us all if Actors' Equity decides to stop by. They can do that, you know, just show up with no warning. They negotiate our salaries and our working conditions."

Cait cringed at the thought of AE showing up at her door. "I promised Sam Cruz the actors would be safe, the police would be here, and to stop worrying."

"Yeah, but that was before Fumié's abduction and LeBow's murder," Ray said.

"Dammit, Ray! What do you expect me to do?" Cait snapped. "Find Wally and kill him myself? Believe me, I'd like nothing better."

Ray reached out and drew her close in a smothering bear hug. "Come here, kid. I'm sorry. It's just my way of blowing off steam. I know none of this is your fault that some scumbag's got a bomb up his ass. You're doing everything anyone could ask. If Tasha were here, she'd be blaming herself for getting you into this mess."

"You're sweet," Cait mumbled into his scratchy work shirt and then pulled away. "If she's looking down on us, she's wondering how her Shakespeare festival can survive under my supervision."

"Not so," Marcus said. "She'd smile and say, 'Praising what is lost, Makes the remembrance dear.' "

Cait smiled, pleased to hear Marcus quote Shakespeare.

"Well said, Marcus," June said. "It's nice Shakespeare's made an impression on you."

Red crept up Marcus's neck.

Cait leaned against the counter. "I can't believe how well the festival is going in spite of murder and constant chaos." She saw a familiar face in the door window. When she opened the door, Betsy Ryder, aka Lady Macbeth, Vanicheque and Perough walked in.

"Betsy, if you're looking for Ray, he's here."

Blond wisps of hair fell in waves around Betsy's face. "These officers flashed their shields when I arrived, so I assumed something bad happened. But you all look fine." She smiled. "Ray, we're waiting to get in the theater."

Ray grunted, "I'm coming."

"I'll go," Marcus said, drawing his modem from his pocket.

"Don't forget about the wigs, Ray," Cait said.

"Something wrong with the wigs?" Betsy asked.

"Someone got into the trunk of wigs at the Elizabethan theater," Vanicheque said. "Don't know if one was stolen, but just make sure you recognize everyone in costume. Give Cait a call or tell an officer if you suspect someone. You might want to have another look at Wally's mug shot."

"Good grief," Betsy laughed. "He wouldn't be difficult to recognize. We don't have a black actor in our play."

"Wally's shown how creative he can be," June said. "So don't hesitate to scream."

"I won't, and it'll be in my loudest stage voice," Betsy said.

"And Betsy," Cait added, "if anyone asks about there being so much security, just tell them it's standard operating procedure. I don't want to frighten them."

"No, of course not," Betsy said.

"Let's go," Ray said, "before the troops break down the door."

"The gift shop is still closed. All the guests need to know is it's being remodeled. Signs have been posted."

Betsy left with Ray, the officers, and Marcus.

June sighed. "Now what?"

Cait shrugged. "We wait."

"Have you talked with Fumié?"

Cait shook her head. "I don't expect to see her today."

"Any word from RT?"

"No." Cait tried not to think about him, but as soon as she laid her head down at night, she always had visions of him.

"At least you know he'll be back. His vehicles are in the parking lot."

A loud bang, sputtering, and the squeal of brakes in the driveway penetrated the house.

They ran to the front and looked out the window.

"Oh, it's Fumié!" June said.

Ilia opened the passenger door of his VW and helped Fumié out. It amazed Cait how Fumié could return so soon after her frightening experience and still be able to laugh.

"Hi," Fumié said when Cait and June stepped out onto the porch.

Cait hurried down the stairs. "What are you doing here? Shouldn't you be home resting?"

"I couldn't stay away. Marcus and I want to finalize plans for the gift shop. He thinks he can have it built in a month."

"Her parents invited me for breakfast," Ilia said. "She insisted on coming here."

Cait laughed. "Marcus will be happy to see you. He's worried about you."

"Be right back," Ilia said. He ran to his car and returned with his new digital Nikon. "I'm going to take her picture with Marcus. For my book," he explained.

June pointed to the yellow bug. "Are you sure that thing is drivable?"

Ilia grinned. "Hey, it's my pride and joy. Could use a bit of a tuneup though."

Cait's cell rang. She recognized Rook's number. "Is it good news?" She frowned. "How could that happen? What about Manning?" She paced the porch as she listened. "Well, damn." She dropped her phone in her pocket.

"Detective Rook?" June asked.

Cait nodded, her gaze sweeping the vineyard. "Wally's gone. Pagan Alley's been cleared out. Rook said to expect a couple more officers. He thinks Wally will come here."

"And Manning?" June asked.

"Don't know."

CHAPTER 47

"Find Manning and you'll find Wally," Cait said when Rook arrived. "What happened at Pagan Alley?"

"Half a dozen of our guys—the best at their jobs—went through the place. They found the usual: drug paraphernalia, empty beer bottles, and empty ammunition boxes."

Cait was quiet for a moment. "Maybe Manning skipped town and took Wally with him."

"You don't believe that, do you?"

"No, but Officer Vanicheque threatened to arrest Manning if he didn't bring Wally in within twenty-four hours. The clock's ticking." She glanced at the time on her cell. "Twenty-two to go."

Rook nodded. "Maybe Wally won't come. Cops will be all over the place."

"That hasn't stopped him before." She touched her Glock to reassure herself it was still there. "I'm going to the Blackfriars to catch a rehearsal. Want to come?"

"You don't think I'd let you go alone, do you?"

She chose not to answer. Instead, she said, "I'll tell Marcus where I'll be." She poked her head in the office and found him sitting on the floor with Fumié, their heads bent over a large set of plans for the gift shop. "I'll be at the Blackfriars."

Marcus looked up and frowned. "You should stay here."

"Rook's going with me. Where's Ilia?"

"He left for an appointment," Fumié said. "He'll be back to

take me home."

Happy to draw a breath of fresh air, Cait forced herself to open her mind to the good things in life: birdsong, the rustle of grasses, the golden hills, and Shakespeare. Niki shot around the corner of the house. She reached in her pocket for a treat and gave it to him.

"He doesn't miss RT now that he's got you," Rook said. He hesitated. "Cait, RT's coming back, maybe as soon as tomorrow."

Her spirits lifted. "You talked to him?"

Rook smiled. "Yes, last night."

Why doesn't he call me?

"Who's with the actors?" Rook asked Perough when they saw him coming toward them.

"Vanicheque and Newman."

Rook nodded. "Cait wants to watch a rehearsal."

"No problem," Perough said. "Caught a few minutes myself. Maybe she can explain it to me. Sometime, I'd like to bring my girlfriend to see a play."

Cait smiled. "Any time. Free tickets for every officer who's been here, and their significant others."

They passed through the gate and turned down the path toward the theater. "When you're ready to leave," Rook told Cait, "snag any officer to walk you back to the house."

Just like a prisoner. "Where are you going?"

"I'll be around."

They made their way toward the front and took a seat. Two actors were on stage with a couple of chairs, two goblets, and the crown—the central image of the play and the reason Macbeth committed the first murder.

Cait whispered, "See the disc in the middle of the stage and the pool of red liquid in its center, and how it appears to glow from within? The disk has been artfully painted to work with the lighting design to convey changing moods." When Perough nodded, she continued. "The costumes are white, simple and elegant, to show the splattered blood."

Perough surprised Cait when he pulled his cell, checked the screen, and said, "Gotta go."

Her attention on the actors, Cait was surprised when June slipped in the row and sat beside her.

June leaned close and whispered, "Compelling, isn't it? More so on this small stage. You can almost feel how Macbeth burns with the desire of becoming Scotland's king, but Lady Macbeth knows the bloody path necessary to attain that crown—a path to disaster."

Cait whispered, "I love the intimacy of the small stage and how it grabs and pulls you in. Why hasn't *Macbeth* always been played in a small intimate theater?"

"It was a risk when it was performed on a small stage for the first time in Ashland," June said, "with staging and action so minimal and abstract, but the director wanted to emphasize simplicity in order to focus better on the psychology of the characters. It worked."

"It does," Cait said, rubbing her arms from a sudden chill. They continued to watch in silence until rehearsal ended and the stark white costumes were splattered with blood.

The lights in the theater remained dim. Cait and June were in no hurry to leave, and they stayed in their seats to muse on the power of the scene they had witnessed.

Then loud, angry voices disrupted their thoughts. They jumped up and ran to the door. An officer Cait didn't know blocked the exit, refusing to let them leave.

"Open the door," Cait demanded.

When the officer still refused, Cait ducked under his arm and pushed the door open. The officer tried to stop her, but she kept going and ran down the path.

Rook, Perough, and Vanicheque ran across the courtyard with their guns drawn.

Cait ran after them.

She froze when she saw Fumié and a light-skinned African-American man circling each other at the ridge of the hill.

"Wally! Stop!" someone yelled.

Cait recognized Manning's voice. Then she saw Marcus on the sideline. The last she'd seen Marcus and Fumié, they were on the floor in his office with a sketchpad. She stared at the guy challenging Fumié. *This average-looking guy is Wally?*

Then the sun flashed on the gun in his hand. Cait inched closer as she removed her gun, shaking with desire to pull the trigger, but training and discipline held her back.

Wally circled Fumié in a menacing manner, ignoring the police and Manning. Cait wanted to warn Fumié to back off, to let the police handle Wally, but Fumié spun, her leg shooting out like a piston, catching Wally's arm.

Wally's gun flew out of his hand. "Bitch!" He charged Fumié.

Fumié whirled, her feet slicing in a flurry of strikes as her long black hair whipped about her face. Wally tried to raise his arm to intercept her kick, but could not. She caught him in the groin.

Wally's face twisted in pain. He collapsed on the ground.

Fumié planted her hands on her hips and stared down at him. "That should even the score."

Vanicheque and Perough rushed to cuff Wally, but Wally surprised everyone by rolling away and jumping to his feet. When he saw Cait, his face contorted with hatred. He spat at her.

Cait jumped back, almost tripping over Niki.

Rook rushed in and grabbed one of Wally's arms from behind and attempted to cuff him. Wally pulled free and screamed in Cait's face. "You bitch! You murderer! Hank was my brother!"

His hand went to his waist as he turned on Manning. He screamed, "You and your shitty idea, using me to do your own dirty work—"

A gunshot echoed across the hills.

Everyone froze.

Wally crumpled to the ground, blood gushing from his neck. This time he didn't move.

Stunned, Cait turned on Manning. "Are you crazy? For God's sake, he was in handcuffs."

"No he wasn't. He was going to kill you," Manning said.

Cait glanced down at Wally. Manning was right. One cuff dangled from the dead man's left hand. Wally had somehow gotten out of the cuffs.

Rook went to Manning and held his hand out. "Give me your gun."

Manning handed the weapon over.

Vanicheque pulled on latex gloves and took out plasticuffs. "Hands behind your back, Manning."

"Wally would never turn himself in," Manning said, desperation in his voice. "He would have fought to the bitter end." He turned to Rook. "Check him out. You'll find he also has a knife."

"Then why didn't he pull it on Fumié?" Cait asked.

Manning shrugged.

Rook stooped and rolled Wally over while Perough, already gloved, searched the body. Perough found a knife strapped to Wally's ankle and held it up.

"Check his waistband," Manning said.

Perough frowned at Manning but pulled up Wally's shirt.

"Careful," Manning warned. "He keeps his knives sharp."

Cait watched Perough unzip Wally's jeans and then pull out a three-inch knife from his waistband.

Rook stared at Manning. "Any more surprises we should know about?"

Manning shook his head. "Not that I know of. Now will you remove these cuffs?"

"Not yet." Rook looked around. "Somebody call the coroner."

After the coroner took the body away and Rook and his officers left with Manning, Cait returned to the theater, where she found June and the actors huddling backstage. She explained what had happened and that Wally was dead, Manning in handcuffs, and the nightmare finally over. They could relax and enjoy the weekend.

Cait returned to the house and took a seat in the kitchen with Marcus, Fumié, and the Harts. She was exhausted but relieved it was over, as if it was the grand finale to her worst nightmare. "Fumié, you amazed me with those kicks, but what were you and Marcus doing there?"

Fumié looked at Marcus and smiled. "Our calculations were off. I wasn't satisfied and wanted to remeasure the area before Marcus cut the lumber."

"But you shouldn't have gone out there." She shuddered at the thought of them being hurt or killed. "How did you happen to see Wally?"

"I saw a movement and when I looked, I recognized him as the guy who kidnapped me." She smiled at Marcus. "I'm sorry, I should have told you I saw him, but you were busy and there wasn't time. I didn't want to lose the opportunity to pay him back for what he did to me."

"You scared the hell out of me. I called Detective Rook when I saw a guy I thought could be Wally," Marcus said. "A lot of help I was."

Fumié leaned over and pecked him on the cheek. "If you hadn't called Detective Rook, the result might have been different."

Marcus grinned and nodded. "I'm glad it's over."

Cait sighed. "I hope so." *But why do I feel unsettled?*

It was after ten that night when Rook called Cait. "How are you doing?"

Cait sat propped up in the bed with her laptop. "Relieved. I hope it's over. What happened when you took Manning to the station? Was he booked into jail?"

A sigh came over the line. "We had to let him go, but not before hours of interrogation. We kept his gun and passport until he comes in tomorrow to sign off on the paperwork. Then he's free to go."

"You let him off too easily."

"It wasn't an easy decision to make. Wally was prepared to kill you. If Manning hadn't told us about the knives, we might not be having this conversation."

Something in the back of her mind nagged at her. "Don't you think it odd, just before Manning shot Wally, that Wally accused him of doing his dirty work for him? Don't you wonder what dirty work he meant? Did you ask Manning about that?"

"Of course. You think we're new at this? Manning said the brothers never took responsibility for their actions, always pointed fingers at someone else. He didn't expect it to be any different with him."

She thought about what Rook said. "So, that's it? Case closed?"

"After the paperwork's filed. Next time you call, make it an invitation to lunch."

"You have an open invitation. I appreciate what you and the officers have done and the time spent working my case. But honestly, I hope I never have to call you again."

He chuckled. "Goodnight, Cait."

She shut her computer down and Niki stretched out beside her. *Maybe after my morning coffee things will begin to feel right again.*

CHAPTER 48

Cait woke at seven, rested, hungry, and ready for a run now that she didn't have Wally to worry about. She slipped on shorts and a T-shirt and then called Shep.

"I was going to call you," Shep said.

"Good news. Wally's dead."

"Hallelujah! And Manning? Has he left town?"

Cait rolled her shoulders to get the kinks out and then curled up on the chaise in the sunny bay window. "That's where it gets interesting. I don't know if he's left yet. He shot Wally yesterday." She explained how it went down, how Fumié used her martial arts skills to get even with Wally for abducting her, and about the police cuffing Manning and taking him to jail. "Manning was later released."

"How do you feel about that?"

"They let him off easy. I'd feel the same way if he were the president of the United States. He killed someone. Shooting Wally wasn't called for. He wouldn't have gotten away because the police were there."

"Has he been in touch with you since his release?"

"No, and I hope I never see him again. I assume he went in this morning to sign papers. It angers me to think Manning was given special privileges because he's a war correspondent. He should pay for killing Wally."

"You're right." He paused. "Manning's mother called the station this morning. Dispatch forwarded the call to my cell phone."

Cait sat up on the edge of her seat. "What did she want?"

"Manning called her after midnight to talk to his daughter, but she was in bed."

"She's three. Of course she'd be in bed."

"Mrs. Manning called because his behavior disturbed her. She's certain he has PTSD, but when she tried to talk to him about it he refused to discuss it."

"Post-traumatic stress disorder. I knew it!"

"Right. You mentioned it."

Cait thought back to when she'd first met Manning. Arrogant, smart-ass, but didn't exhibit signs of PTSD. She later changed her mind after researching the disorder and comparing the symptoms to Manning. "Did she say if he'd been medically diagnosed? A doctor would be obligated to report it. I mean . . . he's not a soldier but he does report news from the front line and could endanger everyone around him."

"It doesn't sound like he's been seen by a doctor, but a friend recognized the signs and suggested he see someone. Manning was afraid he'd lose his job. Concerned, his friend called Manning's mother."

"How long has she known?"

"She said about six months, but remember he's out of the country a lot. She didn't want to believe it, but lately he's been having flashbacks, extreme claustrophobia, and he always positions himself near doors for a fast exit, signs she said he'd never revealed before. She also said he checks under his car before getting in it. It sounds like he fits the disorder."

"I have to tell Rook right away."

"I left him a message after I talked with Mrs. Manning. He probably showed some of these signs during his interrogation."

"Rook knew this before they let him leave?"

"You'd have to ask him. I did a bit of research on PTSD myself and learned that a quarter of war correspondents struggle with this disorder. There are a lot of undetected emotional disorders in the profession, Cait. Policemen and firefighters are also vulnerable because they're exposed to similar violence every day. It's part of the job."

Cait flashed back to when she shot Hank Dillon. Department regulations required her to talk to a professional before she was allowed back on the job. "It might explain why Manning shot Wally in police presence, but I don't buy it entirely. Wally was on the verge of spilling something about Manning. I wish I knew what."

"Manning could have been self-medicating with drugs or alcohol to help cover up the disorder."

"That's true, but if he had drugs in his system when he was arrested it would have shown up during the whole interrogation process."

"You might want to ask Detective Rook about that. Cait, don't let your guard down in case he turns up on your doorstep."

"That possibility crossed my mind."

"You take care. One day I'll come out, play a little golf, see one of your Shakespeare plays, and take you to San Francisco like we talked about."

"I'll look forward to it. Thanks, Shep. I'm sure Rook appreciates everything you've done to help."

"Be safe, Cait."

Cait went downstairs with Niki.

Marcus was at the stove when Cait walked in. "I was going to call if you didn't come down soon."

Cait set her gun on the counter. "Why are you here on a Saturday?"

"I thought you might need help with the festival, especially after yesterday." He set a plate of bacon and toast in front of her. "And I wanted to get back to business as usual without murder on the menu. I'm behind in my work."

She sat on a stool to eat. "I should give you a new title, something like manager and chef, with a raise to match."

He set a steaming coffee mug in front of her, reached for a paper towel, and swiped at a spot on the granite counter. "About that raise—"

"I never say anything I don't mean."

One corner of his mouth turned up. "I'm thinking of going to the ranch to ride."

She grinned. "Get out of here. Say hi to Bo for me."

Cait refilled her coffee mug, slipped her cell in her pocket, and went outside. Niki followed her into the meditation garden and then ran off to explore. She sat on the bench and thought about the last twenty-four hours. Wally was out of her life. Sam Cruz would be relieved when she told him he could stop worrying about his actors. And if not for Fumié, Cait might be dead. She set her coffee down and phoned June. "I'm in the garden enjoying my coffee and the sun, and I wanted you and Jim to know Manning was released last night and is probably on his way back to Ohio."

"He sure caused a lot more trouble than he should have," June said.

Velcro crawled out from under the bench and jumped into Cait's lap. "After this weekend, you and Jim should take a week off, go some place fun."

June laughed. "What's life without a little zip? By the way, if you're looking for Niki, he's with us."

"Poor Niki. I haven't given him enough attention." She held her hand up to shield her eyes from the bright sun. "I'll get him in a few minutes." She set her cell on the bench and sipped her coffee.

"Cait?"

She cringed, her heart raced, and she automatically reached for her gun, but it wasn't there.

Velcro jumped and disappeared into the brush.

Manning stood at the entrance to the garden looking cool and calm dressed in khakis and a bright blue sports shirt under a leather jacket. She rose. "I thought you'd left town."

"Not until I attend to some unfinished business." He took a couple of steps into the garden.

She sipped her coffee to appear at ease. "Oh? What business might that be?"

"Seeing you one more time."

The tiny hairs at the back of her neck tickled. "I thought our business was finished yesterday."

He took a couple more steps and she noticed his bloodshot eyes. *Has he been drinking or is he on meds?*

"Are you afraid of me, Cait?"

Stray bits of windblown trash settled at her feet. "Should I be?"

He glanced over his shoulder. "You're a survivor, Cait," he said with bitter admiration.

With her gun in the kitchen and her cell phone a stretch away on the bench, fear began to consume her, but her police training allowed her to keep her composure. *Did the police return his gun? Where would he get another one without Wally?* Tension gave her voice an edge. "You should go to prison for a very long time for killing Wally."

"You're a sweetheart, Cait. Can't help but admire your tenacity. Still"—he shrugged—"it's time to finish what I came here to do."

A final piece of the puzzle slipped into place. Manning, not Wally, wanted her dead. He used Wally so he could blame him for her death. *This is what Wally was trying to say before he was shot. Manning killed him to shut him up.*

He smiled. "Ah, I see you understand. Don't take it personally, Cait. It was the circumstances we were caught up in." Then, "Damn you! Damn the police! Trigger-happy, all of you."

With tightness in her throat, Cait decided the safest course was to go along with him. It might buy time for June to wonder where she was after saying she'd be over to get Niki. The probability of Manning having PTSD was confirmed by his sudden outburst of anger.

His eyes narrowed as he reached inside his jacket and pulled out a gun. He smiled. "It's just us now. No cops to save you this time."

A chill ran along her spine. *Think of your training. Talk is your weapon when nothing else is available.* "Manning, if you're going to kill me, at least tell me why."

His eyebrows arched. "Because you killed Hank. He was like a brother."

"The adoption never went through."

He frowned. "How do you know that?"

"I know a lot," she said. "Give me another reason. You waited two years to come after me. That's a long time."

He glared at her.

"Then I'll tell you. Your dad, an African-American, was shot and killed by a cop. Then I killed Hank. You hate cops. You think I'm a racist. How am I doing?"

His face white as rice paper, his hazel eyes sparked with hate, he jabbed a finger at her. With rage smoldering in his voice, he said, "A cop killed my dad, an innocent man, as he walked out of a grocery store. My dad died on the street like a common criminal."

Cait felt anger vibrating through his body as he moved closer.

"He was murdered because he was black! Like Hank!" His gun wavered in his shaking hand.

Cait lost track of time and threw everything she had at him. "Tell me about Chip Fallon. Why did you kill him? Because he was white?"

He steadied his gun on Cait. "The guy in the vineyard? That was Wally's doing. His death was a tragic misfortune."

"What about Wally's cousin, John LeBow? More bad luck?"

He shrugged. "A necessary evil. So was the girl's kidnapping."

Her skin crawled at the easy way he dismissed murder, as if the victims were insignificant insects. "Why didn't you kill Fumié?"

"She's hot. I like Asian women."

"You're sick. You used Wally to get to me. Am I the first you and Wally planned to kill, or were there others? How long have you schemed together?"

He laughed. "Schemed together? You don't send a street punk to do a man's job. He already had reason to hate you. A little blackmail from me and he was easy."

"Could have fooled me. He tried to kill me, in case you've forgotten."

"He wanted to play by his own rules and kill you, but I told him not to shoot to kill. That pleasure was going to be all mine."

"He was vulnerable because of Hank."

"Most people are vulnerable, Cait."

She was running out of questions when a phone rang, startling both of them. She knew it wasn't hers; it didn't have a tweety ring she'd programmed into it. "You going to get that? Could be important."

Manning hesitated. He started to reach in his pants pocket for his phone, when Cait tossed her coffee in his face and went for his gun.

Caught off guard, he swiped his face, dropped his phone, gripped his gun, and shoved it hard into Cait's neck, cutting off her breath. "Stupid bitch!" He ignored the rivulets of coffee running down his face.

Cait gasped, heart pounding.

"This ends now," he snarled.

A tree branch swayed in the breeze. *June or Jim? The police?* Cait kept her attention on Manning.

Manning released the pressure on her neck.

Cait shoved him and tried to kick his leg out from under him.

He struggled for balance, his gun wobbling in his hand.

Cait went for it. Both of them went down and rolled in masses of lime thyme. She got her hand on his jacket sleeve, yanked hard, releasing his gun. She dove for it, grabbed it, and struggled to get to her feet. Her ankle turned. She grimaced. Sitting on her rear, she scooted away from Manning and pointed the gun at his chest. "Freeze! I swear I'll shoot you!"

Manning froze and glared at her.

She gave a warning shot into the air, hoping the Harts would call for help. "Go on," she hissed, "give me a reason to shoot you, you despicable SOB."

Rook and RT ran from one side of the house, Perough and Vanicheque from the other side, all with their guns drawn.

She was shocked to see RT, but her twisted ankle along with the fear that Manning could still react and do something she couldn't control kept her on the ground.

"Manning!" Rook yelled as he came up behind him. "Hands behind your head!"

June and Jim ran to Cait as Rook grabbed Manning's arms and snapped cuffs on his wrists.

Shoulders slumped, Manning asked, "How did you know?" as Rook and RT pulled him to his feet.

"Your mother," RT said.

"Mom?"

"Yeah, your mom," Rook said. "The police in Columbus have been in touch with her. She's worried about your mental health. That call just now was from her."

"My mom shouldn't have been involved."

"She didn't have a choice," Rook said. "You need help."

RT helped Cait to her feet. "You okay?"

She brushed herself off. "Never felt better."

A sharp yup-yup-yup echoed overhead. A large bird soared and spiraled on unseen currents.

A golden eagle.

CHAPTER 49

Cait awoke feeling alive, head to toe. Best of all was the man between the cool sheets beside her.

It felt so right.

She wished they could stay together like this all night, but when she glanced at the clock on the bedside table she was surprised to see how late it was. Five o'clock. Two hours until *Macbeth* opened.

Cait slipped out of bed.

"Don't go," RT said, reaching out to her.

The sheet slipped down, exposing his strong, muscular, tanned body. Cait wanted nothing more than to play with the black curly hairs on his chest. The amount of dark stubble on his jaw indicated it had been awhile since his last shave. "There's always later," she said.

RT leaned up on his elbow, his eyes hot with desire. "I sure love the way your mind works."

Cait burned with longing but knew that if she slipped back into bed, they wouldn't make it to the theater in time to see the play.

"RT . . . I need to shower." She pointed to the clock. "We'll be late."

RT rubbed his eyes, then tossed the sheet back. "Okay. The sooner we go, the sooner we'll be back here for an encore."

★ ★ ★ ★ ★

As expected, *Macbeth* was a smashing success. Cait and RT stayed long enough after the play to talk with the actors and Ray before going back to the house. June and Jim offered to stay until everyone had gone and then secure the theater.

The wind picked up and wrapped Cait's long skirt around her legs, making it difficult to walk with her sore ankle. "Your timing on coming back was perfect—Manning's gone and you got to see the play."

He tightened his arm around her shoulders and grinned. "Anything else?"

Cait smiled, heart skipping. "I missed you."

They strolled hand-in-hand to the house. "Rook was uneasy after he released Manning," RT said, "but his hands were tied. Apparently, war correspondents have special privileges. It was touch and go for awhile whether I'd be able to come. I didn't know if I could catch a flight from San Diego in time to help. But when your detective friend in Ohio told Rook that Manning had PTSD, I was angry Manning had been released. I've seen men with that disorder. It's not pretty."

"Where did Manning get the gun?"

"It was his. They returned it to him this morning after papers were signed, but Rook had a couple of officers tail him to the airport. Unfortunately, they lost him in traffic. When he didn't show up to check in for his flight, we came here."

"Thank God you did," she said. "What will happen to Manning?"

"Even though he displays some of the classic symptoms of PTSD, it doesn't excuse what he's done. He'll get treatment for the disorder and serve time. When I think about what would have happened if we hadn't gotten here when we did—"

She covered his mouth with her hand, savoring the warm breath on her fingers. "Don't. It turned out okay. I wasn't hurt."

Carole Price

When they reached the door, RT hesitated. "Do you trust me, Cait?"

Surprised by his question, she said, "Of course. Why would you ask?"

"Because it's important you know I'm here for you, no matter what." He brushed her hair back and tucked it behind her ear. "Anything else in your past I should know about? Ex-lovers? More bad guys? Something that might jump out of the woodwork and bite you?"

She recalled her years as a cop, patrolling the streets, and all the criminals she'd apprehended. She thought about Roger, her deceased husband. "I don't think so."

RT leaned down, his lips grazing her ear. "If you remember anything, I'd rather know now and not when I'm thousands of miles out of touch."

Her heart lurched. "You're not leaving already?"

He pulled her close. "Not a chance."

"How long?"

"Not immediately." He kissed the corner of her mouth.

She wanted to fling herself into his arms.

"Now that your problems are solved, you can get back to the business of running your Shakespeare festival and the vineyard."

"There is one thing left to do."

"As long as it doesn't involve murder."

Smiling, she shook her head. "It can be accomplished with one phone call. I want Kenneth Alt to have the painting of Tasha—*Face in Motion*. I know he yearns for it."

He smiled. "If that's what you want."

Inside, they found Niki sprawled on the kitchen floor, a prisoner in the house while the play was in session. RT leaned down and rubbed his head. "Niki's happy here with you. Where do you keep his treats?"

"In the cupboard under the desk." She watched RT take out

a few treats and offer them to Niki. "I leave him outside most of the time now, except at night when he goes upstairs with me."

RT pulled her hard against him. Cait didn't have to imagine where his thoughts were.

The air crackled between them.

As he kissed her, lust raged through her body, her fingers dug into his back. When he bit her neck with the exquisite touch of a feather, her mind shattered.

"No one is allowed upstairs tonight," he said. "And that means Niki." He turned the lights out, took Cait's hand, and led her down the hall to the stairs.

ABOUT THE AUTHOR

Carole Price is a Buckeye. Born and raised in Columbus, Ohio, she attended the Ohio State University. She worked for a national laboratory in Livermore, California, before turning to writing mysteries. She graduated from Livermore's Citizens Police Academy and is an active volunteer for the Livermore Police Department. Carole fell in love with the Bard after attending plays at the Oregon Shakespeare Festival in Ashland.

Sour Grapes is the second book in her Shakespeare in the Vineyard mystery series and follows *Twisted Vines*.

Carole is a member of Mystery Writers of America and Sisters in Crime. She and her husband reside in the San Francisco Bay Area in the middle of wine country.